COLD TO
THE TOUCH

COLD TO THE TOUCH

A NOVEL

Kerri Hakoda

CROOKED
LANE

NEW YORK

Published in the United States by Crooked Lane Books, an imprint of The Quick Brown Fox & Company LLC.

Crooked Lane Books and its logo are trademarks of The Quick Brown Fox & Company LLC.

Library of Congress Catalog-in-Publication data available upon request.

ISBN (hardcover): 978-1-63910-775-9
ISBN (ebook): 978-1-63910-776-6

Cover design by Nicole Lecht

Printed in the United States.

www.crookedlanebooks.com

Crooked Lane Books
34 West 27th St., 10th Floor
New York, NY 10001

First Edition: April 2024

10 9 8 7 6 5 4 3 2 1

For Sparky and Reggie

Prologue

Her memories float back to her childhood like a drift boat on a gentle tide. In Manokotak, a village on the Nushagak River in Western Alaska, winters are harsh and bleak. Oh, but the summers! In those warm endless days, the river bleeds red with the backs of spawning sockeye salmon. Berry bushes burst from the tundra, throbbing with ripe fruit. That's when her father loads her in front of him on the four-wheeler and they speed along the dirt roads, a plume of dust rising behind them. Mosquitoes whine, and in the humid breeze she smells the sweet musk of beaver and the peaty loam of the tundra.

She smiles at the memory, then jerks awake when something wrenches at her cheeks. She gasps, struggling to suck air through the unyielding barrier of duct tape across her mouth. She tries to move her arms, but they're tied together at the wrists. Her ankles are immobilized. Her heart pounding, she realizes she is not six years old, perched in front of her father on his ATV. She is nineteen, gagged and blindfolded, her arms and legs bound, lying on a scratchy blanket that reeks of manure.

Still, she can't keep her mind from unmooring, bobbing like flotsam between now and then. *When is now, and where is here?*

She tries to grasp at images, events, but everything is hazy. Time is like liquid leaking through her fingers. A rooster crows. *Is it morning?*

Then the memory of her childhood melts like a sidewalk-chalk drawing in the rain. What slowly comes into focus in her mind's eye is her basement apartment in Anchorage. She stares at the blinds that rattle against the aluminum frame and the fairy-like snowflakes that sift through the broken window.

And there, the single pink rose on the kitchen counter, fragrant as a funeral. Her skin crawls with the knowledge that someone has been here, in her apartment, has fondled her clothes, rifled through her drawers, moved through her private space, uninvited.

She shivers.

Her eyes spring open. She sees nothing but a smudge of light through the blindfold. Her head swims as she tries to focus. *Try to focus.* She remembers dropping the Corolla off for servicing and Darla giving her a ride back to the coffee shop. She closed at nine o'clock, like always, when a familiar voice asked for "the usual." She frowns, trying to bring his image forward, but it swirls in her brain like a leaf in an eddy. *Then what?*

She jerks awake on the stinking blanket, freezing. Was she drugged? She must have been drugged. A vague memory of a gloved hand across her mouth, a sharp pain at the back of her neck. *Why can't I remember?* Panic embraces her.

A door bangs open, and frigid air swirls around her. Shuffling footsteps and the sound of ripping fabric echo in the otherwise silent room.

"Who's there?" she asks. She barely recognizes her voice muffled by duct tape.

A man's voice, high-pitched and frantic, speaking gibberish. She tries to shake the fuzziness from her brain.

Then another man's voice. "Hey! What the fuck!" Deeper, angry.

She hears scuffling, boots scraping on the wooden floor, grunting. The first man's voice, high and girlish, begging, "No, no, I promise!" Then a loud explosion that makes her jump. Something heavy falls to the wooden floor.

"Ah, Jesus," the second man says. "Goddamn it."

Her ears ring. "Help me." She is crying, terrified but unable to move, and her muffled voice sounds like a whimpering puppy.

Where are my boots? Her feet are like ice. *I spent two months of tip money on those boots.* Heavy footsteps come toward her then, and she is lifted from the itchy blanket. Strong arms carry her.

"Help me." Her plea is reedy and faraway, like a crow's distant call.

She realizes she is not being carried but slung over a broad shoulder like a sack of flour, a sack of cement. A sack that would sink to the bottom of the Nushagak River.

She tries to scream but hears only desperate grunts. She struggles against the plastic ties that bind her arms and legs and feels them cut into her skin.

"Almost there," the man's voice says.

1

Homicide detective DeHavilland Beans received the call at eight Saturday morning, halfway through an hour-long ride on the stationary bicycle. The jarring ringtone of his cell phone, currently the sound of a barking dog, interrupted his blissful listening to the audiobook *The Art of Happiness* by the Dalai Lama. Sweating and annoyed, he brought the yapping phone to his ear.

"Dead body found a half mile from Glenn Highway," the low smoky voice of the weekend dispatcher reported. After the calming words of peace and happiness he'd just heard from His Holiness the Dalai Lama, this brutal message of violence and death threw his serene karmic balance into a tailspin. He splashed through a quick shower, threw on jeans and a sweatshirt, and slipped on his holstered Glock under his Patagonia jacket. It was Saturday, twelve days before Christmas, and as the detective on call this weekend, he was obliged to respond.

Northern lights swayed above his head like phosphorescent kelp caught in a slow celestial current. At eight o'clock on a December morning in Anchorage, Alaska, it was dark and would stay that way for another three hours. He pulled his Ford Explorer out of the garage, turned on the high beams, and cranked the heater to a gale-force roar.

In this weather, the body was probably frozen solid, and a couple of minutes to order a coffee wouldn't matter either way—at least that's what he told himself. He turned the Explorer down O'Malley Road toward his usual stop on weekdays, the Snow Bunny Baristas coffee stand.

When Beans pulled up to the roundabout, the kiosk was dark and deserted. Even the strings of Christmas lights draped over the eaves were switched off. The coffee kiosk was open seven days a week, he knew, since he bought a twenty-ounce Americano with cream there most mornings.

The standard Snow Bunny uniform was a fur-fringed light-blue velvet minidress, low cut in front and high cut in back. A small white pom-pom on the back of the outfit served as the bunny tail. Black fishnet hose and snow boots completed the ensemble. Sure, it was a corny throwback to the old *Playboy* days of objectifying females, but as long as women consented to keeping the "bikini barista" business model alive and legal, he saw no harm in it.

But this morning, there was to be no twenty-ounce Americano. He peered through the drive-through window. A decal there confirmed the hours of operation. He felt an eerie sense of loneliness, of abandonment. He tried to shake it off, telling himself he had developed way too significant a relationship with these young women, or maybe with caffeine. Even though there was no real emergency, he clapped a flashing blue light onto the roof of the Explorer. The big car fishtailed and set up a spray of frost as he sped away from the kiosk and toward the crime scene, the blue light pulsing and insistent against the snow.

Cross-country skiers had come upon a snow-covered mound they assumed was a moose carcass until a telltale scrap of pale-blue fabric caught their attention. While one young man hurled up his breakfast of eggs and reindeer sausage, the other called 911.

When Beans pulled up, the crime scene was lit up like a burlesque stage, a garish scene playing out against the inky backdrop of a winter morning. Crime scene investigators in protective suits hovered around the corpse like faceless mute performers.

The body was behind a stand of bare-branched shrubs, a few hundred yards from a municipal trail used by bicyclists and pedestrians in the summers and cross-country skiers and snowshoers in the winters.

Forensics investigators had carefully brushed the new-fallen snow from the frozen remains of a young female. It appeared that scavengers had torn at her body, laying her open from her sternum to her pelvis. One arm was attached to her body only by shreds of tendon; her wrists were bound together with plastic ties. Her mouth was sealed shut with a piece of duct tape.

Beans recognized the long chestnut hair, the blue velvet mini-dress, now tattered and bloodied, the limp pom-pom, the ragged black fishnet hose that still clung to her legs, which were bound together at the ankles by the same plastic ties. *Jolene Nilsson.*

He liked all the young baristas at Snow Bunny, but Jolene was his favorite—pretty and petite, with a curvy figure that she'd inherited from her father's Swedish ancestors. She had laughing half-moon eyes and a mischievous grin framed with deep dimples. She'd grown up in a small bush Alaska village, as had Beans, and was the product of a Native Alaskan mother and a white father. Beans himself was a hybrid of Irish/Athabascan on his father's side, Japanese on his mother's, and he and Jolene had hit it off, sharing childhood experiences of village life—berry picking, duck hunting, and muskrat trapping.

If she were a little older, Beans might have asked her out. But he was thirty-three and she was nineteen, and that would be viewed as cradle snatching—if not by her parents, then by his colleagues on the police force, many with daughters her age. Like his fellow detective Ed Heller, who resented him enough already. Beans had often thought of the old Steely Dan song "Hey Nineteen" when Jolene handed him his daily Americano and their hands happened to touch.

Beans felt a rush of nausea and turned away. He took a few deep breaths and, with hands that trembled a little, unwrapped a stick of spearmint gum and popped it in his mouth. She would never again toss him the dimpled smile, giggle at his silly jokes. Never again pick berries or trap muskrat. The lyrics to the Steely Dan song were now on a sinister spool, an evil earworm. His gut twisted, and even with the spearmint gum, he fought the urge to retch.

"You okay, Beans?" Chuckie Hefner, the Anchorage medical examiner, put a gloved hand on his shoulder.

"Yeah." He took another deep breath. "I knew her. I bought coffee from her almost every morning."

Chuckie's ice-blue eyes softened. "Oh shit. I'm sorry." He patted Beans on the back.

Beans cleared his throat and gulped in another lungful of cold air. He turned back toward the crime scene. "Do you want to venture a cause of death?"

"Nah, not yet. I'll know better when I get her to the lab," Chuckie said.

"Time of death?"

7

"I'll have a better idea once I thaw her out. Maybe." Chuckie looked down and pulled off his gloves. "My guess is she was killed somewhere else and dumped." Chuckie shook his head. "This sucks. What was she, twenty?"

"Nineteen."

"Oy vey. Does she have family here?"

"No, her parents are back in Manokotak." Beans' stomach lurched again. It would be his job to tell them.

One of Chuckie's assistants and a tech carefully lifted Jolene and placed her in a black body bag. Her face was untouched except for a small scratch on one cheek. *One small mercy for her parents.* Her dark eyes stared up at the clear cold sky as the technician zipped the bag shut.

"Detective? Doctor?" One of the white-suited crime scene techs called out to Beans and Chuckie. "I've found something here."

Beans and Chuckie walked over to the technician, who stood near a stand of barren trees several yards from the body.

"Take a look at this." The tech pointed to the frozen ground.

On the snow was a single white rose. Long stemmed, reasonably fresh, just a blush of pink. Faint drag marks were barely visible in the fresh snow, from the rose to where Jolene's body had been found.

"Maybe she was dumped here and the wolves dragged her over there? Why the rose? A signature? A sign of remorse?" Beans asked, more to himself than anyone else.

"You can bet 1-800-Flowers didn't drop it by," Chuckie said in a dry voice.

"I doubt you'll find anything, but can't hurt to process it as usual," Beans said to the tech.

"No footprints—it snowed last night," Chuckie said. "Only tracks were left by the guys who found her."

"I'll head back, then. I got a phone call to make."

"Oh yeah." Chuckie frowned. As a small-town coroner in the Lower 48 before he came to Anchorage, he had done his share of notifying the next of kin.

Beans carefully trudged back on the marked pathway to the road and was getting into the Explorer when Chuckie called to him. "Hey, I might ask Raisa to consult."

Beans paused, one leg in the car, the other on the crusty snow. Dr. Raisa Ingalls had been called in on a case a few years ago involving a murdered camper in Denali National Park whose body had been left to be devoured by scavengers. She was the Fish and Game expert on park predators, having studied and observed them for years. Beans and Raisa had worked together on that case and had enjoyed a brief but intense affair until he was sent into the interior to work a triple homicide. During that grueling investigation, they saw each other only when he came home for rare weekends, then slowly, inevitably, not at all.

"Beans? You okay with that?" Chuckie asked. "She's still the best around, especially with dentition."

"Yeah, sure." Fiercely intelligent and passionate, Raisa was like no one Beans had ever known. Just thinking about her quickened his heartbeat and caused stirrings that he thought had long gone. He remembered a warm tingling sensation where her shoulder-length curls brushed against his face, his chest, his belly.

Mixed with his feelings of lust was a sense of guilt. Who had broken it off? He didn't remember any argument or discord, no flashpoint where it all went to pieces. They'd just drifted apart, with their travel schedules and the demands of their jobs. He seemed to remember that she had sent him a text or two. Had he responded? *So much for mindfulness. Oh God, I'm a shit.*

"Okay, so if you're good with that, I'll give her a call and see if she can come in for the postmortem?" Chuckie wrinkled his nose. "Techs are bagging the scat for her. They just love that."

"Of course, Chuckie. She's still the best." He got into the car and turned it onto the highway, the frozen snow crunching under his tires. He gripped the steering wheel hard, steeling himself for the call he would need to make to Jolene's parents.

2

Beans stepped through the swinging doors of the morgue, tying a green gown around his neck.

"You're late, Beans," Chuckie said.

"Only ten minutes."

Chuckie's pale eyes twinkled above his mask. "What? No visions of sugarplums dancing through your head last night?"

"Not even close," Beans grumbled. A half hour of mindful meditation before bed had done no good. The same nightmare of being trapped in his brother Lindbergh's burning truck had shattered his sleep again last night. The old Ford spun on its roof on the frozen tundra, flames licking through the vents while the upside-down cab filled with smoke.

"Lindbergh, get me out!" Eight-year-old Beans shrieked, *pounding his fists against the windows, the glass hot under his touch, the coppery taste of his own blood in his mouth.* In the dream, as in life, Lindbergh staggered drunkenly into the distance, disappearing in the falling snow. But in last night's dream, Jolene had hung upside down next to him, her arms outspread, torso flayed open. She smiled, her dimples deepening like gashes while the scratch on her pale face oozed black blood.

He woke in a cold sweat. He thought he'd probably cried out; his throat felt tight and raw. He splashed some water onto his face and stared at himself in the bathroom mirror. In the harsh overhead light, his Japanese mother's eyes looked back at him. He downed a glass of water, then fell back into bed and into a fitful sleep until he sprang up, realizing he had slept through his alarm. After a haphazard shower and cup of coffee, he'd raced to the morgue, ten minutes late for Jolene's autopsy.

She lay on a table, draped with a sheet. The zip ties and duct tape that had bound and silenced her had already been removed, photographed, and sent to Trace Evidence for processing.

Beans had called the Nilssons yesterday to give them what was probably the worst news of their lives. Jolene's parents had chartered a flight out of the village of Manokotak and arrived yesterday afternoon to confirm identification of the body. Esther Nilsson, a small Native woman clinging to her tall Swedish husband, was inconsolable. Olaf was stoic, patting his wife on the back as she wept.

He set his jaw and looked directly at his daughter's lifeless face. "That's her. That's our Jo." He turned then to Beans, his eyes dry but red rimmed. "We want to take her home."

"We'll release her to you as soon as we can," Beans said. He'd looked away as he recited the canned phrase that seemed so trite in the face of the Nilssons' overwhelming grief: "I'm so sorry for your loss."

"So . . ." Chuckie diverted Beans from remembering his heart-wrenching meeting with the Nilssons. "Where's Raisa?"

"How should I—" Beans began, when the doors swung open and a slender figure in a green gown rushed in, knotting a white mask over her nose and mouth. She set a black camera bag on a rolling chair.

"So sorry I'm late. I forgot about traffic in the big city." Her dark eyes smiled below a fringe of curly brown bangs. "Hey, Chuckie. Long time no see." She approached the body, then stopped when she spotted Beans. "And Beans. Even longer time no see."

Beans found himself fidgeting. "Hi, Raisa. Good to see you."

"What have we got, gentlemen?" She busied herself unpacking her camera and screwing on a lens.

Chuckie switched off the lilting Christmas music that had been playing in the background and switched on the recorder. When the medical examiner uncovered the body, Beans was standing close enough to hear Raisa's sharp intake of breath.

"Postmortem of Jolene Annette Nilsson, Yup'ik and Caucasian ethnicity." Chuckie sighed. "Nineteen years of age."

He was careful with his postmortem, cataloging and bagging every bit of evidence in Jolene's hair and on her skin. He turned her on her side and began to cut away the blue velvet barista uniform, then stopped.

"Well, hello. What do we have here?" Chuckie said.

The back of the uniform was soaked with blood, and there was a single L-shaped tear in it, just above the young woman's fourth rib. Beans and Raisa leaned in closer. A familiar scent made Beans forget the chemical odors of the morgue—not perfume, but a fresh outdoor smell and, faintly, the tea tree soap he remembered that Raisa ordered online from L'Occitane.

"It's not likely a wolf did that," she said. "Not without more ripping of the fabric."

"No other punctures or cuts on the clothing not consistent with scavenger activity." Chuckie cut the uniform off carefully, then gave a low whistle. "Take a look."

He pointed with a gloved finger at the ragged hole on Jolene's back, just where the tear in the uniform was. The cut in her flesh was an equilateral triangle, a scant inch long on each side.

"Knife wound? Maybe a sword?" Beans asked.

"If it is, she wasn't stabbed *in* the back, she was stabbed *through* the back," Chuckie said. "My guess is through the heart as well." He began taking digital photos of the wound.

The traditional Y-shaped incision made during an autopsy wasn't necessary, since most of her torso was gone. Her heart, lungs, liver, and most of her internal organs were also missing, presumably consumed by predators.

"Humans are usually not at the top of a wolf pack's menu," Raisa said. "In the winter, though, pickings are slim. And the organs—the nutrient- and blood-rich components—are generally consumed first." Raisa peered at Jolene's arm, the one hanging by tendons. "Look at the size of the jaw. Definitely wolf. Here, though"—she pointed to smaller gnaw marks—"this is a fox, secondary scavengers."

Beans' stomach lurched, and he had to turn away. This slender arm, now mangled, had handed him an Americano at least three times a week.

"Looks like homicide, but I'm reserving judgment until I see tox results. Any chance the wolves could have killed her?" Chuckie asked.

"Maybe, if she were wounded and bleeding," Raisa said. "If she were on foot, wolves would have nipped at her legs or gone after her throat to bring her down. But her neck is relatively unmarked, and her legs are almost untouched. And again, wolves are usually pretty wary of humans. I'll run a few comparisons with documented wolf kills, but my guess is the predators fed on her remains postmortem."

"That's consistent with the small amount of blood at the scene," Beans said.

Raisa leaned in to take several photos of the body. She stopped suddenly and looked away from her camera's view finder. "Hmm. Look at the back rib, the third or fourth one."

"Looks like it's broken," Beans said.

"Right, but it doesn't seem to be consistent with predation. It's like it was shattered rather than chewed." She zoomed in to take a few more shots.

Chuckie swung the magnifying glass over the rib cage. "Good catch, Raisa. It looks like something struck the bone with enough force to crack it."

"And to cause that exit wound through her back." Beans nodded to Chuckie.

"What's that?" Raisa pointed at what appeared to be bits of debris on the blue fabric.

Chuckie peered through the magnifying glass. "It looks like . . . tree bark? I found some of it in her hair as well."

"Jolene was found on freshly fallen snow. There were no trees within a hundred-foot radius of the body." Beans snapped a photo with his phone. "Bark could be from the murder scene."

"I'll bag it for Trace." Chuckie shook open a plastic evidence bag.

"Are we any closer to a cause of death? Sharp-force trauma?" Beans asked. "Can I tell her parents anything?" He thought again about Olaf and Esther Nilsson in their room at the Captain Cook Hotel, waiting for the phone to ring, waiting for word that they could take their girl home.

"Not yet." Chuckie snapped more photos. "It'll take a while for toxicology reports to come back. But I'm willing to bet that this wound was a contributing factor."

Beans had to avert his eyes again from Jolene's mutilated body. "Sexual assault?" He had to ask, but was afraid to hear the answer.

Chuckie shook his head. "Hard to say, with this level of damage to the remains. Tox and Trace will be able to tell us more."

Raisa sighed. "What a lovely girl. Who would do such a thing?"

"Time of death is a moving target as well," Chuckie said. "She was frozen solid when we found her. The closest I can get is sometime between Thursday and really early Saturday. That would give the killer enough time to kill her, then get her out there to be consumed before she froze."

Chuckie frowned. "Postmortem was concluded at nine fifty-two AM." He clicked off the recorder and covered Jolene gently with a sheet again. "I'll close her up in a minute. I need a little break. Raisa, your scat is in the cooler just outside the door." Without another word, Chuckie padded out through the swinging doors.

Beans knew that meant Chuckie was going out onto the freezing loading dock to smoke his one cigarette a day, the last vestige of the pack-a-day habit he'd kicked years ago. Raisa stared after Chuckie, blinking.

"So, are we done, then?" Raisa started packing her camera into its case.

"Yeah, we are, according to Chuckie." Now that Beans was alone with her, he felt his palms grow sweaty. He threw his latex gloves in the trash and his gown and cap into the laundry bin. Raisa pulled her cap off and shook out her brown curls. They were shorter than he remembered, and he had to fight the urge to touch them.

"So, how have you been?" Raisa asked in a cool, conversational tone. She struggled to unknot the ties behind her neck.

"Here, let me." Beans reached to help her, but she pulled away, face flushed.

"I got it." She worked the ties free and yanked the gown off. Without the oversized garment draped over her, she seemed thinner than when he'd last seen her.

"Raisa—" Beans started to say.

"I really have to go. It was nice seeing you. I'll have the scat analysis to you and Chuckie in a day or so."

"Do you have a minute? Do you want to grab a coffee?" Beans needed to talk to her, to somehow make it right, although exactly where it had gone wrong still escaped him.

She gave him a wistful smile as she shrugged on her coat. "It's okay, Beans, it really is." She grabbed the blue-and-white cooler and pushed through the swinging doors.

Even Beans, an admitted idiot when it came to women, knew it wasn't anywhere close to being okay. He rubbed his face with his hands and realized that in his rush to get out of the house that morning, he'd forgotten to shave. He felt and probably looked like he had slept under a bridge. On days like these, he wished he drank.

He was sitting in the Explorer, scratching at the stubble on his face and considering going back to bed, when his cell phone barked. His heart lurched. "Raisa?"

"Who the hell is Raisa?" a male voice answered. "Beans, this is Frankie."

Frankie Ma, an old friend, helped run his mother's Asian grocery business in Anchorage's Government Hill district. Beans had worked at the store and rented the upstairs apartment from the Ma family while a student at the University of Alaska, and he and Frankie had played college ball together. Through the years, they'd occasionally met for burgers or pickup basketball games. The last time Beans had seen his friend was at the funeral of Frankie's father, two years ago.

"Frankie? Hey, dude, what's up?"

"You gotta help me, Beans." His friend's voice was hushed and tense, without its usual jovial lilt. Beans heard the wail of sirens in the background.

"What's going on?" Beans asked. "Is your mom okay?" Sophie Ma was a tiny Chinese woman whose slight stature was deceiving. She ran the family and the business with a small but powerful iron fist.

"She's fine, visiting my sister in Seattle. I'm fucked, Beans." Frankie sounded on the verge of tears.

"What's happened?" Beans turned the key in the ignition. "Talk to me, man."

"He's missing, Beans. Sevy Concepcion is missing. Maybe dead. They're saying I killed him."

3

The disheveled, unshaven man drumming his fingers on the tabletop was a world away from the handsome scholar-athlete who had been offered a full ride at the University of Alaska. A cold Styrofoam cup of coffee sat on the table in front of him, the surface shuddering with the beat of his thumping fingers. Beans watched him through the small window on the interview room door. Frankie Ma had been the spark plug to their basketball team's offense, the master of the pick and roll. Shaking his head, Beans thought Frankie looked more as if someone had picked his pocket and rolled him in an alley. His dark hair was greasy and flecked with gray, and he wore glasses now.

His own cup of lukewarm coffee in one hand and a file in the other, Beans pushed open the interview room door.

"Oh man, thank God you're here." Frankie leapt to his feet and extended his hand. He winced. "You look like shit."

Beans shook his hand. "Yeah, well, thanks, you too. Jesus, what the hell is going on? Wait, before you tell me, you've talked to a lawyer, right?"

"Oh, yeah, yeah. He's on his way. I got nothing to hide. I told that Detective Heller I had a friend in the department." His palm drummed a nervous beat on the table. "That guy's an asshole."

"Yeah, kinda." Beans and his colleague Ed Heller had a contentious relationship at best. Ever since their partners had retired or transferred south, there had been monumental pressure from the higher-ups for Heller and Beans to partner up, but neither would have it.

Heller was a middle-aged, old-school homicide detective, thickening around the middle, competent but unimaginative. The average second grader, Beans thought, had a better grasp of current technology. And Beans suspected that Heller viewed him as a young upstart who liked to cut corners and had taken advantage of his ethnic minority status to earn a detective shield without paying his dues.

Their lieutenant wanted nothing more than for the two of them to team up. But the caseload in Homicide was heavy enough to allow both detectives to head their own investigations, so Beans and Heller happily evaded the issue.

Beans sipped at his coffee, making a face. *Definitely not as good as Snow Bunny brew.* "So, start from the beginning. How do you know Sevy Concepcion? Wait, don't tell me. Gambling, right?" Beans knew that Sevy Concepcion was a small-time bookie and loan shark.

"Yeah, I'd get into him for a few bucks, pay up, then run up another tab, strictly small potatoes—until I found out about the cockfights up near Eagle River."

"Sevy got you into the cockfights?" Beans asked. He had heard from Vice about a sophisticated cockfighting ring making the circuit of heated barns in the area.

"Oh yeah." Frankie grimaced. "That's how I got into him for ten grand." He began turning the Styrofoam cup between his hands.

"Ten grand? Seriously?" The Frankie Ma he had known in college was frugal to the point of miserly. He hadn't ever spent that much money on a car, much less a gambling debt. "When was the last time you saw Sevy?"

"Three—maybe four—weeks ago at the shop. It was pretty late. Mom wants us to stay open until ten now, you know." His head fell back. "Shit, *Mom*. What am I going to tell her?"

"That's the least of your worries. Go on."

"So, suddenly, Sevy and his brother Manny stroll into the store. Manny is Sevy's muscle, a real loose cannon. They were okay at first, almost polite. Asked for a couple of grand. I told them I didn't have it. Then Sevy nodded to Manny. 'Check the register.'

"Manny came toward me then, and the only thing I could think of was having to tell the old lady that I'd emptied the register to pay a loan shark. I reached under the register and pulled out Dad's old nine-mil Smith & Wesson. I don't know what I was thinking. I've never fired a gun in my life.

"Then all hell broke loose. Manny screamed, 'Drop it!' and pulled out a huge revolver. Just then Ali—you remember, who runs the samosa place next door—came in. He saw the two guns. His eyes got as big as soup plates, and he backed out of there."

Beans tried not to sigh. "So there's a witness who saw you threatening Sevy with a gun. You really are a fuckup, you know?"

"I know, I know." Frankie ran his hands through his hair. "Sevy calmed Manny down. That fucker was ready to shred me. There was only fifty bucks or so in the register. They took that and a six-pack of IPA and left. But not before saying they'd be back and I'd better have some money for them. But now Sevy's gone, right?" Frankie looked hopeful.

"Aren't you a lucky guy?" Beans couldn't keep the sarcasm from his voice. "Here's what we got. Sevy's Lincoln Town Car was found in long-term parking at the airport. Oddly enough, the car's been wiped clean of any prints. Manny Concepcion says you threatened his brother with a nine-mil S&W. Ali Gupta says he saw you with a gun aimed at Sevy."

"I wasn't going to shoot." Frankie's voice was plaintive. "You know me, Beans. I wouldn't kill anybody."

"And you have a motive—you owe the victim ten grand. And you know what else?"

"What?"

"Your dad's gun is gone. They got a warrant and searched the shop and your apartment. It's gone." Beans felt a headache coming on and massaged the back of his neck. "What did you do with the gun, Frankie?"

"I didn't do anything with it! I put it back under the register!" He looked from Beans' face to the two-way mirror, then began pacing. "Where is my fucking lawyer?"

Beans leaned back and watched his friend, in his faded gray hoodie and stained jeans, march jerkily back and forth like a windup toy. All the evidence against him was weak and circumstantial, and Beans was sure that his friend wasn't the only one who wanted to see Sevy Concepcion disappear. Still, the missing nine-mil was not a good thing, and neither were the two witnesses.

Why am I even here? He hadn't seen Frankie Ma in years, and this was Heller's case. He sighed. He was here holding Frankie's hand because he owed it to Sophie and the late Coleman Ma, who had given him a job and a cheap place to live all through college and invited him to dinner when they sensed he was homesick some Asian home cooking.

His cell phone pinged with an incoming text message. *ID'd weapon, I think. Maybe.* The message was from Chuckie, with a thoughtful emoji after it. Beans texted that he would call him in a few minutes. He looked up when Frankie came to a stop and folded his arms across his chest, like he was freezing.

"Shit, Beans, what am I going to tell Mom?" Frankie peered at him with the begging eyes of a starving spaniel. "Would you do it? Would you call her for me?"

Beans' first instinct was to walk out the door, but he had second thoughts. He might be able to soften the blow for Sophie Ma and make it less likely that she would fly into one of her shrill tirades. "Okay, give me her number. I've got an appointment now, but I'll call her after that."

"Thanks, Beans—I owe you, brother. She's at Allison's in Seattle, but here's her cell." He rattled off a phone number, relief bubbling out of him.

As Beans left the interview room, he passed a well-dressed, silver-haired Asian man in the hall, who smiled and nodded at him before he entered the room. Frankie's attorney, he assumed.

He was sitting in the Explorer, about to call Chuckie, when his cell phone pinged again with a text message, this time from his little sister, Piper. Her message had no fewer than ten happy-face emojis and the message *I GOT THE JOB!!!*

Beans smiled at the screen. *Congrats! What's the job?* he typed.

I'M A BARISTA!!!! Followed by fifteen more elated emojis.

4

Beans let his head fall back onto the headrest as he listened to Piper's phone click into voice mail.

"Hi, this is Piper. Leave a message."

"Piper, this is your brother. The one that's not Herc. Call me ASAP."

He rubbed his unshaven face, feeling the sandpaper rasp against the palm of his hand. His eyes felt gritty, and he really could use a decent cup of coffee.

No time for that right now. He had appointments with Jolene's college professors this afternoon, but before then he would find out what Chuckie had discovered about the possible murder weapon. He put the Explorer in gear and made his way back to the morgue through the lightly falling snow.

Chuckie was perched on a rolling stool in the outer office. Still in his green scrubs, he munched on a cheese Danish and sipped from a Starbucks cup. Beans had never figured out how Chuckie could have any appetite at all after opening up several corpses a day, but the medical examiner seemed to have no problem.

"Took a chance you might show up soon and got you one." Chuckie nodded toward a sixteen-ounce cup sitting next to a stack of files.

"Oh, bless you." Beans bowed his head and said a silent sutra of gratitude before he wrapped his hands around the still-hot Americano.

"Sit." Chuckie rolled another stool toward Beans.

Chuckie awakened his computer as Beans sat, and an image flickered onto the monitor. It was a close-up of the triangular exit wound on Jolene's back. With all traces of blood washed away, it looked even more brutal, black and ragged against her pale skin. Now that it had been irrigated and photographed under the harsh fluorescent lights of the morgue, something about it looked familiar. Beans stared at the computer screen. *What is it?*

"Would be easier, of course, if we had an entry wound. This doesn't match the standard knives, swords, dueling épées, ice axes, et cetera, that we see on a daily basis, so . . . I've had to look further." Chuckie clicked to an image of a short sword with a hilt. "Here's a possibility. This is an M1917 Knuckle Duster—issued to US soldiers during World War I. Note the triangular blade, long enough to impale a body and emerge out the back."

Beans peered at the image, sipping his coffee. "So, you're call-ing this the cause of death? This what, bayonet?" He tried to keep the skepticism from his voice. Chuckie deserved credit for using his imagination, but this was a long shot.

"Not definitively at this point, but like I said, it's a possibility. Still waiting on tox, of course. No hyoid fracture or petechial hemorrhage consistent with strangulation either, so sharp-force trauma is the best bet right now.

"And lucky for us"—Chuckie tapped on the monitor with a pen—"I got a contact at a weaponry museum in Pennsylvania who says he can loan me one of these mothers. He suggests I reciprocate with some Alaska salmon." He grimaced. "Do you know what Copper River sockeye goes for these days?"

"Take one for the team, Chuckie."

"Did the CSIs find anything in the girl's apartment?"

"A lot of cat hair, nothing much else. No blood residue or prints of anybody we've got on file."

"You said there was a break-in at her house earlier, right?"

"Yeah, a couple of weeks ago. Nothing taken, according to her landlady and the responding officers. Not sure if there's a connection or not," Beans said.

"Too much of a coincidence, though?"

"Probably."

Chuckie took a huge bite of Danish. "And the car?"

"No blood there either. Nothing to show that either the car or her apartment was involved. She dropped her car off at Fireweed Toyota for servicing after her first shift and got a ride back to the coffee shop for her evening gig. Lots of prints in the car but only one on file. One of Fireweed's guys had an old DUI."

"Not much to go on." Chuckie shook his head.

"I'll keep chipping away at known associates. Her old boyfriend transferred down to Pacific Lutheran University in Tacoma last term. He was pretty shaken up when I told him about Jolene. And last week was finals week, so he had lots of witnesses seeing him taking tests."

"We've got a pretty wonky time of death because of the freezing weather."

"True, but this kid hasn't flown anywhere in the last few months, according to TSA. He hasn't been absent from classes long enough to drive the Alcan. I don't like him for this one."

"Well, crap." Chuckie shoved the last of the Danish into his mouth and washed it down with coffee. He stuck a pen through his thick curly hair and scratched at his scalp.

Beans glanced at his watch. "I gotta go. Jolene's landlady wants me to stop by. Thanks for the coffee, Chuck. Let me know what you find out on the First World War relic, will you?"

"Oh ye of little faith," Chuckie muttered.

Beans was pushing through the exit doors into the frigid air when his cell phone yapped in his pocket. *Piper.*

"Havi! Isn't it awesome?" His sister's voice trilled across the line. Only his family called him Havi; to everyone else, he was Beans.

"If you mean the barista job, I'm less than thrilled." He fumbled with his key fob and unlocked the door.

Her tone was crestfallen. "What do you mean? I thought you'd be happy for me."

"Couldn't you find a different job, like at the DMV?"

"This job has flexible hours, Havi. I can work around my classes. And tips! You don't get tips at the DMV."

"What kind of tips? And what will you be wearing?" Beans felt his palms getting sweaty. The idea of his little sister in a bikini or French maid uniform serving coffee to gawking truck drivers set his teeth on edge.

"What will I be wearing? What the hell are you talking about?"

"You heard me." He realized that he was in danger of igniting his sister's sometimes fiery temper.

"The job is at a Starbucks in the Fred Meyer store on Northern Lights Boulevard. I will be wearing a black shirt and pants. Long pants. And an apron. Probably green." She spoke slowly through gritted teeth.

Beans exhaled. "Well, that's different, then."

"Different than what?" She lowered her voice. "Have you been drinking?"

Without going into detail, he explained that he was investigating the murder of a young woman who worked at a coffee kiosk.

"Oh," she said in a subdued voice. "I heard about her. That's terrible."

"Which is why I asked what you would be wearing, since the gals at this kiosk wear skimpy outfits. But they make great coffee," he hurried to add.

Piper laughed. "Right."

He made her promise to be aware of her surroundings, park in well-lit areas, and report suspicious people or activities. He realized that he sounded like a Neighborhood Watch flyer and reminded himself that Piper was a grown woman.

"Thanks, Havi. And you still owe me dinner at Club Paris, you bum."

He smiled as he hung up. A conversation with his little sister was either amusing or maddening, one or the other, and sometimes both. His smile faded as he remembered that Jolene Nilsson was even younger than Piper, and he still had nothing to tell her grieving family.

He wondered why Jolene's landlady needed to see him again. Hopefully, she'd remembered a detail that had escaped her earlier. Before driving back out to the old woman's house, he reminded himself that he'd promised to call Sophie Ma, Frankie's mother.

Then, suddenly, he knew where he had seen that wound before.

It was a crisp fall day on the tundra, his father Jimmy and old-est brother Lindbergh whooping and cheering after bringing down a caribou bull. Jimmy slung a crossbow over his shoulder and swigged from a silver flask, then passed it on to his eldest son.

"Gave us a run, didn't he?" Jimmy said, a little breathless, wiping a hand across his dripping beard.

"Shit, I thought he'd never drop." Lindbergh laughed and tipped the flask up to take a long drink.

Six-year-old Beans hopped off his father's four-wheeler and cautiously approached the huge animal, two crossbow bolts protruding from its side. Pink saliva foamed at the caribou's mouth. Its eyes were flat and glassy. The carcass reeked of old pee, musk, and blood.

"I got the kill shot." Lindberg yanked at the bolt with yellow fletching.

"Bullshit, he's mine." Jimmy grunted as he pulled at the blue-fletched arrow. It emerged from the caribou's flesh with a sickening squelch.

The memory of the two steaming punctures in the animal's side was now as vivid as a photograph. *That distinctive triangular shape.*

He picked up his phone. When Chuckie answered, he said, "Forget the bayonet. It was an arrow. A crossbow bolt made that wound."

5

A surreal sense of relief washed over Beans after he hung up with Chuckie. He was almost certain he had identified the type of weapon used to kill Jolene. Now he had something to tell her parents, a tiny offering of hope that the police were narrowing in on their daughter's killer.

He felt almost lighthearted as he batted at the Dalai Lama action figure hanging from the rearview mirror. His Miniature Holiness seemed to glare with waxen disapproval at the clutter in the front seat of his police-issued vehicle. Empty coffee cups and gum wrappers littered the Explorer's floor, faded yellow Post-its clung to the dash at weird angles, and dimes and nickels rattled in the cupholder. A snake pit of snarled charging cords lay in the passenger seat.

It never seemed to be the right time to clean the car, and today was no different. Beans picked up his cell phone and, as promised, dialed the number Frankie Ma had given for his mother. After the third ring, a woman's heavily accented voice answered.

"Hallo?"

"Mrs. Ma?"

"Yeah, who is this?"

"Mrs. Ma, this is Beans, DeHavilland Beans, Frankie's friend."

"Oh, Beans!" He could imagine the tiny woman's bright, bird-like eyes disappearing into her round cheeks when she smiled. "How are you?"

"I'm good, Mrs. Ma. Frankie asked me to call you."

"Why? Is he in the hospital?" A note of concern crept into her voice.

"No, he's fine. He is in a little bit of trouble, though."

"What kind of trouble? Did he wreck the car?" The note of concern was replaced by irritation.

"Actually, no. He was brought in by the police for some questioning."

Beans held the phone away from his ear as Sophie Ma screeched in Mandarin. The few English words he could pick out were "no-good asshole."

When she showed signs of winding down, he said, "Right now he's just in for questioning, Mrs. Ma. One of his . . . friends has gone missing. And one of the reasons the police are talking to Frankie is that Mr. Ma's old nine-millimeter gun is gone. Do you know where the gun is?"

"Oh, yeah, I got it." Her tone was matter-of-fact.

"You have it?" Beans wasn't sure he'd understood her correctly. "You have the gun with you there in Seattle?"

"Yeah, yeah. You check with Alaska Airlines. I put it in the suitcase."

"Why did you bring the gun with you?"

"My daughter's husband is no good. He hits her sometimes. She moved out, so I went down to help her. I brought the gun in case he made trouble."

"When did you arrive there in Seattle?"

"Day before Thanksgiving," Mrs. Ma said with her usual confidence.

So she and the gun had been out of the state at least two weeks before Concepcion went missing. It would be easy enough to verify the checked gun and travel schedule—if Sophie Ma's statement was true, it didn't put Frankie totally in the clear, but it meant the department didn't have enough evidence to hold him.

"Okay, thanks, Mrs. Ma. He'll have to stick around in case there are more questions, but he's not a prime suspect right now."

"You tell Frankie I'm coming home next week and he's in big trouble," she grumbled. "Why can't he be a good boy like you?"

After hanging up, Beans left a voice mail for Frankie updating him on the family weapon, tossed the detritus of his front seat compartment into the back seat under the Dalai Lama's watchful eye, then drove across town to Jolene's landlady's house.

The yellow crime scene tape had been removed from Jolene's basement apartment door, somehow making it look sad and abandoned. Beans clomped up the steps to the landlady's upper unit and stamped the snow from his boots before he rang the doorbell.

Anna Kaminski answered the door in a flowered housedress and Seattle Seahawks beanie with a green pom-pom on top.

"Oh, here you are." Her pale eyes were huge behind her glasses as she peered at his face. "Didn't bother to shave, I see. Come on in."

Rubbing at his stubble, he followed her into a dimly lit living room jammed with overstuffed brocade-covered furniture. The arms of the sofa and love seat had been shredded, presumably by the three cats that lounged across the backs of the furniture. She motioned for him to sit, and he perched on a corner of the sofa, aware that every surface in the room was covered with drifts of cat hair.

"I just remembered something last night that Jolene told me after the break-in. She forgot to mention this to the police. She just didn't think it was important," Anna Kaminski said.

"She noticed that something was stolen?"

"No, she remembered that something had been left for her."

"The intruder *left* something in the apartment?" Beans felt his pulse quicken.

"Right. She said the guy left her a rose. A fresh flower."

"Was it in a vase or a holder?" His mind raced. The CSI crew hadn't noted a bud vase among Jolene's effects.

"Oh, no, it was left on the kitchen counter, she said. She threw it away, thought it was just some creep showing off."

The rose found near the body was a "hold-back"—one of Jolene's crime scene details that hadn't been revealed to the press. The rose left here at the apartment was long gone, but it could be a connection between the break-in and the murder.

"Did she describe the rose—the color, a ribbon, any other details?"

The landlady frowned. "No, I don't think so."

Beans made a mental note to review again the police report of the break-in, as well as the CSI's more recent sweep of Jolene's apartment. He stood to leave. "Thanks, Ms. Kaminski. Please contact me if you recall anything else."

"Would you mind doing something for me, Detective?" She looked a little sheepish. "I don't drive anymore, like I told you. With little Jolene gone, it's tough for me to get around."

Here it comes. The ride to bingo night. "Well, I'll help wherever I can, but . . ."

"Oh, good! I can't tell you what a relief this is." Before he could say any more, she shuffled into the kitchen and returned lugging a plastic pet carrier. Its occupant yowled mournfully, and the three cats in the living room hissed with weary irritation. She plunked the carrier down at Beans' feet.

"This is Archie, Jolene's cat. He ran away the day of the break-in. Oh, Jolene was heartbroken, she was. He only just came back the day you all found . . . her." The landlady's voice faltered, and she cleared her throat. "He's been going from room to room, wailing something awful. I need to rent that apartment soon but can't do it with him around. I already have enough cats." She waved at the felines reclined on the sofa. "And her folks are dog people."

Her magnified eyes were beseeching. "You would do me a huge favor by dropping him off at the Humane Society. Here's what's left of his food and his other stuff. He's a good boy. I'm sure someone will adopt him right away."

Archie stared at Beans through the holes in the carrier with a level green gaze, then pressed his eyes shut as if he couldn't be bothered. He was a ginger tabby, with large paws and a V-shaped notch bitten off one ear.

"You could call Animal Control. I'm sure—" he began.

"Please, Detective. It would be a huge load off my mind to know that someone dependable is seeing to Archie. I'm sure Jolene would appreciate it."

Beans suppressed a sigh of resignation as he bent to pick up the carrier, which was surprisingly heavy. *What does this animal weigh—thirty pounds?* He grabbed the shopping bag with the cat food and dishes with his other hand.

Anna Kaminski's face broke into a wide grin that displayed an impressive array of dentures. "I thank you, and Archie thanks you."

Beans set the carrier and the bag into his back seat, then put the car in reverse and looked in the rearview mirror. Archie met his eyes, curled his paws under him, and voiced a series of small conversational meows. By the time the speedometer got up to thirty-five miles per hour, the sounds in the back seat had turned to loud purring.

6

Beans sat behind the wheel of the Ford Explorer, the engine idling, on the icy tarmac in front of the Anchorage Humane Society. The heater roared at full blast and the police radio crackled, interfering with the internal argument he was having with his conscience.

A stooped man in a checked jacket and matching hat picked his way across the slick parking lot, carrying a cardboard box. As he passed Beans' car, the man bent his head and appeared to murmur to the contents of the box. From the opposite end of the parking lot, a young woman coaxed a limping German shepherd at the end of a rope through the automatic doors.

Beans glanced in the rearview mirror at the ginger cat, who stared back at him, an apparent dare in his emerald eyes. The Dalai Lama action figure dangled from the rearview mirror like an accusation.

"Ah, hell." Beans threw the Explorer into reverse and backed out. Keeping the cat wasn't the best idea, that was for sure. He had no time nor desire for a pet. But the thought of handing Jolene's cat over to a total stranger seemed like very bad karma.

As he turned onto O'Malley toward his bungalow, he ran several Archie-adoption scenarios through his mind: (1) Piper could take Archie—she loved animals; (2) Chuckie could take Archie—then Beans remembered that Chuckie owned an Alaskan malamute with a high prey drive; (3) he could run a Craigslist ad—*Overweight cat, free to a good home.*

For now, he would take Archie home until one of the options became a reality or a new one occurred to him. He turned onto his quiet residential street and pulled into the driveway in front of his gray-and-white two-bedroom-plus-den rambler. It was modest and comfortable, with a small front garden and a large fenced backyard. When he bought the house a few years ago, he'd thought that Raisa might be spending more time with him, so he'd chosen a house with room for her sled dogs. *So much for that.* But he liked the house, Raisa or no Raisa.

Once inside, he set up the cat's food and water dishes in a corner of the bright kitchen and the litter box in the mudroom just inside the back door. He closed the bedroom doors and the door to the office—a place of worship and exercise, where he kept his Buddhist shrine and home gym equipment. There was no reason to tempt Archie.

He opened the gate to the cat carrier, and Archie stuck his nose out, sniffing and making a noise that sounded like a questioning "*Prow?*" The cat took quick mincing steps out of the carrier as if walking on wet grass, then sat and cleaned his paws. Next, he found the litter box, made a quick deposit, and kicked up a spray of litter onto the mudroom's tile floor.

Beans ran an electric shaver over his face while he checked emails on his phone. In the back of the pantry, he found an almost petrified energy bar and threw it in his pocket. No time for lunch;

as it was, he would barely make it on time to his appointment with Jolene's employer and colleague. He shrugged into his coat and called to the cat, "Okay, well then, make yourself at home. I'll see you later."

"*Prow?*" Archie said, as he leaped onto the back of the sofa and folded his paws under him.

* * *

April Emmanuelle had been an exotic dancer who entertained oil-field workers on the North Slope until she banked enough money to open a bakery/deli (Snow Bunny Buns) and a drive-through espresso stand, Snow Bunny Baristas. She was a tall, imposing redhead with what Beans suspected were enhanced body parts. Her dark-brown eyes were shrewd and intelligent, and they softened when she talked about Jolene.

"Oh, Jesus, I still can't believe it. How could this happen to little Jo?" She had the remnants of a soft Southern drawl.

"When was the last time you saw her?"

"I guess it was Wednesday morning about nine, the middle of the morning shift. I checked the till and reminded her that she had the split shift that day. She said her car was giving her problems and was going to have Darla . . . You know Darla?"

Beans smiled and nodded at the slender blonde who sat next to April. Darla often worked the kiosk in the mornings with Jolene.

"She said she'd have Darla follow her to the shop between shifts and bring her back here," April said.

"How was she going to get home?"

April's eyes welled and overflowed with tears. "She said she'd take the bus. She said it was really convenient and dropped her two blocks from her apartment. She'd done it dozens of times, she said." April dabbed at her eyes. "That was the last time I saw her. Wednesday evening was her last shift until Saturday morning. She wanted Thursday and Friday off to study for exams."

That explained why the kiosk had been dark on Saturday morning, Beans thought. By Saturday morning, Jolene was already dead and mutilated, frozen solid on the snow.

"Did Jolene or the other women mention any customers who were giving them problems, maybe were too attentive?"

April shook her head. "I don't hire ugly girls, as you know, Detective. They fit the uniform, and they do attract attention. And they know how to defuse most situations. As far as I know, none of them complained about any customers hassling them. Any problems recently, Darla?"

Darla shook her head. She had removed the ring from her nostril, probably because her nose was raw from repeated blowing. She was red-eyed and blotchy-faced from crying.

"I got off at about five Wednesday. I followed her to Fireweed Toyota, where she left her car. Fireweed's just about a mile and a half from here. They were gone for the day, so Jo left the key in the drop box and I brought her back so she could do the late shift."

"What time do you normally close?"

"We close at nine. I offered to pick her up, but she said not to bother, she'd take the bus. Oh, hell, if I'd picked her up . . ." Darla held a tissue to her eyes.

"What can you tell me about her friends? What about boyfriends?"

"She dated Daniel for a few months, but then he moved down to Tacoma last year. She'd hang out with Candace, the other barista, and me sometimes, but she's underage and couldn't get into bars. There might be some kids from school she hung with, but I never met them," Darla said. She agreed with April that there had been no customers recently who had set off warning bells.

Beans' next stop was to speak with Jolene's Continuing Education instructors. Her Intro to Psych instructor was a former social worker, a matronly middle-aged woman who said they were all "shocked and horrified" by what had happened to Jolene Nilsson but couldn't offer any more personal information. Jolene rarely missed classes and was an above-average student, attentive and on time with her assignments. If there were problems with fellow students or instructors, she wasn't aware of them.

Her English Comp professor, a retired newspaperwoman, noted that Jolene had missed her final on Thursday evening, which was unusual. Her Psych instructor had also said that she was absent for the final exam on Friday evening.

By the time Beans left the English professor's overheated apartment, it was after eight, and he had run out of gas, literally and figuratively. After fueling up the Explorer, he swung by Jade Garden and ordered takeout Mongolian beef and shrimp fried rice. He had a club soda in the bar while he waited for his dinner, half watching Monday night football blaring from the TV. Jade Garden had passable Chinese food but was better known for the high-octane strength of its drinks. Beans had pulled his brother Herc out of this bar more times than he cared to remember.

His dinner filled the car with the mouthwatering smell of ginger and garlic, reminding him of Frankie Ma. By now, his friend might be thinking a night in jail was preferable to an earful from his mother.

At home, he flicked on the light in the mudroom and was confronted with the yellow plastic litter box, small rocks of litter sprayed around its perimeter. *Oh, right. Archie.*

"*Prow?*" Archie scampered over to him and wove around his legs, voicing his welcome.

"So, how was your afternoon? Destroy anything?" Beans did a walk-through of the house and saw nothing amiss.

"Not bad. Hungry?" He reached into the shopping bag with Archie's accessories and rattled some strong-smelling kibble into his dish.

Archie leaped onto the counter. "*Prow?*" He nuzzled Beans' hand.

Beans picked him up and deposited him on the floor. "House rule number one: No cats on counters." He wagged his finger at Archie, who followed the movement like a conductor's baton. He set the bowl of cat food on the floor next to the water dish. "Bon appétit."

After he and Archie finished their dinners, Beans picked up his cell and called Piper.

It rang three times, then her breathless voice answered, "Havi, I can't talk now."

In the background, he could hear a PA system announcement: "Cleanup on aisle four."

"Where are you?" Beans asked.

"I'm about to start my training here at Starbucks."

"Oh, right, sorry. Quick question."

"Make it fast, okay?"

"Remember the young woman, the barista who was killed?"

"Of course. You keep reminding me."

"Well, she had a cat."

41

"No, Havi." Piper's voice was firm.

"He's a really nice cat," Beans continued, aware of how lame he sounded. On cue, Archie jumped onto the sofa and settled on his lap.

"I'm sure he is. But my new apartment has a no-pets policy. And besides, my roommate is allergic."

"What am I going to do with him?" Beans already knew the answer.

"Run an ad or something. Sorry, I gotta go." Piper rang off.

Archie kneaded Beans' lap and purred.

"Now what?" Beans scratched the cat behind his ears.

7

The next morning, Beans was awakened by a crushing pressure on his chest. He struggled up from the depths of sleep. Was he having a heart attack?

Aspirin! Take aspirin at the first sign of a heart attack!

His eyes sprang open, and his hand groped for the nightstand, where he kept a bottle of Bayer next to his Glock. A huge furry orange face with luminous green eyes loomed into his vision.

"Holy shit!" He leaped out of bed, and the cat flew across the room, snarling and yowling.

"Fucking cat!" He paced around the bed. If he hadn't been having a heart attack before, he was having one now, he thought. Archie glared at him from the closet door, looking very offended, every orange hair standing on end. He hissed.

"Yeah, well, try to see it from my point of view." Beans looked at the digital alarm clock: 4:02 AM.

By the time he had taken a long hot shower and put on a pot of coffee, he was feeling more charitable toward Archie, who wasn't convinced, slinking around the baseboards and giving him a wide berth. Beans opened a can of smelly cat food and spooned it into a dish along with a handful of dry food. Archie ate, still keeping a wary eye on Beans.

While regaining his resting heart rate, Beans realized that the cat probably had woken him up this early because Jolene was an early riser, working the six AM shift at Snow Bunny Baristas.

"You're getting a pass this time, but tomorrow morning, no earlier than five thirty, do you hear me?" He wagged his finger again, and the cat watched it as if he expected it to fly off his hand. To add incentive to his pronouncement, Beans threw a shrimp from his leftover fried rice into Archie's dish. He could actually hear the cat smack his lips.

His workday began with a call to Delbert Hawkins, his barrel-chested good-old-boy contact at Fish and Game's Licenses and Permits Division. Del chuckled when Beans asked him for a list of all the bowhunters in Alaska. He said he could run a list of everyone who had a license or had completed the ADF&G crossbow certification course, but that was "just a piddly-ass fraction of all the guys plunking arrows into anything that moves."

A few phone calls to the Municipality of Anchorage's bus service gave him the names of the drivers who covered the routes Jolene might have taken on Wednesday night. A visit to the bus barn with Jolene's photo confirmed that none of the drivers had seen the young woman get on their bus that night.

Beans returned to the precinct in a funk. The sky had clouded over and promised more snow, adding to his feeling of gloom. To top it off, the coffee he had purchased from Snow Bunny Darla that morning was long gone, and he was forced to buy the tepid dishwater that passed for coffee at the precinct vending machine.

Ed Heller, hands on his ample hips, stared glumly at the brown liquid dripping into the Styrofoam cup.

"This is some nasty shit, but I keep hoping it'll get better," Heller said to no one in particular. He was Beans' height, but with thinning blond hair and the slackening physique of a former athlete. He pulled the cup out and sipped at the brew, wincing. "Nope, just as bad as yesterday."

Beans nodded to Heller, who nodded back.

"What's new on Concepcion?" Beans asked as he dropped quarters into the machine. It couldn't hurt to see if Frankie Ma was in the clear.

"Not much. Frankie's mother's story checks, as you probably guessed. You know, he never was top on my list of suspects anyway—and with Sevy, it's a long list. Just shaking out his bookmaking homies will keep me busy until New Year's."

"Any chance he just took a flight out?"

"Not according to his brother Manny. Sevy was a no-show at their mother's seventieth birthday party. In that family, you'd have to be dead to miss that. The airlines and TSA don't show him flying anywhere. And the Town Car was wiped clean." Heller took a sip of coffee and grimaced. "No surprise that the close-knit Filipino community is tight-lipped around a big old white boy like me. Hey, maybe I should send you to talk to them."

"Just in case you didn't notice, I'm not Filipino, Heller."

"Well, you're more Filipino than I am."

"Yeah, well, whatever." *Obviously, Heller didn't pay attention during diversity and inclusion training.* Beans took a few steps toward the doorway.

"No, really," Heller said. "Wonder why they didn't give you this one? You know, a high-profile case for the lieut's latest golden boy."

Beans stopped. "Golden boy?"

"Yeah, sure—you gotta admit, you're a poster child for equal-opportunity hiring—half Japanese, a quarter Native, Buddhist and all . . ."

"What does being Buddhist have to do with anything?" Despite Beans' best efforts to ignore him, Heller was getting under his skin.

Heller held his hands up. "To me, nothing. But, you know, especially after the sniper thing . . . some of the other guys were wondering—with most Buddhists being pacifists and all—whether they could depend on you to have their back, you know." He shrugged.

Two years ago, a sniper had haunted Anchorage-area highway overpasses, firing at passing motorists with a high-powered rifle. The first casualty was a gravel truck driver, whose fully loaded trailer skidded and overturned, shutting down Glenn Highway for three days. The second casualty was an Elmendorf Air Force Base service member four days later. Despite a fatal head wound, she somehow spun her SUV onto the shoulder, her nine-month-old baby wailing in her car seat, spattered with her mother's blood but otherwise unharmed. The third victim was lucky enough to suffer only cuts to his face and scalp when the shooter shattered his windows and side-view mirror.

It was the holiday season—*why do all the crazies come out at Christmas?* All holiday leaves had been canceled, and it was "all hands on deck" to catch the sniper before he killed again. Beans and his partner at the time, a veteran named Jake Redbird, were one of several teams assigned to patrol overpasses.

Feathery snow began to fall a few minutes after midnight. Redbird was behind the wheel, steering one-handed while he sipped a gas station coffee with the other. Beans saw the sniper first—a dark smudge against the concrete wall, a long black rod extended in front of it.

"There! There!" Beans screamed and pointed.

They screeched to a stop, lights flashing. Beans practically fell out of the car, slipping on the icy asphalt, gun drawn. "Police! Drop your weapon!"

The shooter, hooded and bundled against the cold, seemed unaware of them and the kaleidoscope lights of the police car as he looked through the rifle's sight at the semi hissing down the snow-slick highway toward them.

"Police! Drop your weapon!" Beans repeated, both hands on his Glock.

At the moment the shooter glanced his way, Beans realized that the gunman was not a man but a slender woman, only her dark, haunted eyes visible above her scarf. She turned her rifle toward him.

Their eyes met, then Beans slowly lowered his weapon. Could he reason with this young woman? Take her peacefully? "Okay, let's take it easy."

"What the fuck are you doing?" Redbird screamed, stumbling out of the car, his gun drawn. "Take the shot!"

For what seemed like an eternity, the young woman stared at Beans. Then she shrugged, swung the rifle toward the police car, and fired. A crystalline spiderweb of shattered bulletproof glass spread across the windshield while the car rocked. Redbird shrieked and ducked behind the car door. Beans hit the pavement, his face in the newly fallen snow.

Before either detective could react, the young woman vaulted over the guardrail and fell sixty feet to the frozen highway below.

The semi's horn boomed through the night, its brakes screeched, and the big truck slid to a stop on the other side of the overpass, dragging the shooter along with it.

Redbird put in for retirement the next day, saying it was about the right time, the end of the year and all. But everyone thought the veteran felt he'd almost cashed his chips that night on the overpass, so he was getting out now.

Although cleared of any wrongdoing, Beans' handling of "Overpass Chick," as the dead shooter was called by bone-weary police officers, made him persona non grata among some in the department. Even now, two years after that incident, Heller and his cronies ragged on Beans about his nonviolent approach at every opportunity.

"You seriously still think I would hesitate to fire my weapon if I needed to?" Beans felt heat rise to his face.

"I don't know. Sometimes that moment's hesitation—that's all it takes. Just sayin'." Heller raised his hands again and sauntered out of the coffee room.

Beans took several deep breaths and loosened his death grip on his coffee cup. *Why do I let that dickhead get to me?* Heller's smug comments made the coffee taste even more caustic.

Back at his desk, Beans did a database search on cases involving flowers. Other than a thirty-year-old case where an old man had killed his wife with an axe and buried her in the tundra with a bouquet of chrysanthemums, he came up empty.

Someone had been obsessed enough with Jolene to leave her a flower at both sites. The only person she'd told about the rose at the break-in was Anna Kaminski; none of her Snow Bunny colleagues knew anything about it.

A quick check of his email showed that as promised, Del Hawkins had sent a database of bowhunters. Beans wasn't holding out a lot of hope for a revelation there, but it required review anyway. He grabbed a yellow legal pad and pen and began making a list in no particular order:

1) *Identify possible witnesses: Jolene was last seen Wednesday afternoon at Snow Bunny Baristas. She did not return home; she did not take the bus. Interview possible witnesses at strip mall within sight of the coffee kiosk.*
2) *Daniel Correa: Former boyfriend with ironclad alibi; source for other known associates?*
3) *Murder weapon/MO: Sex crime?*
4) *Rose: Significance? A gift? Remorse? Courtship?*

He decided to go with the option with the best odds, which was to track down the last people to have seen Jolene alive. He grabbed his coat and keys and tossed the lukewarm vending machine coffee in the trash as he headed for the exit.

Snow Bunny Baristas was nestled in a corner of the parking lot of a well-maintained three-business strip mall. Across the street was an undeveloped snow-shrouded piece of property with a faded FOR SALE sign. *No chance of any witnesses or security video from this angle.* Snow the consistency of confectioner's sugar sifted from the sky as Beans pulled up in front of Silla Cleaners.

A burst of steam assaulted him when he entered the small storefront. A serpentine rack of plastic-encased garments wound its way through the narrow space behind the counter. A middle-aged Asian man, who introduced himself as William Choi, emerged from the depths of the hanging garments. He and his short, stocky wife, Alice, had heard about the unfortunate young woman who "made the expensive coffee." They rarely bought coffee at the kiosk ("Who can afford it?" Mrs. Choi said, rolling her eyes), but they had the contract to dry-clean the bunny outfits.

They hadn't seen anything unusual on Wednesday evening, but they always closed at seven, two hours before Snow Bunny Baristas.

The front door of Happy Tails announced its hours as 6:30 AM to 6:00 PM five days a week, so Beans didn't expect any witnesses here either, but it was worth a try. As he entered, clients barked and howled in unison. The grooming salon was warm and humid and smelled like wet dog.

An attractive willowy blonde came out of the back room, wearing a rubber apron and wiping her hands on a towel. "Magnus! Dolly! Big Head! Quiet!" she called to the back room in a voice of authority. The canine vocalizations immediately stopped.

She introduced herself as Jessie Wilkens, then introduced her wife and partner in the business, Charlotte. Charlotte was shorter, with cropped dark hair and a wide welcoming smile.

"We usually get—got—a latte a couple of times a week from Jolene. Sometimes we were her first customers of the day." Jessie shook her head in disbelief. "I can't believe she's gone."

They confirmed that their business hours ended at six; even after cleaning, they locked up no later than seven. None of the baristas had ever mentioned to them any problems with customers. "We've never seen any suspicious types hanging around either," Charlotte said. "Some kids tagged the building and the kiosk a while back, but building management took care of it right away."

"Just so you know, we groom K-9s too, Detective," Jessie said, a twinkle in her eye. "You could drop your dog off before work and pick him up at lunch."

"I don't have a dog. I have a cat." Beans was surprised at how easily that slipped out.

"A police cat?" Charlotte looked confused.

"No, actually, it's Jolene's cat that I'm fostering until I can rehome him. If any of your customers would like a nice, mature, kind-of-fat orange cat missing part of an ear, he's free for the taking." He realized he wasn't doing a great job of selling Archie but thought it better to be accurate in his description.

He left his card and Archie's info with the two women and went next door to the third business in the strip mall, Mega Teriyaki.

The takeout Asian food restaurant specialized in teriyaki plates, yakisoba, and pot stickers and appeared to be run by Latinos. Joyful accordion accompaniment to Spanish lyrics spilled from the kitchen. The spotless ten-table restaurant smelled like grilling chicken, and Beans could hear his stomach growling.

The owner and manager, Ignacio Fuentes, yelled back to the kitchen, much like Jessie had to the dogs, and the volume level of the music dropped a few decibels.

Ignacio ("Call me Iggy") told Beans the baristas often called in a lunch or dinner order, and the three young men in the kitchen drew straws to see who got to trot across the parking lot with the girls' meals.

The three were Iggy's nephews from Sinaloa, and they spoke halting English at best, so Iggy translated when Beans' high school Spanish faltered. Paco, Reynaldo, and Xavier, pleasant and accommodating, were seventeen, nineteen, and twenty-one.

Last Wednesday evening, they'd closed the restaurant early to attend Iggy's daughter's First Communion party. They were eating and drinking within sight of at least fifty relatives until eleven o'clock. All three young men thought the Snow Bunnies were "muy caliente" but had never asked the young women out because none of them had a car or was licensed to drive. They had closed up the restaurant at five that day and didn't open until ten Thursday morning.

Earlier, the property management firm for the strip mall had told Beans they would make security video of the parking lot available, but the representative there noted that the Snow Bunny kiosk was not included in the surveillance—the camera angle included only the areas immediately adjacent to the strip mall businesses.

"Snow Bunny Barista's agreement," a prim female voice on the other end of the line had said, "includes water, power, and other utilities, but security is not part of our agreement with the ownership."

No shit, Beans thought. If it had, Jolene might be alive today. Still, the video was worth taking a look at, and he swung by Far North Properties to pick up the flash drive the woman had grudgingly promised.

8

The tantalizing smell of charred meat enveloped Beans the moment he opened his car door in the parking lot. All day while enduring fruitless interviews with possible witnesses and the sniffing disdain of the woman at the property management company, the one thing he'd looked forward to was this evening's dinner with Piper at Club Paris.

The Anchorage institution had been dishing up huge portions of beef and seafood to Alaskans since the Depression. He rarely deviated from his usual New York steak, medium rare, with a baked potato, but every now and then he succumbed to the siren call of a platterful of king crab legs.

Tonight it was steak. He didn't even need to look at the menu. He was finally making good on the bet he'd lost to Piper on the Apple Cup game over Thanksgiving weekend. It would set him back some bucks, but he loved dining at Club Paris as much as she did, so losing the wager wasn't very painful.

Beans arrived before Piper and settled into a booth with a glass of club soda with lime. He was trying to decide whether to butter a piece of bread when a gentle hand fell on his shoulder.

"Havi?"

He looked up to see Piper, flushed and breathless. He was struck again by how beautiful she was, with their mother's long dark hair and intense brown eyes behind black-framed glasses. His sister was fair skinned like their father, with a dusting of his freckles across her upturned nose. She wore black jeans, a white shirt, and a gray down vest on her petite frame.

"I'm sorry I'm late. I had to cover for someone at work." She slid into the booth next to him and kissed him on the cheek.

"Yeah, yeah," Beans said, feigning irritation, but they both knew he would forgive his little sister anything short of a Class A felony.

Piper threw a napkin onto her lap and tore at the bread in the basket in front of her. "I'm famished."

"No shit," Beans replied. Piper's voracious appetite was legendary. If he ate as much as she did, he would weigh three hundred pounds, but he knew that Piper always tipped the scales at barely a hundred.

"Haven't eaten since this morning."

"Don't fill up on bread," he warned, although he couldn't remember the last time Piper had filled up on anything.

"Jesus, you sound like Mom."

A gravelly voiced server, a matronly waitress named Madge, took their dinner orders.

"So, how's the job?" Beans asked, as Madge shuffled off to refill his club soda.

"I love it!" Piper's eyes danced. "The pay's decent, the bennies are good, and I get all the coffee I can drink."

Beans thought Piper seemed overcaffeinated. She was practically vibrating in her seat. "Uh, yeah, I can tell."

"Seriously, I'm enjoying it. Everyone's great, and I get to meet all kinds of people."

"What kind of people?"

"Don't look so suspicious. Just kids from college, you know. And guess who came by the other day?" Piper's dancing eyes held a secret.

"Ryan Gosling?

"Hell no! I wish!" It was big news that a spy thriller with big stars was being filmed in Alaska.

"Okay, I give up."

"Raisa. *Your* Raisa."

"So, what was *my* Raisa doing there?" He wiped his suddenly sweaty palms on his napkin.

"Buying coffee. Duh, Havi." She rolled her eyes and sipped at her Diet Pepsi as their salads arrived. "Double grande mocha, no whipped."

"So, did you have a chance to talk?"

"A little. I like her," she announced, as they started on their Caesar salads, crisp and garlicky. "I don't know what went on between the two of you, but you clearly screwed up."

"Did she say that?" The crouton he had been jabbing at shot across the table, coming to rest against the saltshaker. He picked it up and returned it to his plate.

"Of course not."

Madge interrupted their conversation with their entrées. Beans had ordered his usual steak, done to perfection; Piper, the king crab legs. They tucked into their food with silent enthusiasm.

She dipped a long strand of crabmeat in melted butter. "So, did you tell her you loved her?"

"What?" Beans was caught off guard.

Piper dabbed at her mouth with a corner of her napkin, incongruously dainty for someone who could put away such large volumes of food so quickly.

"You heard me. Before you became incommunicado, did you say you loved her?"

Did it come down to that? Did I say I loved her? Sure, that day at her father's house in Homer. Didn't I?

"Maybe. I don't remember."

Piper sat back in the booth and sighed. "If you don't remember, then you didn't say it. How come I know this and you don't?"

"I don't know. I'm an idiot."

"Could be. Or you're just not genetically predisposed. That Y chromosome. Whatever. Did you break her heart?"

Beans felt like he was being interrogated by a colleague. "No. I mean, not intentionally. I cared about her. Still care about her. We just drifted apart."

"Well, that's a crock of shit."

He changed the subject, asking about Piper's college courses, and they continued their meals in companionable conversation. Piper was studying for an MBA, paying her way with student loans and grants and now her job at Starbucks.

It occurred to him, as he watched Piper inhale her third slice of bread, that Raisa's father, Zachary Ingalls, was a hunter of statewide renown, an expert in bowhunting. Beans could call Raisa with the honest intention of getting her father's contact information.

And he could use all the help he could get. Fish and Game records aside, there was no end of places to mine for bowhunters in Alaska. The state teemed with subsistence hunters, rabid out-doorsmen, survivalists, and white separatist militias. Zach Ingalls might be able to narrow the field for him.

Raisa's emailed report on the scat from the area around Jolene's body had been brief and professional. The wolf and fox scat did not contain any human remains, which indicated only that the scavengers hadn't remained at the site long enough for the human tissue to digest. There was no reason to believe that the condition of the body was due to any cause other than scaven-ger activity.

"Have you talked with Herc lately?" Piper interrupted his thoughts. Hercules was their older brother, a lovable alcoholic like their father, whose frequent plunges off the wagon made it impos-sible for him to keep a job longer than a few months. When sober, Herc was an expert mariner, having skippered and crewed on fish-ing boats all over Alaska. He could also operate heavy machinery and fix just about anything when his drinking didn't interfere.

"Not since Halloween. Is he behaving himself?"

"Yeah, for a change. Mindy got him a job at DOT, spreading sand and running a plow. Temporary, but he's hoping it will last until herring season. Maybe it'll develop into something more permanent, if he stays off the booze."

Piper smiled in contentment and rubbed her tummy. Of the plateful of king crab legs, mound of rice pilaf, and steamed vege-tables, the only thing left was a pile of empty crab shells and a small ramekin that held melted butter.

"Dessert?" She flashed him a brilliant smile.

Beans had eaten a Caesar salad, a slab of steak, and a baked potato with the works, and he was full to bursting. He sipped on a cup of decaf coffee while he watched Piper devour a good-sized crème brûlée.

"So, what about your love life, sis? Anybody I need to do background checks on?"

"Nah, I got no time for that these days. I did go out a couple of times with a guy from my Statistics class, just to be nice. He's very sweet, but kind of, you know, wispy."

"Wispy?" He'd never heard a man described this way.

"Very slight. Insubstantial. And he ate like a chickadee."

Compared to Piper, Beans thought, most lumberjacks ate like birds.

She licked her spoon and set it beside the empty crème brûlée bowl with a satisfied smile. "Thanks, Havi. I've been looking forward to this for weeks."

"Me too, sweetie."

As he and Piper left the restaurant, fat wet flakes of snow drifted in front of the red blinking marquee shaped like the Eiffel Tower. The bare trees that lined the streets were festooned with bright red-and-white fairy lights. Piper slipped her hand through his arm as he walked her to her car.

"See you at Mom's for Christmas?" she asked as she started the old Mazda hatchback that had once belonged to Beans.

"I'll be there."

As he waved and watched her drive away, he realized that Jolene Nilsson had been cremated today. In December, the ground was too frozen to receive her simple metal urn, which would sit on the Nilssons' mantel until spring breakup. Then Jolene's family would inter her in the small graveyard on the tundra next to her maternal grandparents.

The meal Beans had just enjoyed couldn't keep the chill away as he trudged back to the Explorer. He turned on the heater full blast and switched on the windshield wipers. The reflection of garish crimson Christmas lights splattered across his windshield, suddenly looking to him like smeared entrails.

9

Zachary Ingalls' "cabin" was a sprawling log structure on ten wooded acres outside of Homer. The split-level home over-looked the frost-shrouded Homer Spit, the home port for much of the area's commercial and charter fishing fleet. The site offered sweeping views of Kachemak Bay, mist rising like a white veil from its frozen surface. Zach Ingalls liked to say with a derisive chuckle that on a clear day, he could see Russia.

But not today. The weather had turned even colder, and a biting wind howled through the leafless trees. The radio predicted seven to nine inches of new snow overnight, and Beans wanted to be home well before then. The snow tires on the Explorer crunched and bit on the recently plowed driveway to the Ingalls house. Beans had been to the Ingalls compound one other time, a few years ago on a hot, humid August day when the mosquitoes and no-see-ums were out for blood. Zach Ingalls and Raisa's "Second Stepmother" Oksana had been hosting their annual Caribou and Salmon Bake, an event to which all the "Who's Who" of the Alaskan hunting community had been invited.

Beans had considered it a milestone in their relationship that Raisa brought him to be introduced to "the folks." Raisa's mother had died in a car accident when she was a teenager, after which her father married the very young "First Stepmother," Svetlana, a union that lasted five years. After the divorce and Svetlana's retreat to Palm Desert, Zach Ingalls married the even younger Oksana.

Zach Ingalls was a "man's man," a fifth-generation Alaskan whose French-Canadian forefather had trapped and hunted his way from the Southeast panhandle to the Yukon River. He organized high-end hunting and fishing excursions that catered to pampered city clients—and was very successful at it. Photos on his website showed Zach as tall and sturdy, with a full head of silver hair and a beard to match—almost a cliché.

That sticky August afternoon, many of his wealthy customers had been in attendance, slathering on DEET and downing Crown Royal on the rocks. They had spilled out onto the large wrap-around deck, raising their drunken voices over the earsplitting country music that thundered from the speakers mounted under the eaves.

Ingalls had hired a valet service to park his guests' luxury SUVs and sedans, but there was no way Beans was going to let a pimply faced teenager get behind the wheel of his then-almost-new Explorer.

He turned to Raisa. "Why don't you get out here, and I'll park down the hill. I'll meet you at the house."

"Are you sure?" Raisa looked worried. "I don't mind walking."

"Not in those shoes," he said, nodding at her feet. She looked fresh and pretty that day in a pale-green sundress and strappy sandals, her dark curly hair pulled back off her neck. "Go on," he said.

She hesitated for a moment, then smiled and laid a cool hand on his cheek and nodded. "I'll wait for you on the front porch."

By the time he had parked a quarter mile away and trudged up the hill to the house, his previously crisp cotton shirt was damp and wilted and a swarm of noisy mosquitoes circled his head.

Raisa was on the front porch, having an animated discussion with a balding Asian man with a suit jacket draped over his arm. When she saw Beans, she broke off her conversation and bounded down the stairs to him.

"Oh, thank God you're here," she said, her lips next to his ear. "Between the Chinese and the Korean guests, I can't understand a single word anybody's saying. Come on." She took his hand. "Let me introduce you to Daddy."

They found Zach Ingalls holding court at his archery range in the large clearing behind the house. Wearing a blinding-white ExOfficio shirt and pressed jeans, he was lecturing a small circle of rapt guests on the finer points of crossbow hunting. He casually aimed and released an arrow, which zinged through the air thirty yards and embedded itself in the red center of the straw target. The guests murmured appreciatively.

Ingalls lifted his steely-blue eyes from his apparently adoring guests and caught sight of Raisa. His face broke into a wide grin, showing brilliant white teeth. "There's my girl!" He opened his arms wide and embraced her. "Folks, this is my lovely daughter, Raisa. When she was thirteen, she took down a ten-point buck with my old Winchester."

"Oh, Daddy," Raisa said, blushing. "That was ages ago."

"It sure was." He gripped her to his side. "And now, you count them rather than shoot them? Despite my best efforts, folks, my own flesh and blood has become a tree-hugging researcher for Fish and Game." The surrounding guests gave a sympathetic groan.

Ingalls gripped Raisa harder, and Beans could tell she was struggling to free herself. He found himself moving in to protect her, an involuntary reflex. Whether Ingalls noticed the movement or not, he released his daughter. Raisa's eyes were flashing, an angry retort about to escape her lips, when Ingalls' attention turned to Beans.

"And you must be the cop boyfriend?"

"Guilty as charged." Beans extended his hand. "DeHavilland Beans, Mr. Ingalls. It's nice to meet you."

He squinted at Beans. "DeHavilland? Like the plane?" Ingalls grasped his hand in an iron grip.

Beans shrugged. He and three of his siblings—Hercules, Piper, and Otter—had all been named after aircraft, while Lindbergh, the oldest, had been named after the famed aviator. "What can I say? Dad was a bush pilot. I go by Beans."

"Beans it is, then. Call me Zach, please. Has my daughter supplied you with a suitable beverage?"

Beans looked down at the ice cubes and lemonade in his red plastic cup. "She's the perfect hostess."

"That's my gal!" Ingalls put one arm around his daughter and the other around Beans, who couldn't help but notice that Ingalls was at least three inches taller than he was. "Let's go inside. The mosquitoes are fearsome today."

Beans and Raisa sat side by side on a leather sofa in the relative cool of the den with the glassy eyes of stuffed wildlife staring down at them—bighorn sheep, elk, antelope, a terrified-looking bobcat. A brown bear rug the size of a pool table lay grimacing on

63

the stone floor. Meanwhile, Ingalls quizzed Beans on his job, his family, and his intentions with his daughter.

Beans answered Ingalls' questions without hesitation. He noticed Raisa's face flush a becoming pink when he told her father he loved her. Wait, had he said this to her yet? Had he breached some unwritten protocol by not saying it to her first? His palms began to sweat.

"Good, good," Ingalls said, and took a long swig from his bottle of Stella Artois. "Because she doesn't bring just anyone home to meet dear old Dad. You must be special."

"I think Raisa's pretty special," Beans said.

Ingalls smiled at his daughter. "He's pretty smooth for a cop."

Beans felt Raisa's hand touch his, and he curled his fingers around hers, thinking he couldn't have screwed up too badly.

They were interrupted by Raisa's Second Stepmother Oksana, a stunning blonde barely older than Raisa, wearing skintight white leather pants and high heels. She gave Raisa a perfunctory peck on the cheek and Beans' hand a limp shake.

"Excuse me for interrupting family time," she said in heavily accented English. "But Zacky, the Chinese buyers are getting ready to leave."

Ingalls shot his wife a warning glance. "You mean *clients*, baby. They're leaving? We haven't even put the salmon on the grill yet. Are the Koreans going too?"

Oksana pursed her lips in a pretty red pout. "You know I cannot tell them apart, Zacky."

In retrospect, Beans thought this encounter should have been an indicator of what was to come for Zach Ingalls. But at the time, he thought it was just Oksana's uncertainty with the English language that had caused her to refer to the Asian guests as "buyers."

Ingalls stood and downed the rest of his beer. "I gotta catch these guys before they take off. Let's continue this a little later. Meanwhile, I'm sure my girl will take care of you." He patted Beans on the shoulder as he strode toward the door.

They never talked again that afternoon. Beans enjoyed an excellent venison steak and barbecued salmon and chatted with some of the other guests, many of whom were customers of Ingalls' Alaskan Excursions.

The contrast between Ingalls' and Jimmy Beans' operations couldn't have been more stark. Ingalls' service was Abercrombie & Kent to his late father's budget "fly and shoot" excursions. With Jimmy Beans' charters, the pilot had almost always been drunk, adding to the sheer thrill and terror of his customers' experience.

When Beans was sure he couldn't eat another bite, Raisa took him by the hand and led him down an access road to an immaculate metal building. Here Ingalls housed his hunting dogs—two yellow Labrador retrievers, two German shorthaired pointers, and three black-and-white spitz-like dogs with heavy coats. The dogs yipped and barked in a happy chorus, wagging their tails and leaping against the chain-link kennels in greeting.

One of the dogs had recently whelped and was nursing a litter of four mewling black-and-white pups—two males and two females. Raisa picked up the smallest puppy, a pink ribbon encircling its neck, and held it in the crook of her arm like an infant.

"Dad promised her to me. Isn't she beautiful? I'm taking her as soon as she's weaned."

"Is she a sled dog, then?"

"Oh no," she said, handing the pup to Beans. "She's a Karelian bear dog, a great breed for hunting big game. They are fearless.

I'm naming her Willow." She picked up one of the other puppies, a larger male.

"Will your dad sell the other puppies?" he asked. Willow began gnawing on one of his shirt buttons.

"I don't think so. He's going to train them to hunt."

"Bear?"

"Yeah, bear, moose, any other large game. Like I said, these dogs are fearless."

Beans held the pup to his face, and she gave his nose a tentative lick. It was hard to think of this little pup with her soulful eyes and milky breath as an aggressive hunter. "Your dad seems to have done very well with his hunting expedition business."

Raisa nodded. "Zachary Ingalls doesn't do anything halfway. Nothing but the best."

"For his daughter too." The puppy tucked her head into his shirt.

She blushed again. He liked this look on her, a little rise of color to her cheeks like the slightest sunburn.

"I'm sorry about the third degree back there. He hasn't liked any of the guys I've brought home."

"How many have there been?" The puppy had managed to wedge half of its chubby body into his shirt.

"Two or three. Jealous?"

"Just curious. Help me out here?" Willow the puppy was now totally inside Beans' shirt. He felt her tiny claws scratching his skin.

Raisa laughed. "She likes you."

As she reached into his shirt to extricate the puppy, her soft hands stroked his chest. Beans had taken the opportunity to steal a kiss in the coolness of the kennel, the warm puppy pressed between them.

Happier times, Beans thought as he stomped his feet to clear the snow from his boots. That had been at least a year before a Fish and Game sting operation caught Zach Ingalls selling bear gallbladders to the Asian black market. According to the F&G rumor mill, only by calling in some valuable markers had Ingalls been able to avoid jail time.

A furry black-and-white blur leaped onto the porch, barking thunderously and wagging his curled tail like a fluttering fan. Startled at first, Beans held out his hand, and the Karelian bear dog gave it an enthusiastic lick.

This was likely going to be the heartiest welcome he could expect from the Ingalls family. When he'd called Raisa earlier to get her father's contact information, Beans had hemmed and hawed and finally spit out what he was after. Raisa coolly and professionally agreed to pass on the message. The phone conversation he had with Zach Ingalls was polite but brief, and Ingalls had reluctantly agreed to see Beans the next afternoon.

Second Stepmother Oksana opened the door in a fur-lined hoodie and skintight black leather pants.

"Thor! You go away!" she scolded the dog, who scampered off around the side of the house. "Oh, the policeman," she said, pursing her red lips. "Come in and I will get Zacky for you. Coffee?"

He accepted gratefully, and she led him into the same study he'd sat in with Raisa, today with a fire crackling in the river-rock fireplace. It might be his imagination, but there seemed to be more stuffed and mounted trophies than before—including some kind of African antelope and a huge moose head.

Oksana entered with a carafe and mug on a silver tray, along with a matching sugar-and-cream service. Zach Ingalls, already carrying a coffee mug, followed her.

He had aged very little in the few years since Beans had last seen him. His shock of silver hair was still full and neat, his back straight, his handshake just as bone-crushing.

"Something stronger than coffee, Detective?" Ingalls asked.

"No, thanks. Coffee is fine." Beans noted that he was *Detective* now and not *Beans*.

Ingalls motioned for him to sit. "Working on a case, you say? How can I help?"

Right to business. No small talk about Raisa or the weather. No chummy conversation about how Ingalls had somehow avoided serious prison time after he was caught with a half dozen coolers of bear organs destined for Asia. No confidences exchanged on whose palms he'd had to grease to escape with only a slap on the wrist. Of course not.

Beans filled him in on the murder of Jolene Nilsson, but without many forensic details.

"We think she may have been killed with an arrow, possibly from a compound or crossbow."

Beans showed him photo enlargements of the wounds from Jolene's body. "We think the bolt entered the body with enough force to break at least one rib and punch through the skin on her back."

Ingalls gave a low whistle and took a close look at the photos. "Did you find the arrowpoint?"

Beans shook his head. "It either passed through or was pulled back through the body, along with the shaft."

Ingalls stood. "Come with me."

He led Beans down the snow-crusted access road to a locked metal barn next to the kennels, where he stored equipment and supplies for his hunting expeditions. Beans was awestruck by the extent and variety of bows, arrows, and firearms lining the shelves and walls. On the floor, four snow machines and a fleet of small ATVs sat under protective covers. An aluminum riverboat on a trailer was parked near the roll-up doors. Three large stainless-steel commercial freezers stood against the far wall, secured with chains and padlocks.

Ingalls pulled several arrows from a display. "Could have been any one of these bolts, I'm thinking. Bolts, unlike traditional arrows, don't have stabilizing vanes near the back."

Beans nodded. He had been on enough of Jimmy Beans' tundra hunts to know the difference. "Judging from the wound, I'm guessing a fixed or expandable broadhead?"

"Looks that way." Ingalls pointed to several lethal-looking tips on the bolts. "You're welcome to borrow these if you think it would help." He pulled several bolts and arrowheads off his wall display, then selected a composition bow and crossbow off the display racks as well.

Beans accepted with a nod of thanks. Back in the warmth of the den, he wrote out a receipt for the bolts, broadheads, and bows. "And please—details of the murder weapon are being held back from the public for now. I'd appreciate you keeping this in the strictest confidence."

Ingalls nodded. "I think I can keep a secret, Detective."

I bet you can. As he packed the borrowed gear into a duffel bag stenciled with *Ingalls' Alaskan Excursions*, Beans said, "With your contacts in the hunting community, I was hoping that you could steer me in the right direction—you know, names and contacts for hunting clubs, blogs, or mailing lists for bowhunting enthusiasts?"

Ingalls helped himself to a cup of coffee from the carafe after Beans declined.

"Well, Detective, this is Alaska, after all. There are probably thousands of bowhunters out here, many flying under the radar."

"I figured as much. But I'd like your read on where to start. There's the state info, but like you say, here in Alaska, many hunters operate off the grid. And, if this suspect happens to be hunting humans like game—well, we're looking for a very specific kind of killer."

"A predator."

Beans nodded.

Ingalls stared at Beans for a few seconds, then shrugged and sipped at his coffee. "You could start with customers and members of the local archery ranges—there are at least a half dozen in the area. You could contact local and online vendors of archery supplies, but that would be overkill. Not sure how cooperative any of these folks would be without a subpoena, though.

"Take my client list, for example," Ingalls continued. "My people value their privacy. I'm afraid it would take a court order to see my list." Ingalls looked smug as he spooned sugar into his coffee.

Beans began to wonder just who was on this list. "We're looking for the savage murderer of a young woman. We'll do what it takes."

"My clients would be a waste of your time," Ingalls said. "Or for that matter, the same goes for anyone who hunts legally in Alaska."

Beans suspected that Ingalls was probably right but felt his patience wearing thin. Zach Ingalls had been cooperative with his expertise on weaponry, but the big man's Great White Hunter act annoyed Beans. The hunting lodge habitat, the trophy wife, the museum of taxidermy, how every reference to Raisa began with "my" as if he owned her—all of it irked him.

Ingalls seemed not to notice and settled into his office chair. "Let me see what I can do." He flicked his laptop computer to life, clicked a few keys, and hit print. As the laser printer in the corner of the room hummed and emitted a sheet of paper, he said, "I don't think this will do you much good, but here's a partial list of the archery ranges and clubs in the area. Like I said, this is a partial list. God knows how many others are around." He handed it to Beans.

"Okay, thanks. This is a good start." Beans zipped the piece of paper into the duffel and rose to leave.

Ingalls stopped him with a hand to his arm and demanded, "I have to know. You and Raisa . . . ?" His blue eyes narrowed.

Beans tried to keep his voice even when he said, "And I have to know—you and the bear guts?"

Anger flared across Ingalls' face, then settled to a smolder. "Okay, I deserved that. None of my goddamn business. But indulge a concerned father, okay?" He walked around the desk to extend his hand to Beans. "She's my only daughter, and I admit I'm very protective of her. I'm sure you understand."

"Don't worry. We only see each other professionally." Beans was disturbed by how sad and final that sounded.

A look of relief crossed Ingalls' weatherworn face. He throttled Beans' hand with his own and saw him to the door, patting him on the shoulder as he had before. Beans fought the urge to turn around to see if Ingalls had anything in his hand. Even without his arsenal of weapons, it seemed dangerous to turn one's back to him.

"And about the other thing." Ingalls held his hands up in sur-render. "That was over a year ago. I've paid my dues."

Innocent act aside, Beans suspected Ingalls was still involved in some form of poaching. Chained and locked freezers in the storage building? *That's a lot of bait, and it's not even fishing season.*

The Karelian bear dog accompanied Beans to the Explorer. After scratching Thor behind his soft ears, he started the car and drove slowly down the driveway. When he looked in the rearview mirror, the black-and-white dog watched him from the shadows, almost hidden in the darkening snow.

10

December 22

The fucking "Waltz of the Snowflakes"—that's the melody jangling through her brain when she opens her eyes. She can't see a thing because of the blindfold, but a faint dull light tells her it's daytime.

She hates all the numbers in *The Nutcracker*. She's been in every Anchorage Ballet production of that holiday standard since she was twelve. At least "Waltz of the Snowflakes" is a number she has a lead in this time, as the Snow Queen. *My God, why do I even care?* She tries to move her legs, but can't. She is lying on her side on a smelly cot with her arms and legs tied. Panic rises like bile in her throat, but she tries to concentrate. *What the fuck happened?*

She remembers buying cigarettes at the Kwik-E-Mart, and Kamal behind the counter flirting with her again. He's kind of cute, but too old. She got the keys to the bathroom, then dropped them in the snow. *Fuck.* It was dark back there; Kamal needed to get some lights. She found the keys and brushed the snow off with her gloves.

"Hey." A voice behind her.

She jumped. "Oh, hi."

"Sorry, I didn't mean to startle you."

"No, it's just—" Then a gloved hand came over her nose and mouth, and everything went black.

Now, on a tiny stage in a corner of her brain, the orchestra is swelling with the "Waltz of the Flowers," another number she despises. She's pirouetting on a mirrored floor like the little plastic figures in her music boxes. Sam Holder, that asshole, stands in the wings, clapping and blowing kisses, and shows her a blue-velvet-lined box with a ginormous diamond ring in it. She almost laughs, but it turns into a sob. *As if.*

Jesus, I must be hallucinating. She tries to focus.

Her head swims as she swings her legs to the floor and lifts her torso into a seated position. *What kind of date-rape shit did he give me?* She still can't see a damn thing but hears heavy footsteps in the snow. And someone humming—not "Waltz of the Flowers," thank God.

Something she should be trying to remember tickles at the base of her skull, but she's still moving through a thick mental fog.

Think, Toni, who was it? Someone you know. Think. The smokes fell to the snow. What happened to her backpack, her phone? How long has she been out? She hears a door squeak open, and a biting wind blows in. It brings back a faded memory of making snow angels in the front yard with her mother, before the years of battling that bastard thief cancer that robbed them all.

Another memory swims into focus—the bouquet of roses that hospice said was okay to leave in her mother's room near the windows. They said that there the scent wouldn't irritate her, but she could still see them from her bed. Then later her father, the burly oil-field worker, nearly doubled over in grief, tossed the withered blooms into the trash.

She smells them still, in this room, brought in with the frigid air. Someone stands in front of her, smelling of cheap aftershave, sweat, and roses.

"Sitting up, are we?"

The voice is so familiar. *Who is he?* Her heart pounds in her chest. Her angry words are absorbed by the duct tape covering her mouth.

"Come along, it's time." He throws her over his shoulder without even grunting. She kicks and bucks, but he holds her fast. "Shit, you're a lively one."

The freezing air is like a slap against her bare legs. *I'm going to die. He's going to kill me.* She takes some comfort in her mother's ancient belief that she will be reborn in the rivers, the wind, the black bear, the hawk. She sobs behind the duct tape as she curls her fingers into talons.

Somehow she engages her well-toned core, swings her bound hands around, and swipes at him. The tips of her French mani-cure rip off, and pain zings through her fingers as she tears through his flesh.

"Ow! Son of a bitch!" He throws her onto the frozen ground.

Her head spins, and she almost vomits behind the duct tape. She scrambles to stand but can't gain purchase with her bare feet, bound with plastic ties at the ankles. He breathes hard, some-where above her. Something warm drips on her face, and she tries to shake it off. *His blood?* She screams, but it just reverberates against the duct tape.

She kicks at him with her bound feet and connects with his shins at least once.

"Goddamn, you're like a fucking mule."

Then, a bone-crunching blow to the side of her head, and she is the Snow Queen, spinning, spinning, to the "Waltz of the Snowflakes" until the curtain falls like endless night.

11

Beans cradled his chin in his cupped hand and gazed at the grainy surveillance video playing in jerky rhythm on his laptop screen. Far North Properties' footage from the day of Jolene's abduction yielded nothing even vaguely interesting.

As the unfriendly woman at the strip mall's property management firm had said, the camera angles did not include the Snow Bunny Barista kiosk or drive-through area. He yawned and fast-forwarded through yet another viewing of the day's footage, watching customers hop and twitch into their cars in comic double time through the falling snow.

SUVs, pickup trucks, and snow plows scraping the residue of the day's precipitation from the blacktop swerved in and out of view. Sweater-clad dogs at the ends of leashes gamboled in and out of Happy Tails, and patrons bundled in hats and scarves carried plastic bags of takeout from Mega Teriyaki.

He stifled another yawn. This was going nowhere. Even with high-tech enhancement, he probably wouldn't be able to get even partial plate numbers on this poor-quality video. He aimed a crumpled wad of yellow legal paper toward the plastic wastebasket beside Heller's desk. It banked off the pale-gray steel, bounced off the rim, and fell to the floor.

Heller glanced up from the file he was reading. "Give it up. There's a reason only a couple of Japanese players have made it to the NBA."

And even fewer fat middle-aged white guys. Beans rubbed his eyes. "I'm going blind watching these security videos, and I still don't have a single suspect."

"I got a different problem. Sevy had his sticky fingers in a shitload of illegal activity. I got suspects up the yin-yang." Heller said this with a smirk. Beans thought he looked like the cat who swallowed the canary, smug that his Japanese-Native-Buddhist golden-boy colleague's case appeared to be stalling out.

Beans sighed. *Or maybe I'm just projecting my own frustrations on Heller.* As Zach Ingalls had predicted, damn him, membership records of the local archery ranges and bowhunter databases were either sadly outdated or overkill, including nine-year-olds who had requested class schedules.

On the positive side, Chuckie had used the weaponry Beans had borrowed from Ingalls to shoot a pig carcass full of arrows and proclaimed the exit wounds a match to Jolene's. Striations on Jolene's broken rib matched the broadhead as well. At least they knew what kind of weapon had killed her.

Beans had another online interview with Jolene's old boyfriend, Daniel Correa, which netted him nothing but a splitting headache. Daniel knew nothing about hunting, with either a gun or a bow, and was a vegan. If Jolene knew anything about bowhunting or knew any bowhunters, she'd never mentioned it to him. In fact, other than her colleagues at the coffee kiosk, she had mentioned no other friends or acquaintances to Daniel.

Beans began to think that Daniel might not have been very involved in Jolene's life at all, and felt a pang of sympathy for her. At this interview, unlike his earlier one, the young man seemed annoyed by the detective's intrusion in his life. Beans noticed photos of Daniel with his arms around a young blond woman tacked up on the wall behind him.

Efforts to locate Jolene's cell phone were fruitless. Her iPhone's last known location was the Snow Bunny Baristas kiosk on her last day of work there.

Christmas was only two days away—and that holiday was the one thing that Beans looked forward to. He'd had to miss last year's festivities in Galena, as he was in the middle of an active investigation at the time. Jolene's case, by contrast, was quickly going cold.

He convinced himself that he could spare a couple of days and fly up to Galena to spend Christmas with his mother, Mari, and Piper and his little brother, Otter. Big brother Herc, he was quite sure, would be spending the holidays this year with his two children in Sitka, where they lived with his ex-wife. Beans' plan was to fly up to Galena on Christmas Eve, then back down to Anchorage the day after. He felt uneasy leaving town with Heller on call, but Ed had given his trademark shrug and conceded that it was his turn, since Beans had covered Thanksgiving, and what, didn't Beans trust him?

He turned his attention back to the surveillance video, watching customers carry plastic-wrapped dry cleaning to their cars, until his cell phone yipped on his desk.

"Oh, Havi!" Piper's voice was close to tears.

His heart leapt to his throat. "What is it, Piper? Are you okay?"

"No, my life sucks." She sniffed. "For the first time, I'm going to miss Christmas at Mom's!"

"Oh sweetie, what happened?" Christmas wouldn't be the same without Piper there.

"I can't get time off from my stupid barista job!"

"What? Seriously?"

"I'm the new hire, so I am totally screwed."

"I'm sorry, sis. Tell you what. I'll cancel my reservations, and we can spend Christmas here together."

"Are you kidding?" Piper's voice was incredulous. "Mom would shit a cow if at least one of us didn't make it home for Christmas!"

She was right there, even with the mixed idioms. Mari was very serious about celebrating the season with her family and expected as many of her children as possible to attend the festivities in Galena.

"Have you told Mom?"

"Yeah. She's majorly bummed, but she gets that I need the job." She blew her nose. "But I can feed your cat while you're gone."

He had forgotten about Archie. "That would be great."

In a small voice, she asked, "Can I watch Disney?"

"Of course. And Hulu too."

"I'll even take you to the airport."

"I'm really sorry you won't be there, sis." He saw another call coming through on his cell. "My flight leaves at noon tomorrow. Come on over at about nine for breakfast, and I'll give you your present. Gotta go. See you tomorrow."

He hung up with Piper and picked up the waiting call.

Carmen Fernandez, the senior investigator in Missing Persons, said, "Merry Christmas, Beans."

He pictured Carmen, a comfortably round middle-aged Latina with a warm laugh, and answered, "Same to you, Fernandez."

"I wish I had some glad tidings. You're still working the barista case, right?"

"Yeah, unfortunately."

She hesitated a moment. "This just came through. Another girl has been reported missing."

"Oh shit."

Merry fucking Christmas to me.

"Yeah. Her name is Antoinette Morelli, goes by Toni. She works at Arctic Foxes Espresso. You can guess the employee attire there."

"I think so. How long has she been missing?"

"About thirty-six hours now, but it doesn't look good. Roommate filed the report. Toni was supposed to work Monday morning but didn't show. She's in the *Nutcracker* production at the ballet. She was a no-show for a performance, which she has never done before, not without letting somebody know."

"Give me her vitals, will you?"

Fernandez recited a description of Toni Morelli—twenty-four years old, blond, blue eyed, five eight, about one hundred and twenty pounds—about as unlike Jolene Nilsson as she could get, Beans thought. Fernandez said she would email her file.

"I'm still hoping that she'll turn up. But I've been doing this long enough now—I doubt it."

He hung up and turned half his attention to the fuzzy surveillance footage again. Plows, pickups, robotic people bundled against the cold. It kept circling in an endless loop, it seemed. No end in sight, no resolution to the murder, just him spinning, like Archie chasing his tail.

Enough. He threw down his pen and clicked off his laptop. He shoved it into its case and zipped it closed. "Have a merry Christmas, Heller."

"Yeah, you too." Heller pointed a gloved finger at him and smiled. "Hey, do Buddhists celebrate Christmas?"

Beans rolled his eyes. "And in the spirit of mindfulness and gratitude, thank you for covering."

"No problem. And besides, you'll owe me one." He ambled out the door, whistling a Christmas tune between his teeth.

Knowing Heller, he would call in his marker the next time a half-rotted floater was fished out of Cook Inlet. Beans rubbed the back of his neck and closed his eyes. White roses, blue velvet, broadhead arrows, and Jolene's lifeless eyes swirled through the darkness like unholy angels. An hour on the stationary bike with the Dalai Lama—that's what he needed to clear his head.

12

The Yukon River village of Galena appeared suddenly, like a mirage in the vast white desert of frozen tundra. Except for a faint pink blush at the horizon, the sun would never fully rise today. Lights from the houses below twinkled like jewels cast onto the snow. The Cessna Grand Caravan made a lazy turn and aligned itself with the runway at the Edward J. Pitka Sr. Airport.

Beans had seen his village from the air countless times, but he was always awed by its stark simple beauty. His younger brother Otter, who had caught an early-morning flight from Juneau to Anchorage and boarded the same flight to Galena, did not share his sentiments.

Otter peered out the window. "Well, folks, we are making our final approach to Deer Scrotum, Alaska."

"Come on, you have to admit you get nostalgic when you see the lights of home."

Otter stared at him in disbelief from under dark bangs. "Only thing that makes me nostalgic is Mom's makizushi and gooseberry pie."

Otter had a disdainful pseudo-sophisticate attitude that Beans sometimes found funny and other times annoying as hell.

Today, because it was Christmas Eve, he did not rise to the bait. He smiled and punched his little brother on the arm, a little harder than he intended.

Otter winced and rubbed at his arm. "Ow, that hurt, yo."

Beans' lanky twenty-three-year-old brother had landed what he considered the jackpot of all jobs for a kid right out of college—a member of the IT staff for the governor's office in Juneau. He proudly stated that he had twice unfrozen the lieutenant governor's laptop and detected a harmful virus in the state's network.

"I mean, consider the source, but they think I'm a hot-shit genius at the state capitol," Otter said, tossing his bangs out of his eyes.

Their mother Mari was there to meet the plane, hopping up and down with excitement, her long braid whipping against her muskrat collar. Beans loved his mother's childlike glee at pretty much everything, but especially at seeing her children. She wrapped them in warm hugs and kissed them on both cheeks. She hustled them into the old Chevy pickup idling next to the log building that served as the passenger terminal.

"Quick, get in. I got pies in the oven."

Beans climbed into the passenger seat, and Otter wedged himself into the back seat with the bags. Beans studied his mother as she leaned forward to clear condensation from the windshield. In her late fifties now, Mari looked much younger, her long black hair barely peppered with gray, only faint tracks of crow's feet near her eyes.

Mari Yamane had come to Galena as a fresh-faced twenty-two-year-old University of Washington graduate. Her one-year contract to teach at the village school was supposed to be an adventure, a lark—after which she was expected to return home to Fremont, in the San Francisco Bay area. Like most Japanese American parents, her folks expected her to establish a career, marry well, and settle down near them—the conventional path Mari's older brother and sister had followed. Instead, she married the wild Irish Athabascan bush pilot Jimmy Beans, who gave her five children—the eldest named after an aviator and the rest named after planes—and settled in Galena.

To her parents' consternation, Mari totally embraced the lifestyle and the culture of her husband's Yukon River hometown. Two generations of Galena children knew "Miss Mari," first as their teacher, then later as the school librarian, a job she loved and that had sustained the family after her husband's death.

Beans and his siblings left Galena for jobs or university at their earliest opportunity, but their mother stayed on. On several occasions, Beans had tried to convince her to move to Anchorage to be closer to her children and grandchildren, or even to the Lower 48, to be near her siblings and aging parents. She always declined, quietly and firmly: "No, I'm just not ready, Havi." Like Piper, Mari was usually cheerful and upbeat, so Beans knew from her tone of voice and the set of her jaw that the subject was closed.

The truck chugged to a stop in front of the family's three-bedroom bungalow, eaves blinking with multicolored Christmas lights. Inside, the house was filled with the mouthwatering aroma of baking pies and ptarmigan stew.

"Gooseberry and blueberry, but not until tomorrow." Mari slapped Otter's hand as he tried to open the oven door.

The traditional Christmas Eve meal in the Beans household was a ptarmigan-and-grouse stew over steamed rice and gingerbread for dessert. Christmas Day was when their mother pulled out all the stops with a braised caribou roast, potatoes and parsnips, wild cranberry relish, and her latticed berry pies.

"Havi, I'm out of butter. Can you run down to the YC Store?"

Beans grabbed the keys to the truck and drove the six blocks to the Yukon Commercial Store. The only major retail operation in town was managed by Victor Paul, a hard-eyed village elder who always glared at Mari and her children when they came into the shop. Victor's brother Lloyd had pursued Mari before her marriage to Jimmy Beans and after her husband's death as well—and the entire Paul family blamed Mari for the fact that Lloyd had left town years ago and never returned to Galena.

Beans paid for the butter and wished Victor a merry Christmas, fighting the urge to say, *And screw you too.* Victor grunted and shoved the box of butter into a paper bag, tossing the change across the counter.

A light snow began to sift down, disguising some of the village's shortcomings, like the landfill and the sewage lagoon. Instead of heading straight home, Beans turned the truck out of town, where so many of his memories lay dormant.

He passed the rusted remains of the hangars that at one time housed the Air Force's tactical aircraft during the Cold War. He and his brothers were responsible for many of the .22 bullet holes that riddled the oxidized sheet metal. Even farther out was the patch of tundra, now coated with snow, where his father had died in the fiery crash of his float plane.

That day, fourteen-year-old DeHavilland had Otter by the hand in the YC Store while the fussy four-year-old tried to decide between a KitKat and gummy bears. Otter wanted both but was allowed only one or the other, a hard-and-fast Mari rule. Victor Paul followed them up and down the narrow aisles with a poisonous glare, as if he expected the Beans children to make away with the store's inventory. Beans dismissed the dull thud in the distance as miners excavating with explosives, until his brother's whines were drowned out by the wail of the village's only fire engine.

Piper had rushed into the store, breathing hard, her face tear streaked. "Havi, come quick."

Beans tucked Otter under one arm and ran after his sister, toward the black smoke boiling into the sky. It was only after hearing Victor's angry but distant "Come back, you little shits! You need to pay for that!" that he realized Otter gripped a KitKat in one hand and a bag of gummy bears in the other.

Twenty years later, he could still feel that shuddering vibration under his feet, the squirming weight of his brother under his arm, his own voice repeating like a mantra, "Please, God, don't let it be Papa." Looking back, he thought maybe this had been his religious turning point, the moment of enlightenment when he realized that his father's Christian God was not listening to the prayers of a teenage boy in a small Alaskan village.

He stopped at the fuel dock, now surrounded by a white expanse of frozen river, where his father's cremated remains had been released. He drove by the little graveyard, where his paternal grandparents, Daisy and Harold Beans, and his eldest brother Lindbergh were buried. He passed the ditch where Lindbergh had rolled his truck with Beans in it. He slowed for a moment at the site of so many of his nightmares, then headed back to the house.

Mari's ptarmigan-and-grouse stew was as good as he remembered, hearty and aromatic. Otter squirted a dollop of sriracha sauce on it, but Beans thought it was perfect without any amendments. Their mother's homemade gingerbread, another of her traditional desserts, was spicy and comforting, complete with a curl of whipped cream from an aerosol can.

Mari poured coffee and Otter sprayed Reddi-wip into his mouth while Beans went out to get more wood for the stove. As he stopped to enjoy the pristine silence of the Yukon night, his cell phone pinged with a text message, startling him.

It was from Chuckie: *Park ranger called in body. AWOL barista? Call me.* This was followed by a grim-faced emoji.

Shit, Beans thought. *More glad tidings.*

Chuckie answered on the first ring, clearly on a hands-free device in his van. "Happy Hanukkah, kid. Sorry to interrupt the festivities, but thought I'd let you know before you saw it on the news. A park ranger in Denali found a young woman's body."

"Fernandez's missing barista?"

"I'm on my way there now and will call you with details. Over and out."

Beans and Otter were bedding down in the room they had shared as children when Chuckie called. Beans went into the darkened living room to take it.

"I think it's her. Just like Jolene. God, she's a mess. The wolves have been at her," Chuckie said.

"Who's there from Homicide?"

"Heller's here."

Oh, great. Now I'll really owe him. "Have him look for the rose, will you? You know the MO."

"Roger."

"I'll be there as soon as I can."

"She'll keep, Beans. She's almost frozen solid."

Beans hung up with Chuckie and sat for a quiet moment with the glow of Christmas lights and the comforting warmth of the woodstove for company. *Another dead barista?* His heavy meal rolled like a boulder in his gut. Another girl dead, left for ravenous wolves, while he spun his wheels, unable to make headway in Jolene's murder investigation. He threw open the front door and stepped out, grateful for the rough slap of frigid air. He sucked in huge gulps of it as his stomach slowly settled. He hoped that Piper was being careful.

To add to his stress level, there was no getting out of Galena on Christmas Day. A snowstorm had hit early that morning, buffeting the tundra with a blinding whiteout.

The one flight out was grounded because of low visibility.

He paced, snowbound in the little bungalow, talking alternately with Chuckie and Heller on his cell phone. Otter binge-watched marathon showings of *A Christmas Story* and *Elf* while Mari basted the caribou roast in the oven and Christmas carols played on the public radio station.

This Christmas, Beans and his siblings had chipped in and bought their mother a new iPad to replace her clunky laptop. As soon as Otter had it up and running, they FaceTimed Piper in Anchorage. She had just come in from work, her green apron draped over her shoulder. She held Archie in her lap and wagged his forepaws in a barely tolerated wave.

"Shit, I miss you guys," she said, her voice catching. "Merry Christmas."

Mari dabbed at her eyes, and even Otter mumbled something about wishing she were here.

Christmas dinner was a subdued affair compared to years past, without Piper's vivacious energy or Herc's off-color jokes. It didn't help that Beans was distracted, leaping up to answer his phone throughout the meal. At one point, his mother made him turn it off while they ate.

"Half an hour, Havi. You can do without it for half an hour." She slipped his phone into her apron pocket.

After dishes were cleared and he was able to retrieve his phone, he learned that the body had been identified by Toni Morelli's father, an oil-field worker whose hopes for a Christmas miracle had been dashed.

He could hear the clinking of silverware and murmured voices in the background when Heller called him. "Chuckie's doing the PM tomorrow so you can be there," Heller said. "The body was found on National Park land, on one of the remote access roads. DuBois says we've got no choice but to call in the feds."

Beans didn't relish working with the FBI, but Lieutenant DuBois, head of the Investigations Division, played by the book. Weather permitting, Beans was scheduled to leave first thing the next day.

Mari was not happy about this turn of events—first Piper not home for Christmas, and now Beans spending Christmas so distracted that he might as well have stayed in Anchorage. She consoled herself by heaping food and affection on Otter, who gorged himself on his mother's attention and holiday treats, including her nori-wrapped makizushi.

The morning after Christmas, Heller picked Beans up at the Anchorage airport in his old Jeep, claiming he needed a break from the in-laws. "I haven't seen anything like this," Heller said, shaking his head, uncharacteristically subdued. "The poor girl was just ripped open."

"Did you find a rose?"

"Yeah, just like you said. A white rose. The evidence boys have it."

"How far from the body?"

"About twenty feet away. She was wearing some kind of skimpy outfit, at least what was left of it. Best guess is that she was abducted on her way to work the morning of the twenty-second. Her car was found at a gas station a block from the espresso stand."

"She stopped for gas or a doughnut and got grabbed?"

"We've requisitioned the surveillance video from the mini-mart."

"Good. Any tracks at the scene?"

Heller grimaced. "No such luck. Fresh snow shortly after she was dumped, looks like. Just prints from the wolves and the park ranger."

Heller dropped Beans by the house so he could clean up and pick up his own vehicle. Piper met him at the door in her pajamas, coffee mug in hand, licking a spoon.

"Hey, what are you doing here? I wasn't expecting you until this evening."

An orange-and-white blur rushed out the door and wove itself around his legs. Beans picked up Archie, surprised at how much he had missed him. Was it his imagination, or had the cat gained a few pounds?

"Any more of that coffee?" Beans asked.

13

Beans gulped down a cup of coffee, grabbed a shower, and promised Piper he'd bring home takeout that evening and they'd catch up. After a two-minute call to assure his mother that he had arrived safely, he jumped into the Explorer and drove through the still-dark Anchorage streets to the morgue.

Beans found Chuckie in his cluttered office, only half-lit from the glow of his computer monitor. As Beans tied himself into a gown and mask, Chuckie tapped at the crime scene photos on his screen.

"She was found two miles from the main highway a little north of Talkeetna. Park ranger on duty found her after hearing wolves."

"Have the feds been notified?"

"Oh yeah. You can bet the Parks people have told them by now."

"Heller said no vehicle tracks were found."

"Nope. Can't catch a break, can we?"

"Not so far."

"This is the same MO, Beans, at least it looks that way." Chuckie looked up with weary eyes and tied on a gown. "But let's see what she'll tell us."

Toni Morelli had long blond hair, blue eyes, and an athletic dancer's build. Mascara ran down her pale cheeks in a horrible parody of tears. Her long, bare legs were latticed with bloody scratches, the soles of her feet scraped and raw. The front of her torso, like Jolene's, had been torn open and virtually consumed by scavengers. Her serene, pretty face was almost untouched except for a few scratches, several drops of blood on her forehead, and a large purple bruise on her left temple. Her once-white fake-fur barista outfit hung from her corpse in bloody shreds.

Chuckie carefully removed these tattered fragments, and young Toni Morelli lay before them like the casualty of a brutal accident.

Except this was no accident.

"Look at this." Chuckie pointed to a front rib that appeared to be nicked and cracked. "If I put a microscope to this, I bet I'll find the same striations as with the Nilsson girl." He irrigated the chest cavity, and pink water trickled down the drain at their feet.

"Fuck," Chuckie said. "Look at the back rib." He swung the magnifying glass over the chest cavity.

Looming into view was a sharp metal broadhead, stopped in its trajectory by Toni Morelli's back rib.

"The murder weapon," Beans breathed.

The broadhead had been snapped off at the shaft, the bolt jagged and splintered at the break.

"It must have broken when the killer tried to dislodge it and pull it through," Beans said.

Chuckie tugged at the bolt head with forceps. "The son of a bitch is really stuck on there."

With a sickening crack, the rib broke, and Chuckie was left holding an evil-looking weapon, dripping bloody water, between his forceps. He dropped it into a stainless-steel pan with an echoing clang.

"Got it," he said. "Thank you, dear girl," he said to Toni Morelli's placid face.

Chuckie continued with his detailed examination, Beans taking occasional notes, until he came to Toni Morelli's hands. On the inside of her left wrist was a small tattoo of a bird of prey, almost prehistoric in its simplicity.

Chuckie clicked his tongue in disapproval as he turned her wrist from side to side. "Beautiful young woman with perfect skin. Why? Looks like somebody drew it on with a Sharpie. Hey, look at her fingertips."

Unlike Jolene's short, close-cut fingernails, Toni's nails were long and manicured, a couple of them broken off at the quick.

"I'm guessing our girl put up a fight, bless her," Chuckie said.

"Maybe she got a piece of her attacker?"

"Could be. I'll send in samples for Trace. Maybe the gods will smile on us and we'll get some DNA."

"Maybe we'll get lucky and we'll have him on file." It was a long shot, Beans knew. If not on file, DNA was good only as a comparative tool, and with no suspect to compare it to at this point, Beans was not optimistic.

"No Raisa on this one?" He could at least hope to see her in a professional capacity, even if she showed no interest in any unofficial contact.

"Didn't think we'd need her expertise this time. The park ranger literally interrupted the wolf pack feeding on the half-frozen body."

Beans' stomach lurched. "No shit, really?"

"He fired a few rounds into the air to scare them off."

"I hope nobody gave her father that gory detail."

"Hey, give us credit for a little bit of class."

They turned Toni's body over.

"No exit wound this time, since the rib stopped it," Beans said. "Similar trace amounts of bark in the uniform again."

"I'll get the lab boys to run a comparison."

After Chuckie closed and covered the body with a sheet, they pulled off their gowns and masks and slumped into facing chairs.

"What's your take on it?" Beans asked.

"Same guy. Has to be. Weapon is similar, if not identical. The flower left at the scene, the pieces of bark, all point to the same killer."

"The only thing we've got going for us this time is the car left at the mini-mart. With any luck, we might have a witness, or at least a video."

"I don't like it." Chuckie shook his head. "The last serial killer of women here in Anchorage that I can remember was that psycho who tracked those poor hookers through the woods."

Beans remembered reading about the Robert Hansen case from the eighties, the man known as the Butcher Baker. Hansen had abducted at least seventeen women, mostly sex workers, from the Anchorage streets and released them in the woods, where he hunted them like terrified game.

"When can we expect the feds?" Beans asked.

"Any minute now, with guns blazing."

"Shit. DuBois wants to have a briefing today."

"I got the memo. See you later."

It was already turning into a long day. First, Beans interviewed the proprietor of the Kwik-E-Mart, the gas station/mini-mart where Toni's car had been found. Kamal Hazim remembered the young woman, who'd bought a pack of Winstons, then asked to use the restroom.

"She came in very early Monday morning, about five thirty, five forty-five. I remember her, very pretty." Kamal smiled. "I told her, 'Why do you smoke? You will ruin your beauty!' She laughed and said that dancers smoke so they don't get fat." He chuckled. "Our bathroom is around the back, so we keep it locked. I gave her the key." Kamal's dark eyes grew sad. "That's the last time I saw her."

"You checked the bathroom?"

"Oh yes, I did, since she never brought back the key. No sign of her. The key to the bathroom was in the lock, that's all. When her car was still here at the end of my shift, I called the police."

Kamal had seen no one suspicious that morning, just a few regulars gassing up or buying coffee or snacks. No one else had interacted with Toni, as far as he knew.

Beans knew that Toni's Subaru had been found locked, with a backpack in the passenger seat. Investigators had jimmied it open and discovered that the backpack contained a pair of tights, well-worn toe shoes, a small bag with makeup, a wallet, and her cell phone, a Samsung Galaxy. In one of the pockets of the backpack was a plastic bag with a half-smoked joint. The trunk held a spare tire and tire chains. Neither the car nor the bathroom had shown any sign of a struggle. In the parking strip near the entrance to the bathroom, an unopened pack of Winstons had been found half-hidden in a mound of snow.

Kamal showed Beans the surveillance cameras, one mounted under the eaves, pointing toward the pumps, and another inside, pointing toward the cashier. Unfortunately, it only recorded activity around the well-lit front of the store, in some of the parking spaces, and by the gas pumps.

Kamal shook his head sadly. "I am sorry. There is no camera at the back of the store."

So no recording of the possible abduction of Toni Morelli as she entered the bathroom. Disappointment weighed on Beans like the ever-present darkness.

Kamal gladly turned over the security video, placing it reverently in a plastic bag that said *We ♥ Our Customers*. "I am so sorry I cannot be of more help."

Beans thanked him and handed him a card. Right now, Kamal Hazim's video was the closest thing he had to an eyewitness. He steeled himself to stare at several more hours of security footage, hoping that it would yield a clue.

He made it back to the office just in time for a briefing with DuBois, Heller, and Chuckie. Heller, as the homicide detective at the Morelli scene, was surprisingly thorough and efficient, without his usual sarcastic commentary. He filled them in on details of the crime scene and his interview with the park ranger. Chuckie reviewed autopsy findings and the discovery of the broadhead, and Beans reported on his interview with Kamal Hazim and the relevance of Jolene Nilsson's homicide to Toni Morelli's.

Lieutenant Nelson DuBois, a handsome, green-eyed Black man with close-cropped graying hair and a military bearing, listened carefully and jotted down notes on a legal pad.

"I don't have to tell you guys that this has the potential of a true shitstorm," he said.

"No, sir," Beans said.

"I think it's safe to assume right now that we are looking for one killer. You drew the Nilsson case first, Beans, so you're lead on both, with Heller assisting."

Heller raised his hand. "Lieut, I still have to wrap up Concepcion . . ."

"Do you have a body yet?" DuBois pointed his pen at Hansen like an accusation.

"No, sir."

"Any more cooperation from the family or associates?"

"Very little, sir." Heller looked at his shoes.

"Then it's back-burner material. Nobody, especially the media, is going to get as excited about a missing loan shark as they will about two murdered young women."

Heller took a breath as if to say something, then seemed to change his mind.

"I'm not saying forget about Concepcion," DuBois continued. "But these two girls take top priority."

Heller shifted in his chair, then shrugged and nodded.

"I also don't need to tell you that the feds have insisted on being involved. It's not every day that a murdered young woman is found on federal land."

Beans grimaced. Heller moaned, "Oh God, please, not Whiz Magnuson."

Both detectives remembered working with FBI Special Agent Norman Magnuson on the Denali camper case a few years ago. Dull eyed and out of shape, Magnuson couldn't walk across the parking lot without wheezing. Because of an enlarged prostate, he spent more time peeing behind trees than analyzing evidence. It wasn't long before Anchorage detectives were calling him "Whiz" behind his back.

"You will be devastated to hear that Norman Magnuson retired last year. They're sending someone up from the Portland region. We'll reconvene when Special Agent O'Reilly arrives tomorrow." DuBois consulted the notes on his yellow legal pad. "I'll run interference with the news folks and work with Public Information on social media. If you want to release any of that mini-mart video and ask for the public's help, let me know. But we'll need to finesse this."

Beans and Heller knew that no one was better at working the media than DuBois, but as he'd said, this could be a shitstorm.

"Two young women have been killed, Lieutenant. Same job description, same MO. The public's going to put two and two together," Beans said.

"Let them add all they want, but right now, we don't want them to come up with *serial killer*. We want people to be cautious, of course. But, if we start caving to public sentiment, start shutting down these bikini barista places to protect these girls, we'll never catch this guy." DuBois began pacing around his desk. "My inclination is, we keep the rose and the arrow under wraps for now."

"We've held back the rose from the media," Heller said.

"Good. Let's do the same with the arrow. We work those angles behind the scenes. We keep a tight lid on the media. And we get him before he strikes again."

Easier said than done, Beans thought as he left police headquarters. He knew the captain was right. Prematurely releasing specific info could drive the suspect underground. But waiting too long could sacrifice more young women. Beans felt like he was walking an ever-narrowing tightrope—and now even more so, with Heller forced to be part of his team. He unlocked the Explorer, slumped behind the wheel, and turned the key.

There was something comforting about sitting in the Explorer in the darkness, feeling the vibration of the engine through the floorboards and the heat whining through the vents, hearing the crackling static on the radio. The Dalai Lama action figure swayed like a hypnotist's watch from his rearview mirror. He shook his head to fight off exhaustion and frustration. Two more calls to make—to the owner of Arctic Foxes Espresso and the director of the Anchorage Ballet's *Nutcracker*—before he called it a day.

14

Spiro Liakos ran Arctic Foxes Espresso from an unfinished plywood enclosure in his heated Eagle River garage. He ushered Beans through the side door into the small office and motioned for him to sit in one of the tattered wheeled office chairs. He fixed the detective a steaming cup of Kona blend from the one-cup coffeemaker on the corner of a paper-strewn credenza, then sat back and peered at him from around a stack of files and receipts.

Liakos was a slightly taller version of Danny DeVito, with dark bushy eyebrows that twitched like animated caterpillars above his beetle-black eyes. He angled his head into a sorrowful tilt. "So, Toni?"

"I'm afraid she's dead, Mr. Liakos. Her body was found on Christmas Eve."

Liakos' chin dropped to his chest, and Beans was startled when a sob broke from him.

"When she didn't show for work that morning, I knew, I just knew that something was wrong. She never misses without calling, never." He pulled a tissue from a box and blotted his eyes. "Jesus, what happened?"

"We're investigating her death as a homicide. That's all I can tell you at this point."

"Oh God," Liakos sobbed into his tissue. "These girls, they are like my daughters." He waved his hand around a half dozen black-and-white headshots and more revealing photos, obviously from these girls' modeling/dancing/acting portfolios, pinned on the walls.

Yeah, right. Beans glanced longer than he meant to at a photo of a vixen with tousled dark hair, wrapped in a satin bedsheet.

"That's Nancy. She works afternoons." Liakos nodded toward the photo.

Beans sipped on his very good cup of coffee, averting his eyes from the photo as his face flushed.

Liakos sniffed and recounted all he knew about Toni Morelli. "Dependable. Customers loved her. She was good for business—personable, friendly, and those long legs, you know." He sighed.

"She was last seen a block from Arctic Foxes, at the Kwik-E-Mart, at about five forty-five AM," Beans said.

"She was never late to open, never." Liakos blew his nose into a tissue. "Who would want to hurt Toni?"

"I was hoping you might be able to answer that. I didn't see any cameras there, but you can confirm—do you have any kind of video security at the coffee shop?"

Liakos shook his head. "No, no cameras. Why? There's never been a problem, never."

When Beans asked if Toni had had any boyfriends, Liakos said he thought she might have been dating someone from the ballet. He frowned and said he could be mistaken, "since most of those guys are poofs."

"And you?" Beans asked. "She is—was—a very pretty girl."

"Me?" Liakos held out his hands. "No, I never mix business with pleasure, never. And my wife"—he lowered his voice—"would kill me."

He told Beans about one of his other businesses, Vendcor, that he ran out of his garage as well. Hulks of vending machines lurked in the semidarkness, and pallets of pop, chips, candy bars, and condoms lined the walls. There was barely enough room to park a small mud-spattered minivan.

"It's good business, cash business," Liakos said, thumping on the side of a vending machine as he walked Beans out.

Beans suspected that Liakos was running a small-scale money-laundering operation out of this garage, but he couldn't imagine that the little entrepreneur had anything to do with Toni's murder.

After leaving Eagle River, Beans was lucky enough to catch Irving Bernson, director of Anchorage Ballet's *Nutcracker* production, between matinee and evening performances. A compact man with a dancer's toned body and a silver man-bun, he encased Beans' hand in a firm grip.

Bernson's shoulders slumped and he sighed when he heard of Toni's death. "I had a bad feeling when she didn't show for the Monday performance. She has never missed a show. And even if she had to, I'm sure she would have let someone know."

Same thing Liakos said.

Bernson knew of no one, inside or outside the company, who harbored any ill will toward Toni. "This is show business, after all, Detective. There are petty jealousies, and, you know, bitchiness. But this company is unusually well adjusted. Probably has to do with the size of the market. And nobody would dream of hurting Toni."

Beans asked about any romantic involvements Toni might have had.

"I heard rumors about her having a thing with Sam Holder, the choreographer, but I don't know how real that is. Holder's moved on, anyway. He's been in Finland since September with a new production."

"And how about you?" Beans thought it was a shot in the dark but fired it anyway. "Did you have anything other than a professional relationship with Toni Morelli?"

"Are you kidding, Detective?" Bernson smiled and, in an eerie echo of Spiro Liakos, said, "My husband would kill me."

Bernson said the best source of information on Toni Morelli was her roommate, Amy Chandler, another member of the company.

"Right now, Amy is probably across the street at that deli. She usually goes there between performances. If she's not, let me know, and I'll get her contact info." He shook his head. "This is really devastating. It's going to hit the company hard."

Beans picked his way across the slick street to the Subs 'N' Salads at the corner. A young woman sat at a booth near the back, plugged into earbuds, munching on a mound of romaine lettuce. She bopped her head from side to side to music only she could hear.

Her dark hair was pulled from her face in a messy ponytail, and her knit hoodie, slumping off one shoulder, did little to conceal her lean dancer's physique. Her face was scrubbed clean of makeup and glowed, even in the harsh fluorescent lighting of the deli. The only other customers were middle-aged men in hooded parkas and heavyset retail workers carrying shopping bags.

The young woman looked up midchew.

"Amy Chandler?" Beans showed her his badge.

Amy dropped her fork on the plate with a clatter and covered her mouth with her hand. Her large blue eyes filled with tears.

"Oh my God," she whispered. "It's Toni, isn't it?"

Beans nodded. "I'm afraid so. May I sit down?"

He slid onto the bench across from her and filled her in with as much detail as he could. The young woman's face grew pale.

"I'm sorry, I think I'm going to be sick." She rushed from the booth to the restroom.

When she returned a few minutes later, she held a paper towel to her mouth. She pushed the Caesar salad away from her and shuddered.

"I'm sorry to have to bring you this news," he said.

"I was going to call her father after dinner to get an update."

"He identified her body late yesterday."

"What? He said he'd call if he heard . . ." She fumbled with her phone. "Oh fuck, I never turned the ringer back on after the matinee." She held the phone to her ear, listening to her messages, and raised reddened eyes to the fluorescent lights.

"Hey, let me get you something." Beans rose. "Coffee or tea, something stronger?"

"A Diet Sprite?"

He went to the counter and brought back a glass of soda. She sipped it gratefully and dabbed at her eyes again. She sniffed and straightened. "What do you want to know?"

She had known Toni Morelli for about five years and lived with her for three. They had shared much of life's sorrows and disappointments, including the breakup of Amy's marriage to her high school sweetheart and the death of Toni's mother to cancer.

Amy knew of no one who would want to harm Toni—a familiar mantra.

"She was a good friend, a terrific dancer. Almost as good as me," she said, with a sad smile. "She would argue that point."

"What about this choreographer, Sam Holder? I understand she had a relationship with him."

"Holder, that prick!" Amy's blue eyes flashed. "The worst kind of asshole—a married asshole. Oh, sorry, you aren't married, are you?"

Beans shook his head and smiled.

She smiled back. "I wasn't making a pass or anything."

Even with her eyes puffy and her nose red and running, Amy Chandler was a stunning young woman, and he was taken aback. He cleared his throat.

"You were telling me about Mr. Holder?"

"Came here last year." She sipped at her drink and blew her nose into a paper napkin. "Toni really cared about him. She thought there might be a future with him, until she found out about the wife and kids in Minneapolis. He's in Oslo or Helsinki or someplace now. I really don't care."

Beans closed his notebook. "We'll need to take a look at your house, if you don't mind. Just standard procedure."

She slid out of the booth and threw some bills on the table. "Let's go now. I can't eat anything anyway. As long as I'm back by six thirty."

She tossed a long wool coat over her baggy knit hoodie and black tights. He couldn't help but notice how graceful she was, the length of her strides in the childlike fleece-lined boots, the way her duffel bag swung rhythmically at her side. There was such confidence in the way she moved through the space around her, like she owned it. Every step, every little gesture was a hypnotic dance in itself.

He held out his hand to help her over a berm of snow piled on the sidewalk. She smiled, a brief, radiant flash like distant lightning, and took his hand.

15

While Beans and Amy Chandler drove down Northern Lights Boulevard, still twinkling with incongruously cheerful Christmas lights, she told him that Antoinette Morelli was the only child of oil-field worker Ray Morelli and his late wife Celeste.

"They both adored her." Amy offered him a Tic Tac, which he declined. "He just lost Celeste two years ago, and now Toni." She stared out the window as she crunched on the mints. "I can't imagine what he's going through."

Toni had grown up in the Anchorage area and always wanted to be a dancer, Amy said. "From the moment she first put on ballet shoes, she knew she was going to be the little spinning figure on the music box."

"How about boyfriends?"

"Oh, she went out on dates, of course. But in the years that I've known her, the only one she was serious about was Sam-the-Prick Holder. Hey, that has a real ring to it, doesn't it?"

As Beans navigated the icy streets in rush-hour traffic, Amy told him that she had grown up in Winthrop, Washington, the daughter of a tavern owner and a nurse.

"Did you always want to be a dancer?" In the closeness of the Explorer, he became aware of the fresh scent of her shampoo and Tic Tacs.

"Oh, Christ no. I wanted to be a barrel racer. My mom was afraid that I would join the rodeo circuit and got me ballet lessons. I was hooked. Toni and I met when we were both cast in *Swan Lake*. Turn here."

She directed him down a recently plowed private drive to a complex of two-unit buildings arranged in a semicircle. She had him park in the driveway of the last building.

"This is us." She pulled out her keys and pointed to the end unit.

The well-maintained townhome complex had only one way in and out, he noted. It would be difficult to stalk someone unnoticed. The backyards of all the units shared a common fence that abutted a greenbelt, now spindly and spare under the snow.

Beans could see that the women had kept the two-level townhome reasonably tidy. Amy blushed as she snatched up a black leotard and sports bra draped over a barstool and kicked a pair of toe shoes into a hall closet.

"It's a two-bedroom, one-and-three-quarter bath unit, pretty convenient. I've got the downstairs bedroom and shower, and the bed and bath upstairs are—were—Toni's." She bit her lip and fought back tears. "Sorry."

He pulled a pair of gloves out of his pocket. "Mind if I look around?" Not waiting for an answer, he climbed the stairs to Toni Morelli's bedroom.

The stairway opened onto a landing with a good-sized master suite to the left and a full bath to the right. The queen-size bed was unmade, with pink pajama bottoms and an Iditarod T-shirt thrown over the rumpled duvet. The walls were covered with large glossy posters of Nureyev, Baryshnikov, and several other ballet dancers he didn't know.

A small desk adjacent to the bed held a MacBook, an assortment of paperback novels, a small notepad with indecipherable doodles, and a handful of ballpoint pens. A photo in a silver frame depicted a tall, sturdy man Amy pointed out as Ray Morelli standing next to a slender, olive-skinned woman she said was Toni's mother, Celeste. Ray Morelli had an arm around a leggy dark-haired teenager with a mouthful of braces.

"This is Toni?" Beans asked Amy, who had followed him upstairs. He pointed at the smiling girl.

"Yeah," Amy said. "Look at those legs. She was destined to be a dancer."

Next to the desk was a three-tiered IKEA bookshelf, displaying at least a dozen music boxes of varying sizes.

"She collected them," Amy said. She opened the largest of the music boxes, dark lacquer with inlaid mother-of-pearl. It began playing Beethoven's "Für Elise" in a slow off-key tinkle while a tiny plastic ballerina spun on a mirrored surface. "Oh God," Amy said, and shut the music box. She stared up at the skylight and blinked back tears.

Beans noted the music boxes, bagged the laptop and notepad, then turned to the bathroom.

This too was reasonably tidy. Shampoos, conditioners, and shave gels stood in an orderly row on the side of the tub. The medicine cabinet was packed with what he'd expect to find in a young woman's bathroom but told him very little—birth control pills, ibuprofen, a few OxyContin tablets cut in half, cold tablets, eye drops, nail polish remover, and various makeup products and skin treatments.

"Do you really need to do this? I mean, she wasn't found here, right?" Amy hugged her arms to herself.

"I'm just trying to get a feel for what Toni was like as a person and why someone might want to kill her. Tell me about Monday morning, the last day you saw her."

She leaned against the bathroom door. "We both got up early, about four thirty. She was going to Arctic Foxes, of course, and I was going to work as well."

"Where do you work?"

"Snowtown Bistro, over on Fourth Avenue. I work the weekday breakfast and lunch shifts. Toni had already had her shower and was getting into her Arctic Foxes gear." Amy screwed her pretty face into a frown.

"You didn't approve of her job?"

"It's not that. She probably made more in tips than I did. It's just that the outfits Spiro wanted them to wear were so . . . so skanky."

"And then what?"

"She stood at the counter and wolfed down a protein bar and a cup of tea."

"Not coffee?"

"Ironic, isn't it? No, Toni doesn't—didn't—drink coffee. She complained that she was out of smokes and needed to get some."

"And then?"

"She got her backpack together and got ready to leave. She said she'd be home in plenty of time for us to drive to the theater together."

"Did she mention if anyone was giving her trouble? Did she receive any hassling phone calls? Anybody at the coffee shop giving her grief?"

Amy shook her head. "No, I'm sure she would have told Spiro if there was. He has a goon who he says is his assistant but is an enforcer of some kind. Bobo would have taken care of any problem customers."

"Bobo?" Beans asked.

"Knuckle dragger. I think he's a brother-in-law." She rolled her eyes.

Beans scribbled the name *Bobo* in his notebook.

She confirmed that there had been no break-ins at their unit or any others in the complex. There had been no flowers delivered to their apartment in a very long time. "Too long," she added.

In one of Toni's bathroom vanity drawers was a hand mirror, dotted and smeared with white residue. Beans showed it to Amy and hoped he didn't sound like her dad when he asked, "If I took this to the lab, would they find cocaine?"

She sighed. "All of us dancers do a little bit of coke now and then. It curbs the appetite and gives you a little pick-me-up, you know?"

He nodded. He knew, having done his share of cocaine before signing on with the police academy. He had to admit that he liked the enlightened buzz. Maybe, if he ever went on a long vacation where there was no danger of drug testing, he might try it again. *Or not.*

"I'm not trying to bust anybody for possession. I'm just trying to find her known associates and see if they could tell us anything. Do you know who she buys from?"

"I'm not getting them in trouble, right?" Amy looked doubtful.

"I'm Homicide, not Narcotics."

"Toni used to occasionally buy a little coke from a guy that runs a Chinese grocery store. He goes by Frankie?"

Beans felt like the top of his head was going to implode. "Frankie? Frankie Ma?"

"Right, Ma's Family Grocery, over on Government Hill."

Holy shit. Beans closed his eyes and tried to regulate his breathing. Since when did Frankie Ma's repertoire of illegal activity include selling drugs? He was ready to drive over there and drag him out in handcuffs, nail him for Concepcion's murder. Maybe Toni's too, while he was at it. He took a deep breath and released it. He shut the doors to Toni's bedroom and bathroom.

"Keep these closed, and don't go in until you hear otherwise. I'll have crime scene technicians go over it more thoroughly."

"I'm not in any danger, am I?" Amy's large blue eyes searched his face.

Good question. "You should be cautious, for sure. But no, I have no reason to think you're in any imminent danger." *But I know someone who is.* He seethed, thinking about Frankie selling dope out his mother's back door.

Beans exited the townhome with the bagged laptop and notepad under his arm while Amy locked the dead bolt behind him. As they headed to the Explorer for the drive back to the theater, he thought of another long shot, but one worth taking. "Did Toni or you know a young woman named Jolene Nilsson?"

"No, I don't think so. Wait, she was the barista—is there a connection?"

"We don't know at this point."

"I didn't know her, and if Toni did, she never mentioned her."

The drive to the theater went quickly, with Amy sitting next to him, filling the car with her minty, soapy smell. Before he knew it, they were pulling up to the stage entrance. She slid out of the car and held out her hand to shake his. Her fingers were long and strong and a little chilled, but she gripped his hand with conviction.

"You'll get that bastard, won't you?"

"I'll do my best." He gave her hand a return squeeze.

She suddenly remembered something and began rummaging through her bag. "Shit! I promised to call her dad!"

"Ms. Chandler?"

"Amy," she said, still distracted by the search for her phone.

"Amy. I said you weren't in any imminent danger, but until we catch this guy, be careful, okay? He's obviously targeting attractive young women . . ."

She stopped rummaging long enough to shoot him a wide smile.

He was flustered but continued. "I mean, be aware of your surroundings. Try not to walk alone, especially after evening performances. Keep to well-lit areas." *Wait, isn't this the same speech I gave Piper?*

"Yes, Officer." Amy saluted. "Just three more performances to go, anyway." She took a few steps toward the theater, then turned back. "Hey, if you come to any of them—the performances, I mean—I'm the third snowflake from the left. And in the 'Waltz of the Flowers,' I'm in blue. The only other blue flower is a blonde, so you should be able to pick me out."

Beans thought now was not a good time to tell her that Tchaikovsky's *Nutcracker* was his least favorite holiday music. In fact, he hated it. He liked Amy Chandler, but not enough to sit through the *Nutcracker*. At least, not yet.

Instead, he said, "Got it. And break a leg."

She looked affronted. "Do not say *break a leg* to a ballerina! To wish a dancer luck, say *merde*."

"*Merde*? Isn't that French for *shit*?"

"Oh, those French. They have a different word for everything. I gotta go." Her cell phone in hand, she punched in a number and waited for the phone to ring. She picked her way over a mound of snow as she chewed her bottom lip.

"Hello, Mr. Morelli? Mr. Morelli, this is Amy Chandler."

Even through the dirty windshield of the Explorer, Beans could tell that she had begun to cry.

16

Frankie Ma was shoveling snow from the sidewalk in front of Ma's Family Grocery when Beans skidded into a spot next to a fire hydrant. He left the engine running and got out, slamming the car door hard enough to spin the plastic Dalai Lama figure suspended from the rearview mirror. Frankie, smiling, propped the shovel against the wall, pulled off his glove, and stretched out his hand.

"Hey, Beans. Didn't know you were stopping by."

Beans ignored his friend's hand. "You son of a bitch." His tone was as icy as the air.

Frankie looked confused, but he was good at that. "What's up, buddy?"

Just then, Sophie Ma swung open the glass door and stepped out, holding her sweater around her tiny frame. "Beans, come inside! It's too cold to be out! You want tea?"

"Hi, Mrs. Ma. No, no thanks. Just need to talk to Frankie for a minute." Beans smiled and gave her a hug.

"Okay," she said, then to her son, "Don't forget to shovel."

"No, Mom, I won't."

"I see your sister at Fred Meyer making coffee." The woman's round face beamed at Beans. "So cute, nice girl."

"Thanks, Mrs. Ma."

As she waved at him and went back into the store, Beans hissed, "Get in the car."

"What?" Frankie looked frightened.

"Get in the car!"

"Mom, I'm going to talk with Beans for a minute," he called into the store.

"Don't forget to shovel!" she called back.

Frankie rolled his eyes and got into the passenger seat of the Explorer. "Shit! The old lady is relentless."

"For good reason."

"What's this all about, Beans?"

"You told me you quit."

"Quit what?"

"The dope. The coke."

"I did. I quit right after you did, remember?"

Beans remembered that quitting had been harder than he thought it would be. Back in college, he and Frankie had drifted into a jock party-boy lifestyle, having a couple of beers after basketball games that turned into a six-pack, then a joint and a pizza. The next morning it took a line or two with black coffee to get going.

It ended for Beans one morning during his senior year at UAA, when he looked in the mirror and saw his dead brother Lindbergh's face staring back at him, bleary eyed and hungover. That was the day he quit—drinking and drugs—swearing he would not end up like Lindbergh, frozen into a snowbank, undiscovered until breakup. He'd applied to the Anchorage Police Academy the next day.

"Yeah, I remember."

"I quit . . . but you remember what it was like," Frankie continued. "Those were good times, Beans."

Good times, my ass. Beans had been flunking every class but PE until the morning he saw Lindbergh's face in the mirror. But he couldn't deny it had been fun. Fun he could never repeat.

"They're over. And dealing was never part of the mix."

"What?" Frankie flashed his Oscar-winning incredulous look.

"Don't bullshit me. I know you're selling." Beans thumped him on the shoulder. "When did you start?"

"Ow! Son of a bitch!" Frankie rubbed his shoulder. "It started the first time I got into Sevy for some money. He said I could help work it off, sell a little out the back, you know?"

"Shit." Beans massaged his forehead. "You know what this could do to your mom, right?"

"She can't ever know." Frankie glanced at his mother, who was arranging bags of chips on a rack near the shop door. "I just have a handful of customers, you gotta believe me."

"I don't care! You're done, and I'm done covering for you!"

"Beans, Beans, listen to me." Frankie moved closer, his beard-stubbled face fearful. "He made me."

"Who made you? Concepcion?"

"Yeah, Sevy. He said he would hurt her." He nodded toward the shop, where Mrs. Ma bagged white globes of turnips for an elderly Asian gentleman.

"Your mother?" Beans watched as Mrs. Ma smiled, nodded, and carefully counted change into the customer's hand.

"Yeah, she could have 'an accident,'" he said. Frankie gnawed at a hangnail on his thumb. "It's not much, Beans, just a little bit of blow, maybe some Ecstasy during prom season . . ."

"I should haul your worthless ass in!" Beans fought the urge to grab him by his collar and shake him.

Frankie chuckled, a high, girlish titter. "You wouldn't do that to my mom, would you?" Beans would do almost anything to protect the little Chinese woman who was like a second mother to him, and Frankie knew it.

Mrs. Ma noticed her son and his friend looking in her direction and waved. Beans smiled weakly and waved back. He pressed his fingers to his forehead, trying to hold back a tension headache. "Awfully convenient for you that Sevy's out of the picture now, isn't it?"

Frankie dropped his head back and whined, "Come on, Beans. This is penny-ante shit. I'm no player."

"I'm saying again, for the last time—I'm done. That's not why I'm here anyway. I'm here because of Toni Morelli."

"Who?"

"One of your customers. Toni. Pretty, tall, blond."

"Oh yeah, Toni the dancing barista, right? Great legs."

"She's dead. Her body was found in Denali Park."

"No shit, really?" Frankie frowned. "Wow, that's too bad. She was a nice girl, real looker." He shook his head. "Wait, she couldn't have OD'd! Not on what little I sold her!"

"No, lucky for you, she was murdered." Beans didn't try to keep the biting sarcasm out of his voice. "What else do you remember about her? When did you last see her?"

"Okay, let me see. Would have been shortly after Thanksgiving. She called and wanted to buy a few grams for the holidays."

"Did she come to the store?"

"We usually met in the alley behind the shop and did our transactions there."

"Was she with anyone?"

"No, she always came alone."

"Notice anything unusual? Did she seem worried about anything?" The questions shot out of Beans like gunfire.

"I'm her drug dealer, not her priest," Frankie said.

"Well, she needs a priest now, fuckwit!"

"Hey!" He looked insulted.

"Did you see anyone follow her?"

"No, but I lost sight of her when she left the alley. Honest, I only sold to her maybe a half dozen times, tops. She was always alone."

"Okay. Get out," Beans said.

"That's it?"

"Yeah, for now. But if I hear any more about you selling, not only am I telling Narcotics and Heller, I'm telling her." He nodded toward the store, where Mrs. Ma picked through a crate of eggplant.

Frankie opened the car door. "Okay, okay. Chill, man. Happy New Year, Beans."

Beans waved him off and put the car in drive. Talking with Frankie had given him a blinding headache but also reminded him that he'd promised Piper he would bring home Chinese takeout for dinner.

When he turned into his driveway at eight thirty, he was relieved to see Piper's battered Mazda parked in front of the house. He took a few deep breaths in and then out, trying to expel the tension from his body with each exhalation. It had been a long day, one that had started at four AM in Galena. He felt a hundred years old and wanted nothing more than to gorge on Chinese food and sleep in his own bed.

Before he could press the garage door opener, something scurried in front of his headlights, and he slammed on the brakes.

Archie. He opened his door, and the cat jumped into his lap. "What the hell? What are you doing out here, boy?"

"*Prow?*" Archie said, and rubbed his face against Beans' chin, then sniffed with great interest at the shrimp fried rice.

Carrying Archie under his arm, Beans went to the front door to unlock it and put the cat safely in the house before pulling the car in. The door was closed but unlocked. "Piper?" He called into the foyer. No answer but the cooking show blaring on the living room TV.

"Sis?" Both the master and the guest bathroom doors were ajar. The back of his neck tingled. Something was wrong. He put Archie down and unsnapped his shoulder holster.

The lights were on in the kitchen and the guest bedroom. Piper's green apron and black jeans lay in a wad on the floor next to the unmade bed. He drew his Glock and held it in front of him. He checked his bedroom and the office—both empty. On the living room TV, Bobby Flay was deboning a chicken.

Adjacent to the garage was the laundry room, the only room he hadn't checked yet. Holding the Glock in both hands, he called into the darkened doorway, "Piper?"

"Yeah?"

The one-word answer was like an explosion in the quiet of the house.

"Jesus Christ!" He whirled around to find Piper standing behind him, holding her trembling hands in the air, a plastic shopping bag hanging from a wrist. His heart pounded as he bent from the waist to catch his breath, dropping his Glock to his side. "What the fuck are you trying to do to me?"

"What the . . . *you're* the one with the gun! You almost blew my head off!"

With shaking hands, Beans holstered the Glock and snapped it in. The thought that he had been a trigger pull away from releasing his weapon's violence upon his little sister shocked his Buddhist sensibilities and made his knees weak.

"What the fuck was Archie doing outside? And why was the fucking door unlocked?" He realized that he was using *fuck* in every possible grammatical form but didn't care. He was simultaneously livid at his careless little sister and horrified at how close he had come to shooting her.

"The hell it was unlocked! Wait, it was unlocked?" Piper looked puzzled. "I could have sworn I locked it!" She fished into her coat pocket for a key.

"And where did you go? Your car's parked outside."

"Just down the street to the little Korean market. I used the last of the shoyu, and I knew we were having Chinese tonight, so I—"

He wrapped her in a tight hug and kissed her on the top of her head, anger draining from him like a retreating tide.

"Remember Jolene Nilsson, the murdered barista? Another young woman has been killed. Remember I told you to be careful, especially after dark?"

He could feel her nodding.

"Wandering down the street at night alone is not being careful!" He gave her another tight squeeze and released her.

She looked sheepish. "I'm sorry. I didn't mean to worry you."

"I know, sis, but Jesus, if anything happened to you . . . Mom would kill me!"

She gave him a playful punch on his shoulder. "Asshole."

"And be careful with the front door. Archie isn't used to this neighborhood yet, and coyotes could get him."

"Just let them try," Piper cooed, snuggling the ginger cat in her arms.

The Explorer was still idling in the driveway in front of the closed garage door. He punched the remote, and the garage door yawned open. When Beans pulled the car in, the headlights shone onto the door leading from the garage to the house. This door was slightly ajar, showing a sliver of light from the laundry room. *Odd.*

He grabbed the bags of still-warm Chinese food and checked the door leading from the garage to the backyard. This one was closed but unlocked. *Even odder.* He locked it, then headed to the house, reminding himself to lecture Piper again on the virtues of home security.

Just an oversight. I'm getting paranoid, seeing bow-wielding killers behind every unlocked door. But as Piper chatted and unpacked cardboard cartons of chow mein and sweet-and-sour pork, an uneasy feeling still gnawed at him. He recognized it as his unrelenting cop's instinct—as devoted as a dog, worrying every shred of suspicion—following him like a curse.

17

The incident with the unlocked doors left Beans restless, and he again had a fitful night's sleep. He lurched out of bed after oversleeping and rushed to the office for the morning briefing. He only had a few minutes to spare, barely enough time to get a cup of the department's foul-tasting coffee. As much as he hated the slightly petroleum-flavored brew that dripped from the machine, he hadn't had time to make a cup at home, nor stop for one on the way. He avoided Snow Bunny Baristas as much as possible these days—he couldn't bear the sad look in Darla's pale-blue eyes when he said he had no news to share on Jolene's investigation.

"Oh my God." A woman's voice came from the break room. She made faint gagging sounds and muttered under her breath. "Jesus, I thought our coffee was bad." Tearing sounds as sugar and creamer packets, at least two of each, were ripped open.

Must be Dolores from Traffic, he thought as he rounded the corner. "Come on," he said, "you're not going to tell me your crap is better down in Traf..."

Despite his best efforts, he couldn't stop his sharp intake of breath.

"Oh, hi," he stammered. "Sorry, I thought you were one of my colleagues . . ."

She smiled, and her green eyes twinkled—actually twinkled, like Amy Adams' in that old Disney movie. Hair like burnished copper was tied back in a ponytail of tousled curls. A slender but curvy figure in a navy pantsuit and sensible rubber boots, she wore a guest pass on a lanyard around her neck and had a laptop bag slung on her shoulder.

"I apologize. I didn't think anyone heard me dissing your coffee," she said.

"It's swamp water, I admit it. I'm DeHavilland Beans, Anchorage Homicide."

"Oh, you're Beans? The lead on the barista case, right?" Her smile widened. "I'm Special Agent Isabelle O'Reilly from the Portland office."

A definite upgrade from Whiz. "We normally work with the Anchorage field office . . ."

"And I'm sure you'll be liaising with the Evidence Response Team here as you usually do," O'Reilly said. "But I'm fresh from a stint at Behavioral Analysis in Quantico, so . . . here I am." Her smile was radiant as she held out her hand.

"Welcome." He gripped her small hand in his own.

"So, maybe you could show me where the briefing is going to be held?"

A cup of awful department coffee in one hand and files in the other, he guided her through the bullpen, past Heller and a couple of the other detectives.

Heller's eyes widened into saucers as he mouthed, *Whiz?*

Beans narrowed his own eyes and shook his head, daring Heller to comment.

The older detective gave his trademark shrug and averted his eyes to his computer monitor.

Because his department was relatively small, Lieutenant Dubois' standard policy was to invite his detectives to casual brown-bag general meetings once or twice a month. Now with two high-profile homicides and the involvement of the FBI, he had made attendance at today's formal meeting mandatory. The tables in the incident room were rearranged to accommodate rows of chairs, each with copies of reports on its seat. Photos of the victims, in life and in death, were taped to a whiteboard. An IT technician cued up Beans' PowerPoint presentation on a large monitor as the detectives filed in and took their seats.

After DuBois called the meeting to order and issued his usual warnings about keeping details of the case strictly within the department, he nodded to O'Reilly. "Before we start, let me introduce Special Agent Isabelle O'Reilly from the FBI's Portland office, here to consult with us. Agent O'Reilly has done considerable work with Behavioral Analysis in Quantico, and we're lucky to have her." O'Reilly smiled and gave a brief wave. "We'll be hearing from her after Beans' presentation," DuBois continued. "Detective, you have the floor."

Beans started with the discovery of Jolene Nilsson's body, inwardly cringing when the PowerPoint slide of her ravaged torso appeared on the screen. With Heller's assistance, he described Toni Morelli's Denali Park crime scene, and both detectives summarized the status of the investigations to date. Next, Chuckie described the victims' wounds and the process by which he had determined the type of weapon used for both killings.

O'Reilly raised her hand. "Your conclusion, Doctor, is that both women were killed by a bow and arrow?"

"A crossbow bolt, yes," Chuckie said.

"Any sign of sexual assault?" O'Reilly asked.

"The remains of both girls were pretty well mutilated, but neither I nor Trace could find any seminal fluid, bruising, or trauma in the usual areas," Chuckie said.

"Thank God for small favors," Heller muttered.

"Anything noteworthy on the ties or the duct tape?" O'Reilly turned to Beans.

"The ties are from the same manufacturer. The tape from both women also match," Beans said. "No prints or other evidence from the perp."

"Same weapon, same restraints, same killer." O'Reilly nodded. "Tox?"

"We're still waiting on toxicology," Chuckie said. "With Morelli, we anticipate finding marijuana, at least. We found some in her backpack."

"I'd like a copy of the full report when you have it, please," she said with another dazzling smile.

"It would be my pleasure." Chuckie smiled back, clearly smitten.

"Thank you, and I apologize for the interruption."

"No apology necessary, Agent."

Before Chuckie could further embarrass himself, Dubois broke in. "Now would be a good time for Special Agent O'Reilly to enlighten us with her insights. Agent?"

She clumped to the front of the room in her rubber boots and pulled an iPad from her messenger bag. "Thank you, Lieutenant. Good morning, all." She looked to Beans, then the whiteboard. "Sorry, I didn't have time to put together a formal presentation, so I'll have to resort to a low-tech option. Okay if I write on this?" Beans nodded.

She consulted her iPad, then tapped at the photos on the whiteboard with a marker. "Okay, so I think we're in agreement that we've got two murders, one killer. In the universe of serial killings, we have a very small sample. As callous as that may sound, this is not a huge well from which to draw info, or from which to perform in-depth analysis.

"With that caveat, here's what I believe we're looking for, based on what we know of the murders of Jolene Nilsson and Antoinette Morelli."

O'Reilly uncapped the marker and began writing on the whiteboard in precise capital letters. "One: male, twenties to thirties. He's probably white, but not necessarily," she continued. "He's a loner; probably lives alone or with a single parent. He is probably working alone.

"Two—and fairly obvious, based on the findings of Dr. Hefner and Anchorage PD: unsub is an outdoorsman and hunter, with considerable expertise in the use of a crossbow.

"Three: the unsub is probably, although not necessarily, working at a blue-collar job, but one which allows him to move freely in an urban setting without attracting attention.

"Four: unsub is probably socially awkward. He probably has feelings of inadequacy sexually or romantically. He targets young women that he finds alluring but at the same time wholesome and approachable. For example, he has not targeted more intimidating women like sex workers. At least not yet.

"Five: we think he might have feelings of remorse for killing these women—hence the rose at the scene. Either that, or he has romanticized a totally fictional relationship with these women. Or a combination of both.

"Six: we think he will most certainly strike again."

While she printed on the whiteboard, her shapely backside facing her rapt audience, it became obvious to Beans that the male members of the Homicide Division had developed a huge collective crush on O'Reilly. *Hell, maybe some of the women too.* What was not to like? She was bright and accomplished, her presentation succinct and informative. And she was easy on the eyes. Heller held his chin in his hand in undisguised admiration. Chuckie looked like he could barely keep from drooling. Someone at the back of the room emitted a soulful sigh.

"So, we've got to get this guy soon or lose other young women," O'Reilly continued, seeming not to notice her roomful of admirers. "None of what I've told you is brain surgery, but that's all we've got to work with at this time. Because of the small sample, some of these points are just assumptions based on past history with similar cases. We'll rely on you to help flesh this guy out. My role here is to help put the Bureau's considerable tools at your disposal."

Special Agent O'Reilly was as unlike Whiz Magnuson as one could get and still be the same species. She was young, energetic, and well versed in current technology—a whole new generation of FBI agent. Beans caught Dubois' eye and nodded his approval.

"For example, I understand that Dr. Hefner has extracted blood and tissue from under the fingernails of Toni Morelli," O'Reilly continued.

"Right, but so far we haven't found a match to anyone on file," Chuckie said.

"With DNA phenotyping, we could determine ethnicity, hair, skin, and eye color, narrowing our suspect base. And we can do it quickly," she added, as if reading Beans' mind.

She stopped in front of a crime scene photo of Jolene's body.

"As soon as possible, let's put together a geographic profile of the unsub. This'll likely be a stab in the dark because of the small sample, but we could give it a shot."

"The abductions occurred pretty much across town from each other. Not sure if there's any kind of pattern," Beans said.

O'Reilly nodded. "We'll need your local knowledge, Detectives Beans and . . . Heller, was it?" She squinted, trying to read Heller's ID on his lanyard.

"Ed Heller, ma'am." Heller shot to his feet and almost saluted.

"Wow, at ease, Detective." O'Reilly smiled, as someone in the room snickered and Heller's face reddened. "But I like your enthusiasm. Maybe the three of us can have a sidebar after this, and we can talk about how I can best aid the investigation."

Beans had been dreading the involvement of the FBI since the discovery of Toni Morelli's body, but now he felt this might be a productive collaboration after all. He collected his files and a large map of the Anchorage area and joined Heller and O'Reilly in the conference room.

18

At twelve thirty Monday, Agent Isabelle O'Reilly strode into the Homicide unit in her rubber boots, bringing with her an intriguing scent combination of maiden-aunt lavender perfume and deli meats. She set down several sacks of sandwiches on an empty desk behind Beans and uncoiled her scarf.

"Well, I just blew through my per diem." She dropped her coat into an empty chair.

"What, no fat expense account?" Beans sat back and rubbed his eyes. He had been staring at security video and spreadsheets all morning and welcomed the lunch break.

"Ha!" She peered into the bags. "Not since Secret Service agents tried to expense their Colombian hookers a few years back."

Heller sauntered up and tossed three twenty-dollar bills on the desk. "I'll cover lunch, Agent."

Chuckie scurried through the doors with a cardboard carrier loaded with drinks. "Hey, I told her I'd buy."

"That's too much, Ed. I owe you some change. Where's my Cobb salad?" O'Reilly rummaged through the bags. "Here's your non-kosher salami on rye, Doctor." She handed a wrapped sandwich to Chuckie.

"Nah, keep the change," Heller said to O'Reilly. "Where's the egg salad on white?"

"Why did I know you'd have egg salad on white?" Chuckie gave Heller a disapproving look.

O'Reilly counted the bills and reached into her wallet for change. Heller waved her off, already unwrapping his sandwich.

"Hey, I shouldn't come out ahead on this." She frowned, staring at the cash.

"You're buying the first round at Muldoon's when this is over," Heller said.

"You're on." She poured dressing on her Cobb salad and speared a cherry tomato on her fork.

They had all gone their separate ways after DuBois' mandatory session, and Beans wanted an update. The best time seemed to be the lunch hour, and no one had objected when O'Reilly offered to get sandwiches for the team.

"This is a really good Reuben," Beans said. "Where did you get it?"

"That little spot near the FBI office—Snowtown Bistro, I think it's called? I've stopped there for coffee a couple of times."

Where Amy Chandler works. Beans' stomach did a little dance around the mouthful of sauerkraut that he'd just swallowed. He cleared his throat and said, "Chuckie, what do you have for us?"

"No surprise, the DNA from the blood on Toni's face and the tissue under her fingernails match," Chuckie said, chewing on a dill pickle. "As we know, there is no match to anyone we have on file. But, thanks to the expedited DNA phenotyping that Agent O'Reilly greased through for us, we have a profile of the killer. Agent?"

"How about you all call me Isabelle?"

"Izzy?" Beans asked.

She smiled. "Nope. The only person who can call me Izzy is my two-year-old niece."

"Isabelle it is, then. Who is this guy?"

"Unfortunately, we don't know a whole lot more than we've already conjectured from the behavior profiling." She looked at her notepad. "He is mostly Northern European but has some Native Alaskan blood, Inuit/Inupiat. He's taller than average, with brown or black hair and brown eyes. And he has hereditary male-pattern baldness."

"That's half the guys in Anchorage," Heller said. "Hell, it could be Beans."

"Hey, I'm not Inupiat. And I'm not going bald. Am I?" Beans asked O'Reilly, who smiled and shook her head. "Okay, that's more than we had before, but not enough to get a composite sketch from."

"Well," O'Reilly said midchew, "no. But on the positive side, we know that he is not Black, Latino, or Asian."

"Trace and tox?" Beans asked.

"The bark fragments found on both the Nilsson girl and Toni Morelli are black spruce. Native to the Denali vicinity where Morelli was found, but not in the immediate area where Jolene was found. Tox is still not back, but my guess is the girls must have been roofied or tranquilized," Chuckie said.

"Nothing special about the roses." Beans took a sip of Diet Coke. "Could have been purchased at any florist or grocery store. As a reminder, the roses are hold-backs, guys. We're not releasing the rose or the arrow info to the media in case we have the usual nutjobs confessing to the killings."

"Got it," O'Reilly said, chewing and scribbling notes on a yellow pad.

"What do you think about the roses?" Beans asked O'Reilly. "A sign of remorse? Mourning? A weird romantic gesture?"

"Could be all of the above. The fact that there's no sexual assault says that he had a kind of respect for them. Like I said yesterday, he could be making up some kind of elaborate fantasy that includes these women."

"As far as security video goes," Beans said, "Far North management's video of the strip mall near Snow Bunny tells us nothing. It was dark and snowing heavily when Jolene was taken, and the video quality is even poorer than usual. I can't imagine even the Bureau's facial recognition software could pick anything out. The Kwik-E-Mart video is pretty much the same."

"We'll give it a shot. I'll have our tech guys look at it." O'Reilly made a few more notes.

"How about the phones, Heller?" Beans asked, pointing a dill pickle spear at the detective.

"Jolene's phone has not been located, but last ping was right there at the coffee kiosk. She had a brief text conversation with Daniel Correa the day before she went missing; longer ones to Olaf and Esther Nilsson in Manokotak and Darla Stayton, her fellow barista. A couple of calls to her landlady, Anna Kaminski. Those are the numbers that come up more than once. All the others are brief calls to the university, takeout Mexican, Fireweed Toyota, et cetera.

"Toni's call history is a little more interesting. Several to Finland, to a Sam Holder, the old boyfriend. He was definitely in Helsinki the day of her abduction, so he's pretty much out of the suspect pool. Texts and phone calls to the roommate, Amy Chandler—and a few to your old buddy." Heller grinned at Beans.

"My old buddy?" Beans was wishing Heller would stop being his usual smug self when it dawned on him, and he shut his eyes. "Frankie Ma."

"Yeah, Frankie Ma, imagine that?" Heller was having far too much fun with this.

"Amy Chandler, the roommate, said that Toni bought an occasional gram of coke from him. He said the last time he saw Toni was around Thanksgiving," Beans said.

"That agrees with her phone records. He had a twenty-five-second call with her at two seventeen PM on November twenty-fifth," Heller said, flipping through phone company printouts.

"Who is this Frankie Ma?" O'Reilly asked.

"Derelict school buddy of Beans." Heller opened a bag of chips. "He was a long shot on the Concepcion disappearance."

"I just found out about this when I talked to the roommate the other day," Beans said. "He's no killer. I don't like him for Toni Morelli. But he did say the only reason he sold drugs was because Sevy Concepcion threatened to hurt his mom."

Heller chewed thoughtfully. "Drug dealing *is* one of Sevy's small business enterprises . . . makes sense that he would make a guy who owes him deal for him."

Beans went on. "Geographic profiling is not conclusive. Snow Bunny is off of O'Malley and Old Seward Highway; Arctic Foxes is across town by the airport. The only common denominators are that neither is covered by video security, and both kiosks are fairly secluded."

"And the attire of the baristas," Chuckie added.

Beans nodded. Even the time of day of the abductions weren't consistent—Jolene had been taken after evening close, Toni before her morning shift.

"Any luck on the arrows?" Heller asked.

"I've requested sales records from local sporting goods stores and online vendors to see if something jumps out," Beans said. "Otherwise, no. The Montec broadhead is very popular."

"I checked the FBI weaponry database," O'Reilly added. "As expected, the crossbow isn't the weapon of choice for serial killers, at least not in this country. In England, though, a criminology student killed three sex workers with a crossbow, then ate parts of them before disposing of their bodies."

Heller set down his sandwich, grimacing. "Oh Jesus, do you mind? I'm trying to have lunch here."

Chuckie grabbed a handful of chips. "No reason to think anybody except the scavengers have eaten these women, is there?"

"I'm not getting a cannibalism vibe from this guy, but it's something to keep in mind." O'Reilly took a swig of Diet Coke.

"So, how many 'bikini barista'–type coffee kiosks do you think there are in the city? How many women do you think are at risk?" Beans reached into a bag for a chocolate chip cookie.

"Metro area?" Heller asked. "I don't know. A dozen coffee drive-throughs, maybe?"

"That might be a conservative estimate," Chuckie said.

"How many do you think have video security?" Beans asked.

"I'll see what I can find out." O'Reilly opened her iPad.

Beans stared at the six colored pins on the large Anchorage map—two blue pins on the locations of the kiosks, two red pins on the dump sites of the two young women, and two yellow pins on their places of residence. He was chewing on a cookie, looking for a pattern in these six points, when his cell phone barked. The display read *Mom*.

He picked up the call with some apprehension. His mother never called him during working hours. "Hi, Mom. Did I forget something at the house?"

"Havi?" Her voice sounded tired and tentative, unlike her usual upbeat self.

"What, Mom? Are you okay?" Beans was conscious of a hush falling over the conversations of his colleagues.

"It's your grandfather, Havi. He's had a stroke. He's alive, but . . . he's at UCSF. I can't get out of Galena until tomorrow. Then I'll catch the afternoon flight out of Anchorage."

Beans had met his maternal grandparents only once when he was ten years old. His mother had brought her three youngest children to see her parents when they stopped through Anchorage on an Alaska cruise. His grandmother, a smiling, immaculately groomed middle-aged Japanese woman, had brought them gifts—a San Francisco Giants baseball jersey two sizes too small for Beans, a fragile Japanese doll in a glass case for Piper, and a jumbo stuffed panda for baby Otter. Beans and Piper had mechanically recited "Thank you" and stared at the inappropriate gifts while Mari tried to jam the toy panda—as large as its recipient—into a diaper bag.

All while their sharp-eyed grandfather seemed to assess them for any genetic frailty inherited from their father, the drunken half-breed Jimmy Beans.

19

Beans had two photographs of his grandfather Ben Yamane—one had been taken that day in Anchorage by a waiter at a sushi restaurant. His grandfather's chiseled face stared, unsmiling, into the camera. By contrast, his grandmother had a forced grin on her face. Baby Otter wailed while Mari tried to console him. Beans and Piper looked fidgety and uncomfortable.

The other photo of his grandfather was a curly-edged black-and-white print of a little boy with a crew cut—a school-aged Ben wearing short pants, a plaid shirt, and a cowboy hat. Cinched around his narrow waist was a child's toy holster with a carved wooden pistol. He stood in a dusty, treeless field, arm in arm with a taller Japanese boy, smiling behind the barbed wire fencing of the Minidoka War Relocation Center.

That evening, Mari yawned as she FaceTimed Beans from her parents' house in the Bay Area. She gestured behind her at the shelves of plastic bins filled with fabric and sewing supplies. "This used to be my old room. Of course, it's now Mom's sewing room. Mom, come say hi to Havi."

His grandmother, still immaculately groomed but stooped and white haired now, peered into the screen. "Is that you, Havi?

All grown up." Her eyes glistened. "And so handsome! Your grandfather would be . . ." Then her face crumpled, and she waved at Beans as she backed out of view. "It's late. You have work tomorrow."

It was well past midnight in California, an hour earlier in Alaska.

"How's Grandpa?" Beans asked, when he was sure his grandmother was out of earshot.

"Breathing on his own, but not conscious. We won't know what the damage is until he wakes up. If he wakes up."

Beans released a long breath. "I'm sorry, Mom. If you need me, I can be there in a couple of days. Piper says she can come too, but not until the weekend."

"No." Her voice was firm. "Stay there, both of you. I'll know more when I talk to the doctors tomorrow." Mari's smile was sad. "You kids never got to know your grandfather at all, did you?"

Beans shook his head. He and his siblings had never had the casual, affectionate relationship with Mari's parents that they'd had with their paternal grandparents, Daisy and Harold Beans. In fact, aside from awkward phone calls and cards at Christmas and birthdays, they had practically no relationship at all with Ben and Michiko Yamane. "I don't remember much about Grandpa Ben except that he kind of scared Piper and me."

"He could be pretty scary. Everything was so black and white, so 'his way or the highway.' The minute he met your father, he decided he hated him—and there was no changing his mind."

Beans knew that what his grandfather had hated most about Jimmy Beans was that he didn't meet either of the requirements for marrying into the Yamane family: being Asian and being a lawyer or doctor. Mari's sister Naomi was married to a Taiwanese ob-gyn, and her brother Roy (an attorney) had married a Japanese American pharmacist. They had followed their father's rules to the letter.

"Your father—no choir boy, as you know, but a good man. My father is a good man too, in his own way, but so . . ." Mari sighed and suddenly looked exhausted. "It's been a long day, Havi. Your grandma and I are getting an early start to try to catch the doctor on morning rounds. I'll say good-night."

Archie jumped off his lap as Beans switched off his laptop. Both cat and owner stretched and yawned. Beans examined the black-and-white print of his grandfather pinned on the corkboard in front of him. In the photo's background were the wooden barracks-like structures typical of World War II Japanese internment camps and blurred figures caught midmovement by the camera. Clouds of dust further obscured details of the buildings and people. In the foreground was a grinning Ben Yamane, pretending to be an American cowboy—pretending, Beans thought, to be part of a culture that had betrayed and imprisoned him.

Beans padded on stocking feet to the small three-tiered Buddhist shrine on a nearby dresser. He lit a few sticks of incense for his grandfather and breathed its distinctive, cleansing perfume while the pale smoke snaked to the ceiling.

20

At the start of the new year, Beans' nightmares took on new, more horrible dimensions. He still hung upside down in the cab of his brother Lindbergh's overturned truck. Pale, lovely Jolene dangled next to him, her torso flayed like a gaping maw. Tangled in a frayed seat belt was Toni Morelli, her blond hair with the dark roots swaying in the heat from the fire. Her mascara dripped across her forehead and into her scalp. In her chest cavity, where the organs had been devoured by predators, a broadhead point lay embedded in a rib.

Lindbergh! Get me out! he screamed, like he always did, and pounded on the hot glass of the window. This time, his hands left bloody palm prints on the glass.

He awoke in a sweat, certain that he could smell burning rubber, smoldering upholstery, singed hair.

The women haunted him in his sleep, while Lieutenant DuBois and the Anchorage media dogged him relentlessly in his waking hours. No one was more adept at handling the media than the lieutenant, but even he visited the incident room daily, inspecting the whiteboard for new leads, wondering what bone he could throw the newshounds.

Reporters, bloggers, and influencers loitered at police head-quarters, ambushing him with questions—no, *accusations*—like, "What have you done to prevent any more killings?"

What have I done? Precious little. Not enough. He ducked his head, muttering, "No comment," as he hurried through the door or out to his car.

For everyone working the barista case in January, it felt like they were holding their collective breath, waiting for the other shoe to drop. It had been a month since Toni Morelli was found at Denali National Park, a month and a half since Jolene lay muti-lated on the snow. According to O'Reilly, the perpetrator most certainly would strike again. Would they stop him in time?

Beans, Heller, and Chuckie regularly convened over bad cof-fee in the incident room to share what meager bits of information they could, and to commiserate.

O'Reilly, who had flown back to Portland for first-quarter regional meetings, had returned to Anchorage, fresh-faced and energized, and arrived carrying a box of doughnuts. "Happy New Year, troops! Ready to hit it running, guys?"

Heller grumbled that the in-laws had finally left. Limping over to grab a glazed doughnut, Chuckie reported that he had gone skiing and twisted his knee badly. Beans and Piper had shared takeout dinners and FaceTimed their mother and grand-mother in San Francisco, getting updates on their grandfather's condition.

Their Grandpa Ben clung to life, thanks to the gastric tube feeding that his wife insisted on—even though his neurologists thought the likelihood of him regaining consciousness was slim. Mari had helped settle her father into a long-term care facility and returned home to Galena in mid-January. "He would have hated being kept alive like a houseplant." She sighed. "But she won't let him go."

In the first few weeks of the new year, the investigation seemed to be paralyzed as well. Barely tasting the doughnut he chewed, Beans stared again at the six colored pins on the Anchorage area map on the wall. *What is it we're missing?* He and his team had rehashed the evidence over and over, shuffling files between them, hoping that fresh eyes would reveal something that had been missed earlier.

"The good news—toxicology is finally in." Chuckie licked glaze off his fingertips. "No surprise—both women had been sedated with Rohypnol, the most common of date-rape drugs."

"But how?" Beans asked. "He can't be slipping it in a drink."

Chuckie stared at the whiteboard. "I'm guessing they were injected with it rather than ingesting it. The date rapers' newest delivery MO is to dissolve the pills and then inject their victims with it. Given the condition of the remains of both these girls, the injection site was impossible to locate, but I'm betting they were jabbed with it." Chuckie wiped his hands on a paper napkin and tapped on his laptop. "Nilsson also had a trace of Xanax in her bloodstream and in her hair, and Morelli had a smattering of THC, but we expected that. Nothing that would raise eyebrows."

Beans was standing in front of the Anchorage map when his desk phone rang. A sinking feeling came over him, and the chocolate éclair he chewed on was suddenly dry and tasteless. *Carmen Fernandez*, the phone display read. *Missing Persons*.

Fernandez's usually jovial voice was stiff and formal. "Another barista didn't show for work, this one at Buffalo Gals Brew on Boniface Parkway. Beans," she said, her voice catching, "her name is Hannah. Hannah Fernandez. She's my niece."

21

Uncle Carlos' chickens squawk and flap their wings in a frenzy. Somehow, they know that they will die. He strides through the backyard toward the faded red chicken coop with his long knife. He chews his cigar and spits, full of purpose to kill some chickens for the pollo guisado that Tía Carmen will make for Hannah's quinceañera feast.

He's quick about it, wringing the necks of four fat white hens and cutting their heads off in deft, practiced strokes. The chickens flop around, sending blood hissing onto the dirty snow.

"Hannah, bring the pot, *ahora*!" Uncle Carlos says.

She always calls her father's brother *Uncle* but his wife Carmen *Tía*. She doesn't know why. She runs outside, shivering in her flip-flops and hoodie, and hands the huge pot to Uncle Carlos, who dumps in the bloody plucked chicken carcasses.

"Here, take it in to your tía."

She looks down, and the chickens are still moving, twitching in the pink solution of blood and melted snow.

Hannah jerks awake, the shrill cries of chickens prodding her into consciousness. She opens her eyes, gummy from crying, but sees nothing except the gray weave of the blindfold. A sob escapes but is trapped in the duct tape across her mouth.

Jesus Maria, where am I?

She tries to focus on the prickly surface of the cot against the side of her face, the faraway drone of machinery, the familiar smells of manure and grain.

But again her mind bobs like an untethered helium balloon to her quinceañera five years ago. Her mama made her the most beautiful off-shoulder formal dress, pale pink, with satin roses on the bodice and across the hem. The gown matched the cake, a three-tiered affair, iced with pink rosebuds. *Dios, it was awesome.*

Uncle Carlos and Tía Carmen's backyard was set up with a huge yellow-and-white heated tent, and her cousin Theo was DJ for the evening. She and her papa danced to "My Girl" by the Temptations, while she stood on his shoes in her bare feet, and Papa had tears in his eyes.

She blinks hard, feeling her own tears squeeze out and blot on the blindfold. She screams, but it comes out as a soft groan behind the duct tape. *How long have I been here?* She has obviously screamed a lot, since her throat feels scratchy and raw. She swallows hard to keep the panic from creeping up her throat.

She rolls herself into a seated position and stands awkwardly, her hands tied behind her and her feet bound at the ankles. After a couple of two-legged hops, she trips over something—a stool, she thinks—and crashes to the floor.

She is in some kind of unheated shed. The floor is damp in spots and covered with what feels like rice. *Mouse shit, maybe?*

145

Her hip aches where she fell. She struggles to remember how she got here, but nothing is clear. Was she drugged, or knocked out?

She remembers bagging up the two-day-old maple bars for Cam, the bus driver. She always gives him leftover pastries, since he's so nice, stopping the bus right in front of the kiosk so she doesn't have to walk so far. *Yeah, he's a little weird, but sweet in a* Rain Man *kind of way.* Got a nice body, at least from what she can tell. So she bagged up the pastries, threw on her coat, locked the kiosk, then what?

She remembers walking toward the curb to wait for the bus. The headlights from the pickup truck idling there almost blinded her. The driver's face was only a smudge behind the wheel of the truck. He rolled down the driver's side window. With that loco taking the baristas, she had to be careful, but she knew this guy; his name was on the tip of her tongue.

"Need a lift?" His face was in darkness.

"No, thanks, the bus will be here any—"

His arm sprang out of the window, a cobra's strike, and she felt a venomous sting at her neck. Then she woke up here, in this freezing shed, with this filthy mouse-shitty floor. She sobs again, snot running down the duct tape and dribbling down her chin.

The door squeaks open and lets in a blast of frigid air.

"What are you doing on the floor?" he asks, as if she can answer. *Hijo de puta.*

She tries to crawl away from the voice, so familiar, so frightening. Another sob catches in her throat.

"No matter, it's time."

He picks her up easily and tosses her over his shoulder. He is a big man, solid under her. She kicks and squirms, trying again to scream.

"Jesus, be still," he scolds, irritated. "Another fighter."

But she can't be still. Like the chickens, she knows she is going to die. She tries to claw at him, but her hands are tied behind her and she groans in frustration. His intense smell of roses and Old Spice makes her gag. She can tell by his staggering steps that he is moving over uneven ground, his footsteps muffled by snow.

She closes her eyes against the grayness of the blindfold and recites to herself, "Hail, Mary, full of grace, the Lord is with thee; blessed art thou among women, and blessed is the fruit of thy womb, Jesus. Holy Mary, Mother of God, pray for us sinners, now and at the hour of our death."

Now at the hour of my death. Amen. She lifts her tear-streaked face to the softly falling snow.

22

Beans balanced his notebook on the weathered arm of the leather recliner in the Fernandezes' overheated living room. Missing Persons officer Carmen Fernandez and her sister-in-law Linda sat across from him on a floral printed sofa. Carmen, a large, maternal presence, seemed to engulf the spindly Linda Fernandez, who looked pale and defenseless. On the wall behind the two women, a small wooden crucifix, suspended by a thin leather strap, hovered between time-faded family photos.

Carmen held one of Linda's hands, patting and smoothing it as if calming a skittish animal. Linda's other hand gripped a strand of rosary beads and a photo of Hannah's pretty, elfin face. Hannah's father, Ernesto, paced from one end of the living room to the other, his hands shoved into his pockets.

"Carmen," Linda said, her faded blue eyes darting from her sister-in-law's worried face to Beans. "Please tell me she's not dead," she begged.

"Dios, don't be crazy, Linda," Ernesto said in a gruff voice. He was a tall, well-built Latino who crossed the small living room in three long strides.

148

"Detective Beans is a friend of mine." Carmen seemed to choose her words carefully. "He's working on the barista cases that you've seen in the news."

"Oh, dear God, you think she's the next victim?" When Linda closed her eyes and made the sign of the cross, she hesitated for a moment, as if she were suddenly unconvinced of a merciful God. Ernesto glided across the room and put a hand on his wife's thin shoulder.

Beans leaned forward and took a deep breath, his hands clasped. He didn't know what was worse: informing a family of their worst nightmare or warning them to prepare for it. A bead of sweat trickled between his shoulder blades. "Of course we want to bring Hannah back home safely," he said. "But if there's any commonality between these cases, we need to identify them right away."

"I knew this barista job was a bad idea, I just knew it. Especially after the Morelli girl . . . but she wanted to do it so bad. And it's been, what, a month since that poor Morelli girl . . . ? I thought this bastard had taken his two girls and was done, or in jail, or, shit, why couldn't he be dead?" Ernesto ran his hands through his lightly graying hair. "Why couldn't we for once, just once, have said no to her?"

"She told us not to worry, she carries pepper spray." Linda's fist clenched around the rosary beads. "And Buffalo Gals has closed-circuit security TV, right?" She looked at Beans.

"Unfortunately, the security system wasn't operational last night."

He didn't have the heart to tell her that Buffalo Gals' security system hadn't worked for months. Earlier that day, Beans had spoken with the owner of the coffee shop, who also owned Ralph's Rentals, the small equipment rental company/hardware store across the parking lot from Buffalo Gals. Ralph Simonov, a grizzled old retired miner, was horrified that "sweet little Hannah" was now missing.

"Sure, I got a camera there. I got one at the rental shop too. Keeps everybody honest, you know?" Ralph sucked on one of his six remaining teeth. "But the one at the coffee shop crapped out on me around Halloween, and I never got it fixed. Cash was a little tight around then." He winced and looked sad. "She ain't been taken, has she, like those other girls?"

"We don't know that yet, Mr. Simonov."

Ralph Simonov sighed and scratched at his two days' worth of sparse gray beard. "I'm sorely upset about that little girl—you tell her parents."

Beans had also confirmed that the night Hannah disappeared, Ralph had been at an Alcoholics Anonymous meeting with a roomful of witnesses who heard him say he had now been six months without a drink.

"Detective Beans is here as a favor to me," Carmen said, jolting Beans' thoughts back to the Fernandezes' oppressively warm living room. "Hannah is not officially missing yet—it hasn't been forty-eight hours. But because we know our girl and that she would never go AWOL without calling us, I asked him here."

"That, and because she's a barista wearing a fucking fur bikini," Ernesto blurted out.

Ernesto was right. Hannah fit the victim profile. She was an attractive young barista in a revealing costume, as were Jolene Nilsson and Toni Morelli. With each hour that passed, it became less likely that Hannah would reappear, sheepish and apologetic.

As much as Beans told himself to keep an open mind, his nagging, jaded cop instinct insisted that she was victim number three. His heart ached for the Fernandezes, the Nilssons, and Mr. Morelli.

"If she has been kidnapped, time is vital," Beans said. "But let's back up a step. Does Hannah have any boy- or girlfriends she could be spending some time with?"

"No." Linda shook her head. "Not without telling us. She hasn't dated anyone seriously since Grady Moreland, and he's out on a NOAA research vessel somewhere in the Beaufort Sea."

"We checked with all of her girlfriends," Carmen added. "No one has seen her lately."

"Does he want a ransom? I have an electrical contracting business. I'm no Jeff Bezos, but I can come up with some cash." Ernesto's eyes had a desperate glint.

"There's been no talk of ransom at this point, Mr. Fernandez," Beans said. "Now, tell me about Hannah's typical routine." He needed to get the family to focus and to work from the assumption that their daughter was still alive.

Linda Fernandez said that Hannah had closed up the Buffalo Gals kiosk at seven PM. She then had caught the bus home. "Silly, isn't it?" she said, with a sad smile. "Born and raised in Alaska, and she hates driving in the snow. She started taking the bus last winter. By the time spring rolled around, it got to be a habit and she realized how much money she was saving on gas. Her little Nissan stays in the garage until her days off."

"The car's here now?" Beans asked.

"Right where she left it," Ernesto said. "Keys are hanging on the hook by the back door."

"She got to be friendly with the bus driver on her route. A young man named Cam something—Christopher?" Linda

151

furrowed her brow as she tried to recall the name. "He picked her up in front of the kiosk every evening—not the normal stop—so she wouldn't need to walk a block in the snow. She usually bagged up the two-day-old pastries to give him, the stuff they would have thrown out the next day."

"Was she dating Cam?"

"Oh no." Linda shook her head again. "Hannah said he was a little sweet on her, but kind of—odd."

"Odd how?" Beans asked.

"Kind of shy, you know, awkward. Rarely looked her in the eye."

"You think this is him? You think this could be the guy?" Ernesto started pacing again.

Beans held out his hands. "It's too soon to tell, Mr. Fernandez. Right now, I'd like to talk to him. He might be able to shed light on Hannah's movements last night." Remembering O'Reilly's profile of the perpetrator as socially awkward, he definitely wanted to pay a call on the bus driver.

After declining offers of coffee or something stronger, Beans stood to leave. The freezing air outside was crisp and refreshing, in contrast to the soul-sapping heat and emotional tension of the Fernandezes' living room. Carmen walked him out to his car.

"I know it's early days," he said, "but I'll get a location on her phone." He paused to study her face. "Are you going to be okay?"

"Yeah, I'll stay with them until Carlos comes by after work with Theo. They'll bring a double-meat pizza." She gave him a sad smile. "With a stuffed crust. That's our family. During times of stress, we gotta eat. The greasier, the better." She covered her face with her hands. "Ernesto is Carlos' kid brother. Hannah grew up with my Theo." Dry-eyed until now, she began to cry.

He drew her into a hug, feeling her soft matronly body shuddering with sobs. He held her for a few seconds until she pulled away, wiping her eyes and putting on a bright, brave smile. A fine dry snow began falling, dusting her plum-colored sweater and dark hair.

"I can't help thinking, what if . . . what if, after the Morelli girl . . . what if we had shut them all down, all those—places—whether it would have stopped this bastard? Would our Hannah be home now?"

"I don't know, Carmen." He took her hands and squeezed them. He knew that if Hannah turned up as the third victim, Carmen wouldn't be the only one asking this question. "Maybe. But maybe he would have started taking other girls. We just don't know right now. I'm sorry."

She nodded. "I know you guys are working hard on this. But Beans, this is my niece, mi sobrina." Her eyes filled with tears again. "Yeah, I'm a cop. I know what the odds are, and they suck."

Beans gave her arm a squeeze. "Call me if you hear anything."

"You too." Carmen pulled her wool cardigan around her, staring straight into the falling snow, as if searching for Hannah's returning silhouette.

23

A quick phone call to Anchorage Transit confirmed that they employed a driver named Cameron Kristovich, not Christopher. He was out on a route now but due back to the bus barn in forty-five minutes.

"And I mean exactly forty-five minutes," the husky-voiced dispatcher said, chuckling.

Beans wondered what exactly that meant but decided he would find out soon enough. On his way to the metro transit bus barn, he checked in with O'Reilly.

"Tech boys haven't had much luck cleaning up the security video." Exasperation sharpened her voice. "Here I am, talking up the technical expertise of our geeks, and all they can say is, 'Does it *ever* stop snowing there?' They managed to pick out a few partial plate numbers that I'll email you, but I'm not sure how much help they'll be."

At the bus barn, he was told that Cameron Kristovich had arrived as scheduled and could be found on a bench in the maintenance warehouse, having a Coke and an Almond Joy.

The maintenance warehouse, across a snow-crusted alley from the office, smelled of diesel exhaust and motor oil. Just as the receptionist had said, a sandy-haired young man sat on a wooden bench in a far corner of the warehouse, a can of Coke in one hand and a half-eaten Almond Joy in the other.

"Cameron Kristovich?"

The young man looked up at Beans with pale-blue eyes. He set the Coke on the bench beside him and balanced the candy bar across the top of the soda can. He stood, as if being called to attention. He was Beans' height, slender but muscular. Beans thought that girls would probably find him attractive except for the expressionless cast to his face.

"Yes," he said in a loud, flat voice.

"Mr. Kristovich, I'm Detective Beans with the Anchorage Police Department."

Cameron Kristovich looked somewhere over Beans' left shoulder, which made Beans turn to see if someone was standing behind him.

"Am I in trouble?" Cameron said, with the same robotic delivery.

"Trouble? No, I'm here because I'm hoping you can help me. We're afraid that your friend Hannah Fernandez may be missing."

"Missing?" The mention of Hannah's name seemed to spark interest. He wiped his hands on his jeans-clad thighs as his eyes flicked, just for a moment, across Beans' face.

"You know Hannah Fernandez, don't you?" Beans asked.

"Buffalo Gal Hannah."

"Yes, she works at Buffalo Gals Brew coffee shop."

"On Boniface Parkway and Twenty-Fourth Street."

"Yes, that's the one. She didn't come home last night and didn't show up for work this morning."

"Yes, I know."

"You know? How do you know?"

"I know because she wasn't waiting for the bus last night. On the days she works—Tuesday-Wednesday-Thursday-Friday-Saturday—I pick her up at seven ten PM at the corner of Boniface Parkway and Twenty-Fourth with the number-thirty bus."

His recitation was without pause, and he ran the days of the week together as if they were one long word. This was an odd one, Beans thought. "You seem pretty sure," he said.

"She's the only one I pick up there. Every night she works, she is there at seven ten PM. But she wasn't there last night. The shop was dark, all locked up. I thought maybe she got sick, because she is always there Tuesday-Wednesday-Thursday-Friday-Saturday. She gives me maple bars and cheese Danishes, but I like maple bars better. There are one hundred and twenty more milligrams of sodium in a maple bar than a cheese Danish."

Beans scribbled in his notebook so he wouldn't stare. More information than he needed on the nutritional composition of a pastry. "How long have you been picking her up?"

"Since March third of last year."

"What normally happens after you pick her up at the usual spot at"—Beans consulted his notes—"Boniface Parkway and Twenty-Fourth?"

"I take her to the Muldoon Transit Hub, where she transfers to the twenty-five heading north. She catches the seven thirty-two bus."

Cameron Kristovich remembered intricate details about a young woman who was one of many riders he saw daily. "You sure know a lot about Hannah's schedule."

"Is that bad?"

"No, not at all. I'm just wondering how you manage to remember all this when you must have dozens of riders throughout the day."

"At that time of the day on the eastbound thirty, there are usually five or maybe seven people on the bus, and they all get off at the Muldoon Transit Hub. That's the end of the line." He looked down at his scuffed work boots. "And Hannah is very nice. And very pretty."

At last. The boy's not an android after all.

"Do you ever see Hannah any other time?"

"Other time?"

"Other than the evening bus."

"No."

"Did you ever ask her out?"

"Out?" *Is there an echo?*

"Out on a date? To get a bite to eat, or see a movie?"

"No, no." Cameron looked down at his boots again and rose briefly onto his toes. "No."

"Did you ever want to?"

Before Cameron could answer, a nearby door labeled EMPLOYEES ONLY opened and a bearded middle-aged man in a plaid shirt stepped through.

"Sorry to interrupt. Ingrid said there was a police detective here to talk to one of our drivers." He extended a calloused hand to Beans. "Ted Baylor, I'm the shift supervisor." His handshake was firm and confident. "Cam, would you mind letting the detective and me chat for a minute? Ingrid could use some help with the spreadsheet she's working on."

Cameron nodded and left through the same door Ted Baylor had entered. Beans was about to ask about this interruption when

Baylor interjected, "I apologize for barging in, but I thought I should give you some background, so you don't draw the wrong conclusions. Please, have a seat, Detective."

Beans sat on one end of the bench and Ted Baylor settled on the other. Metal tools clattered to the cement floor somewhere in the building, and a diesel engine revved.

"Cam Kristovich has Asperger's syndrome. Are you familiar with it?"

"It's a high-functioning form of autism, right? I've heard of it but don't think I've met anyone with it."

"Right. Cam is incredibly bright and has an eye for detail that would amaze even a detective like yourself. But you've probably noticed he's a little—different."

"A little." *This explains a lot. The awkwardness, lack of eye contact, strict adherence to routine.*

"I'm telling you, this guy knows the times of all the bus stops—and not just his routes, mind you, but all the buses that transit through the Muldoon Transit Center. He has a photographic memory for numbers—faces too, and patterns. It's uncanny. Can I ask why you're talking with him?"

"Right now, we're trying to find a missing young woman. She's one of Cameron's regulars on his thirty route."

Baylor's pleasant demeanor faded. "Not the nice kid at the coffee shop? The one who gives him pastries?"

Beans nodded. "It's too soon to confirm her as a missing person, but we're trying to get as much info as possible on her activities last night."

Baylor stroked his beard. "Oh, Jesus, you think she might be another victim . . . ?"

"As I said, it's too soon to tell."

Baylor stood. "I'll send Cam back in. Sorry for the interruption, but I wanted to explain his situation to you."

"Understood, and thanks. You're welcome to stay while I talk to him."

"Not necessary. But I'll trust you to tell me if he needs a lawyer. Cam's folks are elderly, and we all pretty much look out for him around here."

"He's lucky to have such good friends and colleagues."

Ted Baylor smiled sadly. "I hope she comes home safely, for Cam's sake as well as hers. He doesn't make too many human connections, especially with girls." Baylor shook Beans' hand again, took his card, and stepped through the EMPLOYEES ONLY door. Cameron poked his head through a few seconds later.

"Just a few more questions, Cameron. May I call you Cameron?"

"Cam." He sat down next to his Coke and Almond Joy.

"Okay, Cam. Do you ever remember anyone talking with Hannah when you picked her up? Anyone hanging out at the coffee stand?"

Cam shook his head. "She's always alone. I pick her up where I do because I don't want her to wait on the street, alone in the dark."

Beans was touched by Cam's straightforwardness. It seemed that he really liked Hannah and cared about her safety. At the same time, O'Reilly's bullet point echoed in his memory—that the unsub could be socially awkward, and Cam definitely was. *Could this young man who accepted day-old doughnuts from Hannah have orchestrated her kidnapping? Maybe even her killing?*

Beans made a mental note to check Cam's bus routes against the locations of Snow Bunny Baristas and Arctic Foxes Espresso.

He asked a few more questions, then got Cam's contact info. He passed his business card to Cam, who studied it, flipped it over, and tucked it into his pocket.

"If you think of anything that might help us find Hannah, please let me know. Her family is very concerned."

Beans stood and extended his hand. After a beat, Cam shook it with his own cool, dry one.

"Thank you for your time," Beans said, and turned to leave.

"She would have told me," Cam said to Beans' back. "She would have told me not to stop at Boniface Parkway and Twenty-Fourth Street. She always has before when she went on vacation."

Beans turned again to face the young man.

"Something bad has happened." Cam's strange, flat voice clanged like a falling wrench in the echoing warehouse.

24

Snow began to fall again as Beans left the bus maintenance facility, not the cornmeal-like precipitation that had covered the streets this morning but large wet flakes that lay on his dark coat like wax shavings. Even by Alaska standards, it had snowed a lot this winter. For the past few months, mounded berms of the gritty white stuff lay like glacial calves on curbs and parking strips.

Cam Kristovich's parting words echoed in Beans' brain as he picked his way across the parking lot. *Something bad has happened.* Probably the understatement of the century. Beans had no doubt that something bad had happened to Hannah Fernandez.

Brushing the snow off his coat, he ducked into his car and turned the key. While the Explorer warmed up, he turned on his phone, which he had silenced during his interview with the bus driver.

There was a gruff voice mail from Heller: *"Pulled in your homeboy Frankie Ma for additional questioning. No more to add on Toni Morelli. Still don't like him for Concepcion; he's too gutless. He spit out a little more intel on Sevy's loan-sharking activities in exchange for letting him skate on the selling, so it wasn't a total waste of time."*

Before Beans headed back to the office, he had a quick errand to run. Archie had finished all the cat food from Anna Kaminski and this morning had looked woefully at the empty bag in the trash can. It wasn't grocery-store-stocked Purina or Little Friskies but some kind of God-awful-smelling salmon and sweet potato formula for finicky eaters. As far as he could tell, Archie ate pretty much anything, but Beans really did not want to upset his digestive system—not as long as he was the one cleaning out the litter box. He remembered seeing a Back to Nature pet store a few doors from the FBI building and stopped in.

A few minutes later, a faintly fishy-scented bag of premium cat food under his arm, he stepped onto the sidewalk as a light dusting of snow began to fall again. As he checked traffic to cross the street, he saw a red-and-blue neon sign a half block away— Snowtown Bistro, the restaurant where Amy Chandler worked.

She stood framed in the front window, her dark hair pulled into a chignon at the back of her neck. She wore an ivory-colored fisherman's knit sweater, a blue down vest, and fitted jeans tucked into her snow boots. She smiled at a woman and her young son as she took their orders.

What the hell. He could use a decent cup of coffee, and perhaps he should have lunch as well.

The bell on the door jangled as he wiped his boots off and took a seat at the counter. Amy looked up from pouring coffee, and her polite smile broadened into a welcoming grin, her blue eyes dancing. They darted to the cat food he had propped on the stool next to him.

"Hungry?" she asked.

Beans suddenly felt embarrassed, a grown man with a bag of cat food perched on the stool next to him like a silent, smelly lunch companion. He hurried to stow it on the floor near his feet.

She slid a laminated menu in front of him. "Coffee, right?" She started filling his mug before he had a chance to answer. "Of course you want coffee. It's really good here. Brazilian." She set the coffeepot down and met his eyes. "Any news on Toni's case?"

She was right about the coffee, it was hot and rich, but there really was nothing he could share with her.

"It's an ongoing investigation, so there's not a lot I can say right now. But more evidence has come to light recently."

"Wow, that's telling me a lot of nothing." Amy smiled, but the note of bitterness in her voice betrayed her true feelings.

"Yeah, we go to police academy to learn to say as little as possible." He held up his hands in surrender. "I know it's frustrating, but we're working hard on it, as is the FBI."

"I get it, I just want this guy caught." She picked up her pad and pen. "What'll it be, Detective?"

He ordered a BLT and a cup of tomato basil bisque. Bacon and hot soup were a couple of Beans' go-to comfort foods, and between the weather and the sluggish progress of his investigations, he was in dire need of comforting.

After placing his order and closing out another customer's tab, Amy brought him his meal, then sat on the stool next to him. "There, you are officially the last order of my shift." She nodded to a young blond woman behind the counter. "Maddie, I'm off. Holler if you need help."

Her colleague waved dismissively. "Nah, I'm good."

Amy poured herself a cup of coffee and stared down into the mug. "Just so you know, we're finally having a memorial service for Toni in the rehearsal room at the ballet—just the company, a few non-ballet homies, and Mr. Morelli. Irv Bernson offered the space, and her dad was glad to accept. Toni was happiest there, dancing, among her friends." She swiped the back of her hand across her eyes. "Sorry. Anyway, it'll be Sunday at two, if you want to attend."

"I'll plan on being there." *Will the killer be there as well? A member of Toni's close-knit ballet family?*

Amy told him that Ray Morelli had been by to pick up Toni's belongings after the police completed processing the townhome for evidence.

"It was so sad. Mr. Morelli, this big strong guy wearing Carhartts, pulls up in a U-Haul truck—a big box truck—to pick up her stuff. I packed her belongings in a half dozen boxes. Other than that, she had her bed, a dresser, a tiny desk she's had since grade school, a couple of lamps, and some bookshelves from IKEA. Most of the furniture and housewares in the townhome are mine. It made me cry, seeing her few things being swallowed by the huge emptiness in the back of that truck. Like that was all there was, all that was left of Toni."

Beans nodded. He and Heller had spoken with Ray Morelli, a large, bearded man with rough hands and a gentle way of speaking. Morelli couldn't understand who would have done this, taken this lovely young woman, his only child, from him. Beans and Heller let him ramble, speechless in the presence of his grief. He reminisced about Toni, his little ballerina, and how later, after her mother's death, she had held their small family together.

"Who could have done this? Why did they do this?" he asked, looking at the lighting fixture on the ceiling, tears in rivulets down his weatherworn face. After swearing to the grieving father that they were doing everything they could, Beans and Heller sat in the Explorer in the man's driveway.

Heller, the father of three girls, one close to Toni's age, staring at the lightly swaying Dalai Lama figure, had broken the silence. "No parent should survive his child, ever."

"So, is the sandwich okay?" Amy asked, concerned. Beans was aware that he had stopped chewing.

"Oh, yeah, it's great." And it was. The bacon was warm and crisp, the bread lightly toasted. A BLT, in Beans' mind, was Nature's Perfect Sandwich—but he didn't want to tell this young woman that his mind had been miles away just then, in Ray Morelli's living room, reliving a father's heartbreak.

She went on. "Anyway, he drove away with her whole life in four feet of a cold, sad moving van. I had a good cry, then started cleaning to get ready for my next tenant."

"Another tenant?"

"I can't afford the townhouse on my own. Toni was paid up until the end of the month, but after that . . ." She sipped at her coffee.

"You've got someone lined up already?"

"Yeah, another dancer."

"When does she move in?"

"He. He'll start moving in next week."

"He?" Beans wiped his mayo-greasy hands on a napkin and pulled out his notepad. "What's his name? I'll check him out."

"You will not!" She smiled and slapped his arm. "His name is Brady, and I've known him since he joined the company the same time I did. He and his boyfriend are lovely people and great cooks, and I will not have you . . . screwing up this arrangement." He could tell that the f-word was on her lips before she substituted it with *screwing*.

He closed the notepad. "Okay, just saying the offer's open anytime you want a background check."

"Thanks, Officer Krupke."

"Krupke?"

"You know, from *West Side Story*."

He actually did know that musical, one of the few he liked, and had seen it performed live several times. He hummed a few bars from the "Officer Krupke" number.

She gave him a wide grin. "Not bad. If this cop gig doesn't work out, you might have a future in musical theater."

That made Beans smile. "Thanks, I'll keep my day job."

She topped off both their coffee mugs. "You didn't show up after all, did you?" she asked.

"Show up where?"

"To see *The Nutcracker*."

"No." He felt guilty that he didn't feel worse about it. He probably should have gone, but he really didn't like the music. "I'm sorry," he heard himself say.

She laughed like he was the funniest guy on the planet. "Don't apologize, Detective, I'm just yanking your chain. Anyway"—she arranged the salt and pepper shakers in front of her on the retro yellow Formica countertop—"we're in rehearsals now for Shostakovich's Ballet Suites. You can redeem yourself then. I'm supposed to be dancing one of the pas de deux with Brady, so Bernson tells me. You can come to that one. It's a great date ballet, really short. Bring your girlfriend."

Beans was taken aback by that. *WTF?* His last uncomfortable phone conversation with Raisa rewound and played through his memory. All the confusion, the crazy uncertainty of their relationship, returned like a painful relapse of a chronic disease.

He must have had a stricken look on his face, as Amy smiled and nodded knowingly. "I thought so. Guys with girlfriends have that deer-in-the-headlights look." She looked at his empty plate and put a bright professional tone to her voice. "Anything else? Dessert? The hot apple pie is to die for."

He said no, that he was ready for his bill. As he left a generous tip on the counter, he said, "See you Sunday at the memorial?"

"I'll be there," she said, clearing his plate and coffee mug.

He stepped out into the brisk air, which for a change wasn't laced with falling snow. The bell on the café door jangled again, too cheerful for the weather or his mood.

"Detective?"

Amy stood behind him, playing the role of the smiling waitress, politely reminding a customer of his forgotten doggy bag or hat or gloves. She held his bag of salmon and sweet potato cat food. When their hands touched briefly on the cat food bag, Amy's fingers were warm, while his felt far too cold.

25

He was upside down in the cab of Lindbergh's burning truck again, his ankle wedged painfully between the seat and the gearshift console. Flames licked around the hood. The cab began to fill with smoke.

A phone rang, over and over, insistent.

"Answer it," Jolene said, *her ashen face set in a frown.*

"It's for you." Toni *pointed at him with her index finger, its manicured nail broken off at the quick.*

It was coming from the glove box, barely reachable above his head. He managed to tip the lever to open the compartment. Empty airline-size bottles of booze cascaded around him, and so did an older-model iPhone, the cracked screen lighting up *Unknown Caller.* He grabbed it and swiped to answer it.

"Hello? Hello?" He heard himself say. The phone kept ringing.

Then there was a rapping at the window. His brother Herc, in faded navy coveralls, squatted outside the upside-down truck, holding a phone out to him, motioning for him to roll down the window.

"Havi? Havi, wake up."

Beans eyes sprang open. His older brother Herc stared down at him, bleary eyed, stinking of last night's booze. He shoved the cell phone at Beans.

"You left your phone in the living room. Hell, you sleep like the dead." He shuffled away, mumbling, "And I'm the one who was drunk."

The display read *APD Dispatch*.

He put the phone to his ear. "Sorry about that. Beans here."

A cool professional female voice said, "Farmer just south of Eagle River called in a DB in his cabbage field. Young female."

It was the call he had been waiting for but dreading at the same time, ever since the discovery of Hannah's iPhone yesterday. The phone had just enough juice for them to track it to Hannah's canvas messenger bag, which they found in a ditch less than a mile from Buffalo Gals Brew. Although the bag appeared to have been dragged and mauled by scavengers, the cell phone had been protected in an inner pocket and weakly pinged its location. Scattered around the bag were her wallet—complete with credit cards and cash, a purse-size can of pepper spray, and a torn paper sack, sticky with maple frosting.

Beans lay in bed until the vision of the burning truck cleared from his mind. Then he threw on some jeans, a flannel shirt, and a down vest. He ran a toothbrush around his mouth, the minty flavor of the toothpaste shocking him into wakefulness. He started to tiptoe past the guest room, but the door was ajar, the room empty. Herc stood in the kitchen in his striped boxer shorts, cracking open a Gatorade in the light from the open refrigerator, while Archie wove around his legs, purring.

An amiable but incorrigible drunk, Herc had gone on a bender the night before. His live-in girlfriend, the well-inked

Mindy, did not tolerate his insobriety—so Herc had Ubered to Beans' house to sleep it off.

"Thanks for letting me crash here, bro. Mindy'll come around. She always does." His two days' growth of dark beard, a grooming attribute he swore drove women mad, made a raspy noise as he rubbed it. "Since when did you get a cat?" He scratched the base of Archie's tail with his bare foot, and the cat arched his back, purring.

"Since the first murdered barista. What time is it?" Beans yawned as he fired up the Keurig to brew a cup of coffee.

"I don't know, three? I got up to piss and your phone was ringing."

Beans screwed the lid onto his thermal mug. "Gotta go, bud. Stay as long as you like, but don't let the cat out." He poured some foul-smelling kibble into Archie's bowl.

"Another dead body?"

"Afraid so."

"Another barista?"

Beans sighed and nodded.

Marvin Chambers' ten-acre cabbage-and-beet farm, just outside of Chugiak, was blanketed in snow. Chambers, in sweats and gum boots, his gray hair standing in uneven tufts, greeted Beans at the front porch and beckoned him into the warm kitchen.

"Bruno got me up a little after one, whining and pawing at me." At the mention of his name, the gangly Belgian Malinois sitting at Chambers' side pricked his ears and cocked his head. "Since our old dog Elsie died a month ago, Bruno's been really needy, so at first I was just going to ignore him."

"But he was so insistent, very unlike him," Chambers' wife Tammy added. She was a wholesome-looking fifty-plus-year-old who had insisted on brewing a huge urn of coffee and baking some Pillsbury biscuits for the responders.

"I went to this window, the one that faces south towards the fields, and saw a couple of parking lights," her husband continued. "It was a good-sized rig; I could tell by the distance between the beams. I left the kitchen lights off so there wouldn't be any glare."

"Any way you could identify the truck?" Beans asked.

Chambers shook his head. "Sorry, too far away. But it was at least a Ford F-150 or bigger. It went slowly down the access road, then stopped. A light came on in the cab. The driver must have opened the door. Then it went off. Then the overhead light came on again, which went off after a couple of seconds. Then a strange thing—a flash of light, like somebody took a picture?" The farmer ran a hand across his unruly hair. "The light in the cab came on again, just for a second, and the truck continued down the road, headed toward the freeway.

"We've had some vandals, kids probably, tagging my barn and burning trash on the property, so I thought I might catch them red-handed. I piled the dog and the shotgun in the Gator and went out there." He pointed to where techs had just illuminated the area with blinding lights.

"Bruno jumped out before I came to a complete stop and ran straight to her before I could stop him," he said. "Sorry about that. I know you guys want as little disturbance as possible." He scratched the dog behind his ears.

"First, I thought someone had hit a moose calf and dumped it in my field, which got my goat too, I don't mind saying. But when I got closer, I saw it was a girl." Chambers shook his shaggy head. "Just a tiny thing, wearing practically nothing at all."

Tammy Chambers handed Beans a plastic shopping bag, which she'd packed with a large thermos, cups, and warm biscuits. "Take this out there with you."

The crime scene again was lit like a theater, white-suited techs lumbering around like clumsy prop masters. Chuckie shuffled up as Beans brought Chambers' utility vehicle to a stop.

"It's her," Chuckie said. "It's Hannah Fernandez."

She lay on the crystalline snow, a pristine white rose across her chest. Under a stained down coat, she wore the fake-fur bikini that was her uniform at Buffalo Gals. Salty tears had frozen in crusty patches down her face, and a slash of duct tape covered her mouth. She was barefoot, chipped dark toenail polish the only color on her opalescent feet, bound together at the ankles with plastic ties. Her pretty heart-shaped face, framed by wisps of dark hair, was peaceful. Other than the duct tape and the plastic ties binding her hands and feet, she could have been a sleeping princess, awaiting true love's first kiss. That and the ragged triangular hole in her chest.

The memory of the Fernandezes' stuffy living room and the rustic wooden crucifix hanging on the wall flashed through Beans' mind. He unwrapped a stick of gum and jammed it in his mouth, trying to calm the queasiness that threatened to overcome him.

"Thankfully, the farmer stopped his dog from licking the body, the only thing the dog did *not* do," Chuckie grumbled. "Two distinct footprints—one set belongs to Marvin Chambers, obviously. The other has to be the killer's." He pointed to where crime scene techs were making casts of shoe prints. "And of course, dog prints everywhere."

The only positive note about this crime scene was that Hannah's body had been discovered before predators had a chance to scatter or consume the remains. Her body, pristine in death, might be able to tell them much more than Jolene's or Toni's. The fact that it had been clear and cold before the discovery of the body also worked in their favor. Snow cover had not compromised tracks and trace evidence.

As if reading Beans' mind, Chuckie said, "We're also casting the truck tire tracks."

The short access road ran south through Marvin Chambers' beet patch to the spur that led to the Glenn Highway. It would have taken the perpetrator five minutes to get to the highway, another fifteen to get to Eagle River. The suspect would be long gone by now.

"First body with a recognizable entrance wound," Chuckie said, shining his penlight on the bloodless hole in the young woman's chest. "Look like an arrow to you?"

"Can we turn her?" Beans asked a tech who was snapping photos.

"Let me finish bagging her hands and feet first," Chuckie said. "There's some trace stuff I don't want to lose."

After securing plastic bags on Hannah's hands and feet, Chuckie and his tech carefully turned the body onto its stomach. The exit wound in Hannah's upper back was similar to that of Jolene's. A faint pink staining of snow had blossomed under her.

"She wasn't killed here, obviously," Chuckie said.

"Not anywhere near enough blood."

"If I were to guess, I'd say no sexual activity, like the others. But I'll run the full kit on her. There's some bruising here on her hip and upper arms, separate from the lividity. Obviously incurred before death." Then Chuckie said softly, "Poor little girl."

"Time of death?" Beans asked.

"She's cold, but Jesus, who isn't?" Chuckie shivered. "Impossible to tell at these temps. Best guess, she's been dead at least twenty-four hours."

Beans walked around the cordoned area, his boots sinking in the snow. He looked back at the Chambers farmhouse in the distance, the kitchen a well-lit and welcoming beacon. The killer had driven a good-sized vehicle to this spot, stopped the truck, pulled out Hannah's body, and dumped her in the field. Taken the time to flash a light or take a picture, then driven off again. *Who? Why?*

"Hey, got something here," one of the techs casting shoe prints said. He held something up to the light at the end of a pair of tweezers. "It was ground into the boot print. Looks like a feather. Maybe from a chicken?"

"Does Chambers raise chickens?" Chuckie asked.

"Not that I could tell, but I'll find out. Could it be something wild, maybe? Ptarmigan, or grouse?" Beans asked.

"Can't be sure, but I'll take it back to the lab for comparison." The tech placed the feather in an evidence bag and sealed it.

Chuckie's assistants placed Hannah in a plastic body bag and zipped it up. The grating sound of the zipper was a harsh reminder. He needed to make a call to Hannah's aunt, his friend and colleague Carmen Fernandez.

He slumped into the Gator and pulled out his cell phone. He had earlier programmed Carmen's cell number into his contacts so he could find it right away. He imagined the phone on her nightstand, throbbing in the darkness, as he listened to it ring.

26

That Sunday, Beans received a text from Chuckie as he was leaving Toni Morelli's memorial: *More Fernandez info.* He loosened his tie as he exited the rehearsal hall at the Anchorage Ballet. He had felt out of place in his scratchy outdated wool suit and tie, while the other attendees, mostly dancers, were dressed in more comfortable and flamboyant attire. Amy Chandler's handsome new roommate Brady poured wine and beer, while the rehearsal pianist played music from the soundtrack of Toni Morelli's life. Irv Bernson was there, encouraging attendees to share memories of Toni, as were Spiro Liakos and a silent mountain of a man who was introduced to him as Bobo.

And Amy too, of course, graceful as a swan in a diaphanous black dress. She was polite but cool, and Beans felt even more like an outcast. Toni's father got drunk and weepy and hung on his shoulder.

"You gotta find the fucker who did this, you gotta," Ray Morelli said, as he sloshed red wine on Beans' lapel.

Beans could only promise to do his best, using the same lame words he had with Esther and Olaf Nilsson and Linda and Ernesto Fernandez.

175

He had downed three Diet Cokes at the service and arrived at the morgue overcaffeinated and needing desperately to pee. After stopping to relieve himself and to slough off the red-wine-stained suit jacket, he tied on a gown and entered the exam room.

As he did before every autopsy, he folded a stick of spearmint gum into his mouth, feeling the coolness calm his slight nausea. Advanced decomposition and its characteristic smells, fluids, and disfigurement were bad enough, but to him, an autopsy of the newly dead was infinitely more disturbing.

He hated the way they looked like they were sleeping, like they were just grabbing some quick shut-eye in the morgue drawer. Their features were still recognizable, frozen into a peaceful mask, eyes still in their sockets, skin still holding everything together.

This girl, Hannah Carmelita Fernandez, barely twenty-one, without a blemish on her—not even an appendectomy scar—lay splayed open in front of him. Chuckie had completed the basic weights and measurements and cataloged all his findings by the time Beans arrived.

"Closing now at"—Chuckie glanced at the clock on the wall—"sixteen thirty-seven." He clicked off the recorder, then sewed the classic Y incision that started at each shoulder, intersected at the sternum, and continued down the center of the abdomen.

Beans looked down with profound sadness at Hannah Fernandez's sweet elfin face. "Anything I should know?"

"In the autopsy? No surprises, really. Healthy young woman. Cause of death was sharp-force trauma through the chest, piercing the heart and exiting just south of the scapula. Nicked a rib on the way out. Exit wound is similar to those of Morelli and Nilsson. For the first time, though, we have a clear look at the entrance wound."

O'Reilly came rushing through the swinging doors, her maiden-aunt smell of lavender following her like a memory. She tied her gown on behind her neck as she asked, "What did I miss?"

"Glad you could make it, Isabelle. I was telling the detective here that this is the first good look we're getting at the point of entry." Chuckie pointed to the ragged triangular hole above Hannah's left breast. "I'll compare it to the arrowhead we took from Toni Morelli, but my guess is that we've nailed down the type of murder weapon for all three women." He shook his head. "It does deepen the evidence pool."

Beans wondered if at any time, years from now, Hannah's family would ever regard her senseless death in this light. It had been two nights since Beans had leaned against the farmer's ATV in the harsh lights at the crime scene and found Carmen Fernandez's number in his contacts.

She had answered on the third ring, her voice hoarse with sleep. "Beans? Have you found her?"

He had, he said, and he was so, so sorry. Carmen gave a soft wail and spoke in a muffled tearful voice to someone nearby—her husband Carlos, he assumed. He gave her what details he could and said they would bring Hannah back to the morgue later in the day to be identified.

"Thanks, Beans," Carmen said, a sob catching in her throat. "I'll let Ernesto and Linda know."

"I can call them if you like."

"It'll be better if I tell them."

That afternoon, Ernesto and Linda, with Carmen at their side, had confirmed the identity of their daughter Hannah. Linda had insisted on coming, refusing to believe that her daughter was dead until she saw so with her own eyes. Her face as pale as her daughter's, she whispered a quiet prayer over Hannah's body, then bent to kiss her cold forehead.

Now, with the death of the third young woman, the media had coined a new term for the series of brutal murders—"The Baristacides." Beans would have thought it clever if it didn't target the department's inadequacies and seem to trivialize the women's deaths. Under increasing pressure, his team had doubled their efforts. Heller, surly and argumentative, had reinterviewed the known contacts of the victims as well as the coffee kiosk suppliers. O'Reilly had mined the FBI's serial killer databases for possible insights. Beans requested and was temporarily assigned two rookie detectives to work the bowhunting supplier lists and tip lines, both exercises in futility. Cam Kristovich, who had been either driving a bus or at home with his parents when the women were abducted, was eliminated as a possible suspect.

For the first time in Beans' memory, the normally unflappable Lieutenant DuBois looked stressed. Between dealing with demands from the higher-ups and deflecting the rabid media, DuBois had lost much of his smooth demeanor and looked rumpled and frazzled on his daily—sometimes twice-daily—visits to the incident room.

The team was putting in long hours but coming no closer to finding the killer.

Beans and his colleagues had felt like they were desperately treading water—until Hannah Fernandez's body and the dump site were found. Because her body was discovered so soon after its disposal, all the human, animal, and vehicle evidence was well preserved.

After eliminating Marvin Chambers' size 10.5 XtraTuf boots, CSIs had determined that the only other human footprints were from the perpetrator, a size 11.5 Sorel hunting boot, available at numerous outdoor stores and online.

Ground into one of the size 11.5 prints had been a tiny black-and-white speckled feather.

"And stuck onto it, a trace amount of chicken shit." Chuckie was triumphant.

"Does the owner of the farm raise chickens?" O'Reilly asked.

"No, he doesn't. He bought the farm ten years ago from a guy who also did not raise chickens," Beans said. "I think we can assume that the perp raises chickens or had been around chickens."

"How about the tire tracks?" O'Reilly asked.

"Wheelbase would indicate a vehicle the size of a Ford F-150 or similar, just like Chambers said. Unfortunately, the tire tracks are to a garden-variety Firestone snow tire—half the pickups in the state probably have these on in the winter," Beans said.

"Ah, but you haven't asked me about the pièce de résistance," Chuckie said with a gleeful look.

"Okay, what is it you're dying to tell us?" O'Reilly accepted a stick of Beans' spearmint gum.

"Unlike with the previous victims, we were able to extract trace evidence—from her feet."

"Her feet?" Beans asked.

"Hannah's remains weren't compromised by either the weather or scavengers, so we were able to gather biological evidence that had adhered to her bare feet." Chuckie flicked on his computer monitor, and an enlarged image of a dark shape, tapered at both ends, loomed onto the screen. "We found several of these stuck to the bottom of Hannah's feet and between her toes. This is enlarged of course, about a hundred times."

"What is it?" O'Reilly squinted at the screen.

Chuckie grinned at O'Reilly. "It's mouse shit! The feces of *Mus musculus*, the common house mouse! None too fresh, I might add. Our Hannah was held, at least for a while, barefoot in an area that has or had rodent activity."

"Attic or basement? Abandoned building?" Beans suggested.

"Could be, except for this, also found on her feet." Chuckie projected what looked like broken shells and sand-like granules on the computer screen.

"I give up," O'Reilly said.

"Actually, two different substances. This"—Chuckie enlarged the slide of what looked like a rough sand-like substance—"is what's called chicken grit and given to poultry to help them digest their food. And these"—he switched to the other slide—"are oyster shells."

"My grandmother used to give her chickens oyster shells." O'Reilly pointed at the monitor. "I remember! She said the added calcium would give the eggs stronger shells."

"Exactly!" Chuckie beamed at his star pupil.

"So, she was held in a chicken coop?" O'Reilly frowned. "She'd have more evidence on her than that, wouldn't she?"

"My guess is that she was held in a shed or barn where chicken feed and supplies were stored. That would explain the mouse excrement as well as trace amounts of grit and oyster shells on her feet," Chuckie said.

"Yeah, that makes sense, but there must be dozens, maybe hundreds, of folks raising chickens out here. We've narrowed the suspect base down, but still not to a workable level." Beans pulled his tie off and stuffed it into his pocket. "We have three dead women now. We have to get closer than 'any chicken farmer in the Metro area.'" He tried unsuccessfully to keep the irritation from his voice.

"You're just a little ray of sunshine, aren't you?" Chuckie looked deflated.

"Don't get me wrong, this is great, Chuckie, but we aren't there yet." Beans paced around the table. "And we need to figure out why. He doesn't appear to be sexually assaulting them, at least not yet."

"Oh, there's no penetration," O'Reilly said, frowning, "but there's definitely a sexual element. Look at the women he's chosen—young ones in suggestive costumes, 'virgin whores,' if you will. And the roses, of course." She looked down at Hannah Fernandez's passive face. "What makes him choose these girls, anyway? He doesn't seem to be gravitating to any particular physical type, except they're all young and attractive."

"If you ask me, Toni Morelli is the anomaly," Beans said. "She was the only blonde, the only white girl without any obvious Latino or Native ethnicity. She was the only one not taken from the coffee kiosk. Why?"

"Opportunity?" O'Reilly chewed her gum thoughtfully.

Maybe another visit to Spiro Liakos is in order, Beans thought. *Was Toni Morelli a last-minute substitute?*

The three of them were silent for a minute, lost in their thoughts. Beans tried to exorcise the memory of Ray Morelli's red-eyed devastation, and the breathless feeling that he was running a losing race against time.

27

Beans stood in front of the microwave, watching a Stouffer's frozen entrée revolve on the glass carousel. His mind had wandered to the trace evidence on Hannah Fernandez's feet (mouse turds, oyster shells, chicken grit), and he couldn't remember what he was heating up anymore—lasagna? Shepherd's pie? It was an unrecognizable freezer-burned lump under the cellophane cover that he had slit according to the packaging instructions.

Archie purred and weaved his way between Beans' legs. The ginger tabby was more dog than cat, Beans thought. He scampered to greet Beans when he returned home, wolfed down his foul-smelling food, and even engaged in a game of fetch now and then with a small felt mouse. He perched on the back of the sofa while Beans watched TV and slept curled up at the foot of his bed.

Beans had more or less given up on finding Archie a new home. Having the cat was good for him, he decided. A pet and the associated responsibilities would ground him, maybe give his world more karmic balance. In lieu of a woman sharing his life and his bed, a cat would have to do for now.

"No woman, no cry," he crooned in his best Bob Marley.

"*Prow?*" Archie asked.

Now I'm singing to a cat. "Never mind."

Archie leaped onto a kitchen stool and began to lick his crotch.

The microwave beeped that the frozen entrée was done, and Beans slid the plastic tray onto the kitchen counter.

The doorbell chimed. Probably kids selling magazine subscriptions to win a trip to Disneyland, he thought, shuffling to the front door in his fur-lined moccasins. He glanced over to the hook near the door, where his holstered Glock hung within easy reach. He couldn't help that a deadly weapon was now part of his identity, even though it conflicted with his Buddhist pacifist beliefs. *Yeah, and I have a cat who's a dog; I'm a study in contrast.*

He peered out the peephole and was stunned when he saw the face that glanced nervously from side to side, grotesquely shadowed under the harsh porch light. It was unmistakably Raisa. She drew her coat closer to her and rang the doorbell again.

"Raisa?" He held the door open, and she rushed in, bringing a wave of cold air in her wake.

"Thank God you're home," she said, throwing herself against him.

He folded his arms around her. She was so familiar—her smell, her touch. She felt thinner, even through her bulky coat and down vest.

"Oh God, Beans." She drew back, and he could see that she had been crying, her eyes sunken in her pale face like black holes in the snow.

"What is it? What's wrong?"

"It's Dad, Beans. He's dead." The backpack fell from her shoulder and hit the floor with a hollow thud.

After a moment of stunned silence, he guided her to the sofa and made her sit. "Let me get you some water."

"How about something stronger?"

"I have a little bit of brandy here." Beans rummaged in the small china hutch in the dining room. "And I mean a 'little bit,' since Herc stole it from an airplane."

He returned with the miniature bottle, broke the seal, and poured it into a tumbler. Raisa wrapped shaking hands around it and took a sip. Beans draped the multicolored afghan his mother had crocheted around her shoulders. He flipped the switch to the gas fireplace and was grateful for its comforting warmth. "When?"

"Two days ago. I flew into Fairbanks yesterday to identify him."

"Tell me what happened." He hated that he sounded like a cop, but he couldn't help it. "Sorry, police instinct. How are you?"

"I'm fine. Or I'm unhurt. I am not fine." Fresh tears rolled down her face.

He sat next to her and pulled her to him. Zach Ingalls, vibrant macho outdoorsman, could not have succumbed to anything as pedestrian as a heart attack. Maybe an overturned snow machine, a misfiring rifle, or a crazed-moose attack?

"I'm so sorry, Raisa. Was there an accident?"

"Not by a long shot," she said. "You know where Harding Lake is, just south of Fairbanks? A park ranger found him on the frozen lake, dead, more broken bones than they could count. They moved him to Fairbanks, where the closest medical examiner is. Beans, I could hardly recognize him."

"Oh God." Beans was horrified. "I'm so sorry."

"When I went to see him, he was wearing the L.L.Bean pajamas I got him for Christmas and a bathrobe! What the fuck was he doing on a frozen lake, miles from home, in his pajamas?" She swigged down the rest of the brandy, then stared at the bottom of the empty glass.

"Who's on it? Fairbanks Homicide?"

"Them and a bunch of Department of Interior flunkies. Maybe even the FBI, I don't know."

"Shit, that's terrible, Raisa."

"All kinds of suits hovering, asking questions, telling me how sorry they were. I barely heard a word they said. I finally escaped, stopped at a doc-in-a-box for some Valium, and curled up in the hotel room with the minibar."

He hugged her to him and kissed the top of her head.

She sniffed. "I know you don't—didn't—like him much."

"It's not that I didn't like him." He shrugged. "But his history—"

"It's not like you think!" Angry red splotches rose on her face.

"Okay." Beans tried to calm her. "Tell me what happened."

"Well, you know that last year he got caught dealing bear parts and bile to the Chinese," she conceded.

"Right."

"What you don't know is that Dad negotiated a deal with the feds to go undercover. He offered to wear a wire, to try to bring down the honchos of the poaching ring. That's how he got off with just a slap on the wrist the last time."

Of course, Beans thought. This made perfect sense.

"Dad was found on the lake with no footprints or tire prints leading to his body. It's like he . . . fell from the sky. It was awful, Beans. He was so—broken. The wire the feds had given him was jammed into his mouth," she wailed.

"Christ." Zach Ingalls had thought of himself as a high roller, but Beans wondered if he had realized just how high the stakes were.

"Can I stay here tonight, Beans? I won't be a bother. I'll stay in the guest room, and you won't know I'm here, I promise. I just can't bear the thought of going home to an empty house."

"The dogs?"

"A gal from work, a fellow musher, is taking care of them, thank God."

"How about Oksana? How's she taking it?"

"She and Dad had a huge fight, and she flew home to Babushka a week ago. I called and left a message. I don't even know if she knows yet."

"Of course you can stay here." He patted her hand.

"Thank you," she whispered, and gave him a wan, grateful smile.

He coaxed her into eating part of his Stouffer's entrée while he remade the guest bed with fresh sheets. The room probably still retained some of Herc's residual masculine funk—including a pair of insulated work gloves under the bed—but he didn't think that in her current state she would notice. He tossed the gloves onto the dresser, next to the stocking cap Herc had also left behind. When he returned to the living room, he saw that Archie had curled up on Raisa's lap and was squinting contentedly.

She stroked the cat as he purred. "When did you get a cat?"

The same question Herc had asked. "He belonged to the first barista, Jolene Nilsson."

"Oh, poor boy," Raisa said, and hugged the cat to her. "Another orphan." Archie flexed his huge feet and rumbled.

After Beans settled Raisa in the guest room, he made himself an unsatisfying bowl of instant miso soup and powered up his laptop. He found a few news items on the body that had mysteriously appeared on Harding Lake. No other information was available online. He made a mental note to contact Denny Singer, an academy colleague who worked Fairbanks Homicide.

At eleven thirty, the ache in his neck and a hollow sense of loss convinced him that it was past time for him to go to bed. Too much death, too much sadness. He grabbed the Glock from the hook by the door. Another anti-pacifist habit was to put the gun in his nightstand drawer before he went to bed. He stood for a moment outside the guest room door, waiting for a sob or any sign of life, or mourning, or anger. It was silent inside. He shuffled down the hall to his bedroom, rolling his shoulders and yawning, Archie close at his heels, and shut the door.

He was awakened by Archie standing on his chest, sniffing at his upper lip. Then he heard it—a metallic snicking sound, like something being opened, then clicked shut as quietly as possible. A milky slit of light escaped from under the bathroom door, as if someone were using a flashlight. Small, muffled noises came from the bathroom, and the slit of light under the door seemed to flicker on and off. Someone was moving quietly in the master bathroom.

Without a sound, he set Archie on the floor and shoved him under the bed. He slid his nightstand drawer open and was about to pull out the Glock when he remembered that Raisa was overnighting in the guest room. Clad only in his Jockey shorts, he stood in front of the bathroom door.

Then a tinkle and crash of glass.

"Shit!" came Raisa's whispered voice.

Beans sighed. He tapped on the door, and Raisa opened it, her deep-set brown eyes apologetic.

"Are you okay?" he asked.

When Raisa opened the door further, he saw that she wore one of the old Great Alaska Shootout T-shirts that he had given her years ago. In the baggy shirt that draped down to her mid-thigh, she looked especially fragile, her shoulders jutting out in sharp angles against the thin cotton. He struggled to keep his eyes on her small face, pretty but bladelike, a pale weapon.

"I'm sorry," she stammered, holding up her iPhone. She had been using the flashlight feature rather than turning on the overhead light. "I was looking for some aspirin or ibuprofen or something. There's nothing in the other bathroom. And sorry," she said again, wincing. "I accidentally broke a glass. I think all of it is in the sink, though, so you shouldn't have to worry about walking barefoot." She looked down at his feet, and he felt her eyes traveling up his body, appraising his legs, the glaring white of his Jockeys.

Archie rubbed against his shins. "Oh right. Aspirin." He pulled the nightstand drawer open and removed a bottle of Advil from among other pill containers. "Will this do?"

"Perfect. I've got a pounding headache."

He held the bottle of Advil out to her. They were standing close enough now that he could feel the heat from her body. Instead of taking the bottle from him, she ran her fingers across the old scar that extended in a keloid slash across his chest. Her fingers were warm, but he still shivered under her touch.

Her soft fingers stroked the scar tissue. "Like a road map home."

She moved into his arms like it was the most natural thing in the world, like they hadn't been apart for more than two years. His hands roved under the T-shirt against the small of her back, then cupped her small breasts, her nipples hard against his palms. Her hands moved too, feverishly, against his scar, his chest, under the elastic waistband of his Jockeys.

Making love to her was familiar too, comforting and sweetly satisfying. He knew her body almost as well as he knew his own—what made her moan, or sigh, or cry out loud. She did all of those as they clung to each other in the darkness. When they came apart finally, panting, slick with sweat, a feeling of well-being washed over him.

This is how it should be. She will ground me. He was so drowsy with postcoital bliss that only until much later did he realize that this was the same thing he'd thought earlier about Archie. He fell asleep spooned against her slender back, one hand on her belly, feeling the gentle rise and fall of her breathing. In that delicious moment before sleep claimed him, he thought he felt her shudder.

His eyes sprang open again to the sound of running water, light again from under the bathroom door. He yawned and smiled to himself. *Raisa, of course.* There was still a warm spot on the bed where she had lain, and he ran his hand across it.

The sound of water stopped, and just as Beans was drifting back to sleep, he heard a clunk, like the toilet lid dropping into place. Then a softly muttered, "Fuck."

He wondered if the toilet was running again. Occasionally, the flapper would get stuck and cause the toilet to run until the handle was jiggled or the chain that held the flapper unkinked.

He struggled to a sitting position and yawned again. He heard the clacking sound of plastic hitting the floor and what sounded like a spray of gravel, then Raisa's voice.

"Shit."

Maybe she needs more Advil. He grabbed the bottle of ibuprofen from the nightstand drawer, his fingers brushing against his Glock.

He rapped gently on the bathroom door. It was ajar and swung slowly open. In the light cast by Raisa's iPhone, Beans saw her on her hands and knees, reaching behind the toilet. At first, he thought she was sick, maybe about to vomit, but then he saw her groping behind the bowl. His stomach did a somersault when she picked something off the floor and popped it into her mouth, like a chimpanzee harvesting grubs in the rain forest.

"Raisa, I thought you might need more Advil," he heard himself say.

She started, then sighed and rubbed her face. "Fuck no, Beans. I don't need an Advil. No, thank you."

Beans' eyes traveled to the orange pill canister that sat on the toilet tank lid. The label read *DeHavilland Beans.* The prescription was for Percocet that his doctor had prescribed years ago after arthroscopic knee surgery. He knew there had been several pills left, but now the container—which he kept in the bottom drawer of his nightstand—was empty.

"Raisa . . ." He moved toward her.

To his alarm, she reached into the toilet bowl and retrieved a pill before he could stop her. She went to the sink, rinsed the pill quickly under the tap, chewed it with a grimace, and swallowed it. Beans' stomach did another lurch. "Jesus," he whispered. He felt frozen in place, gripping the bottle of Advil in his hand.

Raisa seemed to ignore him completely and crouched on the bathroom floor again, collecting the half dozen pills that had settled against the dusty baseboard behind the toilet. She cupped a hand under the faucet and slurped water in loud gulps. Then she splashed water over her face and dabbed it dry with a hand towel, all the while clutching the lint-covered pills. She was again wearing the Great Alaska Shootout T-shirt, now damp across the chest and wrinkled from being tossed on the floor.

She sighed again. "Go ahead, say it."

"Say what?" He was suddenly aware that he was standing in his bathroom doorway stark naked.

"Say that I had no business taking your Percocet."

"All you had to do was ask."

"So you could grill me on *why* I need a Percocet so bad I would pull it out of the toilet?"

"Are you in pain? I can take you to . . ." Realization dawned like an icy winter morning. "You weren't looking for aspirin before, were you?"

She shook her head and peered at him from her sunken eyes.

He shivered. He was chilled, standing there, buck-ass naked, and still queasy from watching her swallow a pill that had most recently been in his toilet. "Can we maybe talk out here?" He grabbed the first article of clothing he could find, the London Fog overcoat he had draped across a nearby chair after changing from his memorial service attire. He wrapped the coat around him, still feeling cold, and sat on the bed.

"Okay, talk to me," he said.

"You almost destroyed me when you left for Kaltag, you know."

"Wait, you're telling me that I broke your heart, so a couple of years later you started sticking your arm in toilets looking for drugs? Seriously, Raisa?" He held his hands out in a *Give me a break* gesture.

She paced in front of him, barefoot, her hands crossed over her breasts.

"Okay, okay. Shortly after you dumped me—"

"Hey."

"We split up, whatever. Shortly after that, I screwed up my back dogsledding. My doc prescribed PT and painkillers."

"I didn't know."

"How could you? You broke up with me. Anyway, I did as the doctor ordered. Did all the PT, but the pain never totally went away. So I kept taking the painkillers. Until the doc wouldn't give me any more."

Beans shook his head, suddenly feeling very sad. "Oxy?"

Raisa nodded. "I remembered that you had knee surgery a while back and you had a prescription for some kind of narcotic painkiller."

"So you came here looking for it." *Forget the fantasies of reconciliation, of completeness, of coming home again.*

"I couldn't find it the first time."

"What first time?"

Raisa buried her face in her hands. "I came here just after Christmas. I had the spare key you gave me, remember? I saw Piper leave, then used the key to get in. But I couldn't find it."

"Shit." He remembered Archie being outside and how angry he had been at Piper for leaving the house unlocked. He shuddered, thinking that he had almost shot Piper when she returned home. *All for some pills.*

"Yeah, how desperate can you be, right? Breaking into a cop's house to look for drugs?" She wiped her eyes with the back of her hand.

Not just a cop—her boyfriend, Beans thought. "So, tonight— you and me—that was just so you could get some Percocet?" His voice sounded flat and expressionless, even to him.

"Oh, Beans." She reached forward to run her hand through his hair, but he caught her arm and brought it gently down to her side. He didn't want her to touch him, not now.

"So, you just came here for some drugs?" he repeated, his voice strangely calm, not betraying the hurt and anger that roiled inside him.

She gave him a sad smile. "I needed it, Beans. I'm really hurting right now. Ten milligrams of Valium from urgent care doesn't cut it. But it's not the only reason I came here." Her eyes welled with tears. "My dad died, Beans. I didn't want to be alone."

"You and me, then—I was a warm body, just a diversion?" The woman he thought would save him was herself foundering in stormy seas.

"Just a diversion?" Her voice broke as she took an angry swipe at the tears trickling down her face. She hurried into the guest room, pills still clutched in her fist, and slammed the door.

When Beans went into the bathroom, the empty pill container suddenly made him furious. He swept it off the toilet tank with the back of his hand, and it bounced off the tub. He stared in the mirror and rubbed at the stubble on his face. There was that two days' worth of beard that Herc said women found irresistible. *What the fuck do you know, Herc?* He picked out the glass fragments from the sink and threw them into the trash with enough force to shatter them further. A pointed shard pricked his index finger. He watched numbly as a drop of blood ran in a jagged red line down the side of the sink.

After a few minutes, Raisa appeared, again dressed in jeans, down vest, and snow boots, backpack slung on her shoulder. She took a deep breath and announced to the room, "I have to go now." She swept by him and grabbed her coat from the hook by the door.

He suddenly felt like a flasher, standing in the hallway in an overcoat with his junk hanging out. He fumbled with the belt of his coat. "Raisa . . . there's a clinic, just south of here . . ."

Raisa spun around, sudden anger flashing in her damp eyes. "Christ, couldn't you just love me instead of trying to save me?"

"What the hell is that supposed to mean?" The bitter anger, the painful disappointment, barely controlled earlier, welled to the surface.

"Fuck yourself, Beans." She flung open the front door, letting a flurry of snowflakes in, and slammed it behind her. Her old Range Rover sputtered to a start on the third try, and he stood there, listening to its snow tires crunch down the icy street.

Beans shuffled into the kitchen and looked at the oven clock. Four forty-five. He knew there was no way he'd get back to sleep, so he decided to brew a full pot of coffee, not just a single cup this time. He slumped onto a kitchen stool, watching the coffee drip into the carafe. His anger ebbed and he felt empty, defeated. Her body next to his, the nostalgic feeling of wholeness that she had given him, had lulled him into a misguided sense of equilibrium. For a few breathless hours, his life had seemed in perfect balance, defying the brutal gravity of the barista killings and the weight of the police-issue Glock, sometimes too heavy to bear.

And he'd been so distracted by his own sense of balance that he had overlooked Raisa's burdens. How could he, a cop and professional observer, have been so blind to her physical pain, her sadness, her loneliness? How could he have mistaken this thin, desperate woman for the fresh-faced Raisa he had loved?

Was she right? Was it easier for him to want to save her than to love her? Did he just not care for her enough? Even now, he wasn't sure he could answer any of those questions honestly. And why not?

He clicked the remote for the TV on the kitchen counter and watched as the weather girl in the tight sweater advised Anchorage residents to brace for more cold snowy weather. *So what else is new?*

The acid from the hot coffee seemed to eat into his stomach, but he swallowed another scalding mouthful. He sat in his chilly kitchen in his overcoat, confused and dyspeptic, the bittersweet memory of Raisa still on his skin.

28

Ironically, the hold music that played while Beans waited for homicide detective Denny Singer to answer was an instrumental version of "Killing Me Softly." He tapped his pen against his knee as he half listened for Denny and stared at enlargements of mouse excrement and chicken grit on his computer monitor.

"Beans, my man!" a raspy voice boomed over the line. Tall and athletic, Denny Singer was every NFL team owner's dream of a blocking tight end, with close-cropped hair and a cherubic face. A police academy classmate of Beans, Denny had been with the Fairbanks Homicide Division now for several years.

"D-Man!" Beans smiled as he pictured his friend's wide gap-toothed grin.

"So, to what do I to owe this pleasure, my man? I know it's not to tell me that you're going caribou hunting with me." Denny's deep chuckle rumbled across the line.

"Actually," Beans continued, "I wanted to see what you knew about the Zachary Ingalls case."

"Ingalls? The Harding Lake body?"

"Right."

"It's not my case, but it's got us all hopping, let me tell you."

"How so?"

Denny lowered his voice. "Body was found on the frozen lake. No footprints except for the park ranger who found him. The body is barefoot, wearing pajamas and a bathrobe. Autopsy's being done now, but preliminary looks like extreme trauma consistent with—get this—falling from a great height."

"Shit," Beans said. *Raisa was right. He fell out of the fucking sky.*

"No shit," Denny said. "Know what else? He had a wire jammed in his mouth—a government-issued wire."

"I heard that he was working with the feds . . ."

"Whoa, wait. Is Ingalls your dogsledding lady's dad?"

"He's Raisa's dad, yeah." Beans winced, the image of her fishing a pill out of his toilet leaping unwelcome into his mind.

"Wow, I'm so sorry, man."

"Yeah, me too."

"We've got Fish and Game and Department of Interior guys crawling all over this. Not every day that a civilian working undercover for them gets thrown out of a plane."

"Jesus."

"The DOI guys were pretty freaked out about it. There'll be hell to pay, as you can guess."

"What did the ranger have to say?"

"He made his usual rounds yesterday morning and saw the body on the lake. Called us immediately. It's been too cold to snow much up here. There were no tracks that would have been covered up with snowfall other than the ranger's."

"Any leads?"

"DOI thinks they know who did it; they're tracking them down now. Speculation is that they escaped into Canada or even Big Diomede, into Russian jurisdiction."

"What do you know so far?"

"Ingalls was staying at the Millennium Hotel near the airport. He was last seen three nights ago having a nightcap at the bar at about ten thirty."

"Alone?" Beans asked.

"Looked like it. He was chatting up the bartender. Security video shows him going up alone in the elevator at eleven fifteen. At eleven thirty there was a power outage on the floor."

"Convenient."

"Right. Power came back on ten minutes later. By then, we're guessing that Ingalls was already out of the building."

"Professionals?"

"Definitely. No fuss, no muss, no collateral damage. No trail either. Hell, they haven't even found the plane yet."

By the time Beans hung up with Denny, his mood was even darker than before. Should he call Raisa and give her the cheery news that her father had likely been thrown from a plane by professional assassins? Maybe he should send her a text, or an email, since she probably wasn't speaking to him. *Maybe ever again.* He started writing a carefully worded email with the details he could reveal about her father's case and saved it as a draft.

He glanced at the time on his computer monitor. Nine o'clock. Carmen should be at her desk. He took a deep breath and released it slowly, then stood and headed for the elevator.

Missing Persons was housed in a corner of the basement, too brightly lit, probably meant to offset the general dinginess of the offices. Carmen Fernandez and another officer, Roberta Gorman, took most of the missing persons calls from two paper-stuffed cubicles, but today Carmen was alone. She raised her red-rimmed eyes to Beans, and he folded her in a tight embrace.

"I don't know what to say, Carmen. I'm so sorry."

"I know."

"How are her folks doing?"

"Her brother's home from college now, so that's a help. Linda is crushed, and Ernesto is trying to hold it all together."

Beans nodded. "I need to ask a couple of questions that you might be able to answer."

Carmen dabbed at her eyes and sat back down, motioning Beans to the chair across her desk. "Anything to help, Beans."

"Confidential, of course. You know the drill."

She frowned at him. "I'm a cop, Beans."

"Yes, but you're also a bereaved family member." He patted her hand. "Sorry, but I had to say that."

She nodded. "Ask."

"There was trace evidence on Hannah's feet that is very specific to a certain environment."

Carmen leaned forward. "What was it?"

"Chicken grit and oyster shells. Oh, and mouse shit."

"The killer had chickens?"

"We think so. Looks like Hannah was held somewhere that stored chicken feed or supplies."

Carmen's eyes widened. "We have chickens."

Beans nodded. "That's why I need to ask the next questions."

"I know you have to do this, but we had nothing to do with Hannah's . . ." Her voice broke. "You must know that."

"I do," Beans said gently. "But I have to cross Carlos off the list. There were boot prints at the scene. What size does Carlos wear?"

"Twelve and a half," she said promptly. "Triple E. He has feet like paddles, and I have to special order his shoes."

Beans sighed in relief. "Good. Not the same size as the prints we found. What about Ernesto? Does he have any connection with chickens or poultry?"

"Not that I know of. He has big feet too. He and Carlos often trade shoes."

Carmen assured Beans that she knew of no acquaintances of Hannah's who raised chickens but said her parents would have more information. Beans nodded; he would stop by the Fernandezes' and find out for himself.

He gave Carmen another quick hug and took the stairs two at a time to the second floor. After talking with the Fernandez family, he would consult with someone at the Department of Natural Resources' Agriculture office, hoping for more data on chicken farmers in the area.

When he reached the second-floor lobby, Heller was about to step into the elevator.

"There you are. Reception is looking for you. Guess someone's here to see you."

"Me?" He wasn't expecting anyone.

"He asked for you by name, she said." Heller held the elevator door open, and Beans stepped in.

"So, where are you going?" Beans eyed Heller suspiciously. Heller had performed all duties asked of him on this barista case, but grudgingly. He was usually on his best behavior when O'Reilly was in the room but made no bones about his displeasure when he and Beans were alone together.

Heller stared straight ahead. "Off to knock heads with Sevy's tight-lipped compadres."

Stress and sleepless nights made Beans snap. "Isn't that a back-burner case? Didn't DuBois say the baristas were top priority?"

Heller glared at him. "Listen, I did my part. I did your grunt work. I talked to that Spiro guy at least twice and Ralph at the rental place as many times."

"How about the bowhunters? The security videos?"

"Even the FBI geeks won't watch six fucking weeks of video! And I don't have to tell you how many fucking bowhunters there are!" Heller's raised voice reverberated in the elevator.

"We only need to find one! The fucker who's killing these girls!" Beans shouted back.

When the elevator dinged and the door slid open, Beans and Heller exited, red-faced. One of the clerks in Records, a young Native Alaskan woman holding a carrier with takeout coffees, stood aside, her eyes downcast behind horn-rimmed glasses. She had obviously overheard their heated, profanity-laced exchange. Heller strode to the front doors without looking back.

"Sorry," Beans mumbled. He veered toward Reception, wanting to put as much distance as possible between himself and Heller.

Beans was surprised to find Cameron Kristovich sitting erect on one of the uncomfortable plastic chairs, his beanie folded in his lap.

"Cam? What are you doing here?" Beans extended his hand. Cam paused before he took it in his own cool, dry one.

"Hannah is dead," Cam said in his trademark flat voice. He reached into his coat pocket and retrieved a neatly folded printout of an online news story. Beans inwardly cringed when he read the "Latest Baristacide Victim" headline.

"Yes, I'm sorry. I know she was a good friend to you." Beans thought that Cam carrying around a clipping describing the discovery of Hannah's body was a little creepy, but he didn't say so.

"I want to help," Cam said, without inflection.

"Is there something else you remember about the night she went missing?"

"No, but I want to help. You said I could help."

Beans was aware that Barb the receptionist had lifted her handset and was giving him a *Should I call for backup?* look. He shook his head and gave her a reassuring smile.

"Come with me, Cam. Let's go to my office."

After he settled Cam across from him, Beans said, "I appreciate you coming here, but what I meant when I said you could help was that you could maybe supply new information that you forgot to tell me earlier."

"I didn't forget anything." Cam unfolded the article and pressed it flat on the desktop.

"Okay then, how do you think you can help? I'm open to suggestions here." Beans tried to keep the frustration from his voice.

"I don't know. There must be something I can do." He examined the article in front of him.

Despite the maddening aspect of dealing with Cameron Kristovich, Beans realized he liked the young man and respected his affection for Hannah Fernandez.

"I have to drive the thirty route at eleven," Cam stated. "I can help until then."

Beans looked up at the wall clock—nine thirty-five. He sighed. "Would you like a cup of coffee?"

"I don't drink coffee," Cam said, then as an afterthought, "No, thank you."

"Excuse me while I get myself a cup."

While the department's wicked brew dripped into a Styrofoam cup, an idea struck him. Cam's supervisor at the bus barn had said that he had an eidetic memory, with an uncanny ability to remember numbers and patterns. What if Beans put Cam to work viewing the hours of security videos from the mall across from Snow Bunny Baristas, the Kwik-E-Mart near Arctic Foxes, and the hardware store adjacent to Buffalo Gals? Who better than Cam Kristovich to pick out common images? It was highly irregular, of course, but he thought he could get it by DuBois, especially since nobody had the time nor the inclination, in the case of Heller and the FBI, to look at hours of eye-numbing security video right now.

Across from Beans' desk was a workstation with a computer terminal occasionally used by visiting officers.

"Sit here," he said to Cam, and pulled the chair out from behind the workstation.

He made a couple of phone calls, the first to Lieutenant DuBois, who approved the arrangement, with the caveat that Cam be set up in the system as a one-time contractor.

"We might find a little money in it for him. And for Christ's sake, do a security check on him too. And," he added, "you are responsible, Beans. The whole time he is here, he has to be supervised. We can't have a civilian wandering around here by himself."

Beans' second call was to the IT department, who set Cam up with limited permissions to view only the folder with the security videos.

Cam's background check came back spotless. He was issued a temporary ID badge with his unsmiling photo to wear on a lanyard around his neck.

"Here's how you can help." Beans clicked on the folder on the secure drive. In it were numerous links to closed-circuit videos from the areas around the three coffee kiosks.

"These are videos that were taken near where Hannah and the two other baristas were kidnapped. They go back several weeks before each of the abductions. We are looking for any common elements—license plates if you can read them, vehicles, faces, people, anything."

Beans showed him how to bookmark certain frames and gave him a yellow legal pad and several pens so he could make notes. Cam looked almost happy as he fingered the ID badge around his neck.

"I can come for two hours every Monday-Tuesday-Wednesday-Thursday-Friday. I have to leave by eleven every day to drive the thirty route," he said, almost by way of an apology. He looked up at the clock. "I have to leave now, but I will be here tomorrow at nine AM," he said, standing. He pushed his chair in flush with the desk and headed toward the elevator. Then as an afterthought, he strode back to Beans' desk and stuck out his hand. Surprised, Beans took it.

"Thank you," Cam said, and turned back toward the elevator. He faced forward, staring straight ahead at nothing in particular, as the elevator doors closed in front of him.

29

It was well after nine by the time Beans decided to call it a night. He had spent the last few hours staring mutely at chicken farmer data until his eyes felt gritty and lost focus. He leaned back in his chair and yawned. There was nothing more to be accomplished this evening. He would go home, drown his eyes in Visine, find something to microwave, and fall into bed.

But first, he would swing by Herc and Mindy's place on his way home. He'd been driving around with Herc's insulated work gloves, beanie, and thermal underwear in the back seat of the Explorer since his brother had spent his "sleep-it-off" night at Beans' a few days ago. As Herc had predicted, Mindy had forgiven him his fall off the wagon and allowed him back home.

Beans had just turned into his brother's driveway when his cell phone pinged with an incoming text. The message from Lieutenant DuBois read *Chief wants update. See me in AM. Bring good news.*

Beans sighed and slouched in the driver's seat, his eyes closed. Good news? There were still leads to follow up on from Hannah Fernandez's forensic evidence but no viable suspects yet. On the same depressing end of the good-news scale, there was the dumpster fire in his personal life—his recent disastrous encounter with Raisa.

Since last night, he had tried several times to call her, but she wouldn't pick up. He'd left rambling voice mails about her father's murder investigation. He'd left more messages with her long-suffering colleagues, who no doubt had been instructed to tell him that she was "in the field." He knew he was only trying to keep intact the tenuous connection he had with her, since after his initial conversation with Denny Singer, he'd found out practically nothing new about the DOI inquiry into her father's death.

Raisa's father had almost certainly been killed by the Chinese smugglers the DOI was investigating. The feds knew them by name, but the suspects had pretty much vaporized shortly before Ingalls' body was found.

Online news agencies had already posted glowing obituaries of the intrepid Alaskan outdoorsman Zachary Ingalls, allotting only a couple of column inches to the federal inquiry into his poaching operation. Raisa was listed as his only child, and the three past and present wives were mentioned—Irina, Svetlana, and Oksana.

He drifted off, autopsy photos of the three dead young women and Zachary Ingalls' publicity headshot swirling in and out of his consciousness as the heat roared into the Explorer's cab. He was jerked awake by Herc tapping on the driver's window.

He rolled down the window. "Jesus, you scared the shit out of me." Beans rubbed his eyes.

"What are you doing out here? Mindy saw your car running and had me check it out."

Beans yawned. "I just came by to return the stuff you left at my place." He reached into the back seat and handed Herc his bundle of apparel.

"Cool. I wondered where those went. Thanks."

Beans had begun rolling up the driver's window when his brother rapped on the window again.

"Hey, come in for a second. You haven't seen our new place."

Beans shook his head. "I don't know, it's getting late . . ."

"Come on, just for a few minutes. Mindy put on a pot of decaf."

Herc and Mindy's ranch house was warm and inviting, with a gas fireplace in one corner of the great room and comfortable overstuffed furniture. Mindy's tuxedo cat, Pussy Galore, lounged languorously across the back of the sofa.

Mindy Weisskopf, smelling of molasses and liquid smoke, gave Beans a quick hug. She was a tall and sturdy German beauty with ice-blond hair that cascaded down her back. Her pale skin was adorned with a variety of colorful tattoos, the most notable being Mount Denali at sunset emblazoned across her chest.

"You should have come earlier. We had barbecued ribs." She handed Beans a steaming mug. "Don't worry, it's decaf."

He gave her a weary smile. "Yeah, I sleep badly enough already."

Mindy gave him a worried look. "This case . . . it must keep you awake at night."

"We have some promising forensic leads, but we're still not close to arresting anyone." Beans sipped at his coffee and took a bite of one of the Oreo cookies Mindy had set out on a plate. *This might be dinner.*

"Yeah, and I'm sure you can't talk about it." Herc popped a cookie in his mouth.

"You know I can't," Beans said. "But you folks with normal jobs can talk about them, right? They keeping you hopping at the DOT, Mindy?" As a human resources manager at the Department of Transportation, she had helped Herc land his snowplow driver job.

"Go figure, we had *so* much snow! A record year, even for Alaska! We had to hire a bunch of temps to take up the slack . . . I mean, we're still plowing around the clock."

"Which is how I got my job," Herc said. "It was a sweetheart deal too. Union wages, dude."

Mindy smiled at Herc. "You did good, babe."

"Yeah, but now what? They're predicting a warming trend—an early breakup?" Herc said. "They've already told me to start looking. Not just contract guys like me. I bet a lot of gyppo operators will be looking for work."

"Well, that sucks," Beans said. Herc needed structure more than anything else, and lack of a job could send him into a drunken tailspin.

"Yeah, but I'm pretty sure that Ingmar would take me back on the *Elsinore*." Herc was referring to the herring seiner he occasionally skippered. "Other than Ingmar himself, nobody can run that boat better than me."

Mindy looked worried. "I might be able to find you something, you know, long-term. Maybe running a paver or compactor . . ."

"Or flipping the sign between SLOW and STOP, like a crossing guard?" Herc chuckled, but without humor.

"Baby, you know I always worry about you out on the ocean. Don't you want a job where you could be home every night?" Mindy propped her stockinged feet across Herc's lap and wiggled her toes.

Herc rubbed her feet. "Course I would, Mins. But this winter has been a pretty good run for me, you gotta admit."

Mindy sighed. "If only they were all like this."

When ten o'clock rolled around, Beans stood to leave, thanking Mindy and accepting another warm embrace.

As Herc walked him to his car, Beans' cell phone buzzed. *Piper.* "Pipe? You'll never guess where I am," Beans said.

"You'll never guess where I am either, Havi." Piper's voice sounded tense and far away. "I'm on the shoulder on Fifteenth, near the convention center. I'm stuck in the snow, and my battery is toast. Can you give me a push and a jump, please? Pretty please?"

"What's up?" Herc asked.

"Sis's car died," Beans said.

"Remember, this is *your* old car," Piper grumbled.

"Yeah, but I expected that you would replace the battery at some point. It *is* twenty years old."

"Whatever. Can you give me a jump?"

"Okay, okay. You're at Fifteenth and what again?"

"I'm next to the vacant lot and the Denny's that. . . ." Piper's voice started to cut in and out.

"I'm just leaving Herc and Mindy's. I can be there in about twenty minutes. And Piper, lock your doors until I get there." It was late, and that wasn't the safest neighborhood after dark.

"Yeah, yeah, don't worry. And can you . . . ? The battery on . . . phone . . . die . . . too," she said, and hung up.

Great, Beans thought. *Here's why Piper was never a Girl Scout.*

Herc emerged from the doorway to the garage, holding jumper cables. "I'm coming with."

Beans was glad for the company. Herc was a large and congenial presence, drunk or sober, and was comfortable around any kind of mechanical device.

Mindy waved from the porch under the snow-laden eaves as Beans backed the Explorer out of the driveway.

"She's the best," Beans said to his brother. "Don't screw this up." He was grateful that Herc didn't remind him who, between the two brothers, the real fuckup was when it came to relationships.

30

Damp snow engulfed Piper's disabled Mazda like white icing on a car-shaped cake. Beans pulled a U-turn and pointed the front of the Explorer toward the hood of the small hatchback. This time of night, traffic was light, and he was able to swerve into the oncoming lanes without having to wait for an opening.

He popped the Explorer's hood while Herc stepped out and trudged through the snow to rap on the driver's window of Piper's car. Beans attached the cables to his battery and turned to see Herc scraping the snow off the driver's window, then the windshield.

"Havi, she's not here," Herc said in a strange soft voice, not at all like his usual hearty self. He tried the door. "It's locked, but she's not in the car."

Beans' stomach felt like it was plummeting down an elevator shaft. "I told her we were only twenty minutes out." He pulled out his cell phone and called her number. It went directly to voice mail.

He rubbed his forehead with a gloved hand. Piper, a mixed-race girl like Jolene, long dark hair, pretty. *Oh my God.* He hated that he jumped to that conclusion, hated that fatalistic cop part of him. Hated that he was right more than half the time.

"Try to text her. She said her battery was dying, but maybe she's got enough juice to receive texts."

Herc texted Piper while Beans retrieved a Slim Jim from the Explorer and slid it into the door lock mechanism of the Mazda. In a few minutes, the driver's door clicked and he pulled it open.

The car was littered with the detritus of Piper's life—college textbooks, Starbucks coffee cups, her green apron, lip gloss, energy bar wrappers, earbuds, hair scrunchies of every conceivable color. In the glove box was her iPhone in its pearlescent case, its battery totally dead.

Beans' chest went cold. "Oh, Jesus fucking Christ."

"Where do you think? Would she have taken off walking somewhere?" Herc asked, sifting through more debris in the back seat.

The snow started not so much falling off the car as thumping to the ground in clumps. Beans picked up his phone to call Carmen Fernandez, then stopped himself. *We don't know she's missing yet. Calm down.*

But images leaped to mind like flickering frames from a horror movie—of Jolene Nilsson's ravaged body, Toni Morelli's bloody hands with broken nails, and sweet-faced Hannah Fernandez with the jagged hole in her heart. He had to fight back the urge to scream. Then he realized that Herc was staring at him, pale and worried, holding Piper's green apron in his hand, looking to him for direction.

"Okay," Beans said, trying to sound calm, realizing that his voice seemed foreign, even to himself. "Put that back where you found it. Let's not touch anything we don't have to."

Herc dropped the apron like it was on fire. "Oh my Christ, you don't think something's happened to her? Oh fuck, Havi, has something happened to her?"

Beans carefully replaced the iPhone in the glove compartment. "We don't know that, do we? Maybe she got tired of waiting; you know how she is." Beans tried for a chuckle, but it sounded like a desperate cackle. "Maybe she caught a ride with a friend. There's her roommate—Brenda Patterson or Peterson, something like that?"

"I think it's Pederson. Wait, I remember Piper saying Brenda was the last person of her generation with a landline."

Beans called the listed number for *B Pederson* at the address he knew to be Piper's. A young woman answered on the third ring, the theme song of a popular reality show thundering in the background.

"Oh, yeah, her brother the cop. No, she's not here. I haven't talked to her since she left at about seven thirty for some frat party. Doesn't she answer her cell?"

This is getting worse, Beans thought. He and Herc sat in the Explorer with the hood up and the heat roaring, trying desperately to come up with names of Piper's friends—even if they could charge up her phone, he knew it would be locked. More wet snow smothered the landscape.

Beans realized how little he knew about his little sister's life, her relationships. Why didn't he have a list of emergency contacts for her? He would be at the top of that list, along with their mother, brothers Herc and Otter, and who else? He slammed his hands on the steering wheel in frustration.

Herc stared at him, wide-eyed. "Should we call Mom?" His voice was tentative, a whisper.

"No!" He didn't mean to shout, but his voice was loud and shrill in the confines of the car. Herc was sometimes childlike— endearing at times but exasperating at others. Beans said more calmly, "We will absolutely not call Mom until we have more information. Promise me, Herc, we will not worry her with this. Not yet."

Herc nodded. "So, what do we do now?"

The lights of a pickup truck seemed to peer through the dense curtain of wet snow and loomed behind Piper's little Mazda. Beans sat up and shielded his eyes from the glare.

The passenger door opened, and a slight figure with long dark hair hopped out. Beans and Herc reached her just as she was saying to the driver, "Thanks for the coffee, Tom. Looks like my brother—"

Beans grabbed her arm and spun her around. "Where the hell have you been?"

"Hey, you made me spill." Piper stared down at a steaming stain in the snow.

"We were worried sick, sis," Herc said, in his official big-brother voice.

"Oh, for chrissakes. I was sitting here freezing my ass off, and Tom here . . ." Piper pointed at the red-haired young man behind the wheel of the pickup. He smiled and waved feebly. "Tom pulled up. We work together at Starbucks. He asked me if I needed a lift, and I said no thanks, my crazy-ass brothers were on their way, but I would kill for some heat."

"I'm sorry we worried you, sir," Tom said.

Sir? Beans thought, annoyed. *I am maybe seven years older than this kid.*

"I thought we could get a quick cup of coffee at the Jitters drive-through and be back before you got here," Tom added.

"Jitters is literally down the block . . . and holy shit, did you break into my car?" Piper's mouth fell open in indignation.

"When I said lock your car, I meant with you in it. I didn't mean you should leave and then lock the car." Beans realized he was babbling. "We thought you were . . . *taken*, Piper. We thought—" He heard his voice break. "I told you to wait! I told you to lock your door!"

"And I did! Which is why you had to jimmy it open!"

"Listen, I should go," Tom said. "Nice meeting you." He looked from Herc to Beans. "I'll see you at work, Piper."

"Thanks again, Tom." She turned to her brothers. "Please jump my car so I can get the hell out of here."

While the battery charged, she explained in icy tones that she had been invited to a party at Statistics Boy's fraternity. "I'm not even dignifying him with a name," she said. "He got drunk and passed out. Meanwhile, his roommate tried to get his hand up my dress." She opened her coat to show them her silver-tasseled go-go girl minidress and white boots. "The theme was seventies disco," she said, rolling her eyes. Beans winced.

"So, I said, 'Fuck you very much,' and left," Piper continued. "The car was dicey getting started, but I got it going. So I'm cruising along by the convention center when a fucking fox ran in front of the car! I slammed on the brakes and spun out and got stuck. On top of that, the engine died, and I couldn't get it started again. That's when I called you."

Now that Piper had showed up, Beans felt exhausted. He had not slept well for days now, his dreams full of flaming trucks and flayed women. He rested his forehead on the steering wheel.

"Listen," he said. "I don't want to be that big brother who is overprotective and never lets his little sister do anything fun. I leave that to Herc." Herc wiggled his fingers and sipped at Piper's coffee. "But what I've seen the last few weeks would give you—has given me—nightmares."

"Of course what's happened to these women is horrible! But you can't . . ." Piper protested.

"Listen to me. Piper, listen. There is a killer loose in Anchorage. A killer that targets young women. And you, sis, look enough like the first victim to be her sister." Beans nodded at her dress.

Piper pulled her coat around herself and chewed on her thumbnail.

"When we couldn't find you, we thought . . . I thought . . ." He took a deep breath. "I thought that I would find you in a farmer's field, or in Denali Park after the wolves got to you. I thought I would have to tell our mother . . ." Beans couldn't go on. His throat had tightened up. *I couldn't save my baby sister.* Herc, sitting in the back seat, put a hand on his shoulder and squeezed.

Piper held her hands to her face, her eyes suddenly glistening with tears. "I'm so sorry, Havi. I didn't mean to freak you out."

"Again," he said. "I pointed my Glock at you the first time."

"Again." She nodded. "I'm a thoughtless bitch."

He held her for a moment, feeling her sob and sniff against his coat, then pulled away to look at her.

"Promise me. Be very careful. Don't go anywhere alone at night. Get that Tom guy to go with you, if you like him enough."

"He's a nice guy." Piper blushed and fingered the buttons on her coat.

"Just promise me." Beans lifted her chin to look her in the eye, and she didn't waver.

"I promise, Havi."

He held his hand to her cheek, looking into her dark eyes and the sprinkling of freckles across her upturned nose. The best and brightest of them all, and he'd thought he had lost her forever. "Good. Let's get you home."

Beans followed her home, Herc driving the Mazda with Piper in the passenger seat. Herc promised to pick her up to go battery shopping the next day and install the new battery for her. She kissed each of them on the cheek and told them, teary-eyed, that she loved them more than anything.

Herc was silent as Beans drove him back to the cozy home he shared with Mindy. Then, as they turned into the driveway, Herc blurted out, "What if the worst had happened, Havi? I don't know what I would have done."

"Me neither, buddy," Beans said, and clasped his brother around his neck. Herc's eyes, damp and luminous, met his.

At that moment, Beans envied Herc, with his childlike good nature and his simple view of the world. In bed tonight, Herc would put his arms around Mindy, and any thoughts of this evening's near-disaster would drain from him. Beans, however, would be alone with his grisly visions of Jolene, Toni, and Hannah as soon as the lights went out.

31

February 5

Sarah Yancey jerked awake, but her eyes, her arms, and legs felt as if they were encased in hardening plaster. She realized the woman's moaning voice she kept hearing was her own. She was not rescuing a bathrobe-clad woman from a burning building, as she was dreaming, but lying on the back seat of a vehicle, barreling through the darkness. She smelled him, in the car with her, the heady, overly sweet smell of Old Spice and motor oil.

She remembered, slowly, like swimming through black water toward the surface, closing up Petting Zoo and heading to her car through the slushy parking lot. She had her keys in her hand, about to unlock the pickup, then remembered that she'd left her phone in the kiosk. Just as she was about to put the key in the coffee stand's door, a stabbing pain in her neck almost brought her to her knees. She felt crushed between the door and a man's thick chest, his breath heaving, the cloying smell of aftershave filling her nose and mouth.

"What the . . ." She struggled against him, stomping on his instep, trying to jab her elbows into his sides.

"Fuck! Stop already!" He had pressed against her, her breath leaving her in steaming bursts against the glass of the door. Then everything went gray, and she lost consciousness.

In the car, she almost gagged with the memory of the sickeningly sweet smell. Where was he taking her? She tried to roll onto her side, but then her eyes grew heavy, and she descended into blackness again.

Then something like cannon fire exploded, and she was thrown forward, caroming off the car seat and hitting her head on the floor.

"Oh fuck!" a man's voice screamed. The vehicle beneath her shuddered and skidded to a stop.

Sarah groaned and tried to get her eyes to focus. Through the dim light from the console, she saw a dark blotch, a man's head, pressed into the white parachute-like expanse of a deployed airbag.

Her knee was wedged painfully under her, but she pulled herself back to the seat, her head swimming. She had no idea where she was, but she knew she needed to get out. She slid to the door and pulled the handle. Miraculously, the door sprang open and admitted a rush of cold air. She dragged herself out the door and collapsed onto the slushy snow at the side of the road.

She staggered to her feet and crossed the two-lane road, the slick pavement seeming to move under her. She shook her head, trying to throw off the grogginess. What kind of drug had he given her? The moonlight swirled around her like a kaleidoscope, and she grew dizzy, falling to her hands and knees in the wet road.

Get up, the voice inside her muddled brain screamed at her. *Get up or die.*

She rose, sobbing, and stumbled to the shoulder of the road. "Help!" she cried into the darkness. No headlights or streetlights or welcoming porch lights from nearby homes. "Oh, please, help," she whimpered. She looked back at the truck. The only signs of life were the glow from the console and the back door, still swaying slightly from when she'd shoved it open. She needed to find cover—if she stayed on the road, he would find her.

She tripped and fell into the ditch at the side of the road, gasping at the knee-high muddy water, swift and icy from the snow-melt off the nearby hillside. The frigid water was a rude awakening, but it shocked her into lucidity. *Get off the road.* She repeated it to herself like a mantra as she splashed out of the ditch and toward whatever cover the trees and shrubs on the hillside could offer. The terrain was steep and crusted over with icy slush, but the more she moved, the more confident she felt in the strength of her legs, the conditioning that she had worked so hard to achieve.

She dared not glance back for several minutes, but when she did, she saw the white pickup she had exited, its headlights shining on a moose cow, bloody and thrown to the side of the road. The back door still yawned open. *Where is he? Unconscious, still in the truck? Is he behind me?* She quickened her drunken gait, getting farther away from the truck.

The hillside was thick with leafless brush and berms of melting snow.

She realized that tears were streaming down her face as she groped in her raincoat pocket for her phone. She had left it in the kiosk. No phone, no purse, nothing. She choked down a sob as she scrambled up the rise, tripping, scrabbling at the bare branches with her hands. *Who is he? The son of a bitch who killed those girls?*

There was enough moonlight to dimly define a muddy trail through the woods. She slipped and fell to her knees, sobbed as she struggled to get purchase. *No time to be a wuss now, Sarah.* She wiped at her face with a grimy forearm and half stumbled, half jogged along the trail.

At the top of the ridge, the moonlight illuminated glistening threads of barbed-wire fencing. She stumbled along the fence line for a few hundred feet.

Shit shit shit. Nowhere to go.

Then, in what seemed like the second miracle that night, she saw just ahead of her that a fallen tree had bent a section of barbed wire down to the ground. Carefully, she stepped across the felled fencing. Barbs seemed to claw at her, ripping painfully at the flesh on her calves, her knees, her palms. The hem of her coat got caught by its spiny talons, holding her fast.

My new North Face coat, fucked. She took a deep breath and yanked at her coat with all her strength. A tearing sound and she stumbled forward, freed, and found the path down the hill.

In the distance, like a mirage, she thought she saw a peaked roof, then she was sure of it. The third miracle of the night—a small A-framed house, dark except for the moonlight glinting off the eaves. She broke into a clumsy trot, grasping at low-lying branches to pull herself forward.

In a clearing to the side of the A-frame was a chain-link structure at least seven feet high, with separate enclosures that she recognized as kennels. She had seen enough dogsled races to know that these structures probably housed Alaskan huskies. Dark shapes moved within the enclosures, some pacing along the fence line, some sitting or lying on the patchy snow or on mounds of straw.

Sarah slowed and approached the kennels cautiously. She had been raised with dogs, so she wasn't intimidated, but she didn't want them to raise the alarm.

Her legs felt like lead. The drugs he had given her and the adrenaline that had coursed through her body after her escape ebbed from her. Her head throbbed. She stood in the darkness, swaying slightly, listening for heavy splashing through the slushy puddles, the ragged breathing of the big man who had snatched her. She heard nothing except the jingle of dog tags and the scratching and pacing of restless dogs.

She must have lost the bastard, unless he lived in the A-frame. She was almost too tired and numb to care. As she neared the kennels, a few of the dogs rose up on their hind legs and yipped. Another dog howled, and a second dog joined him in unison.

The enclosure at the end appeared to be unoccupied. She crept in and latched the door behind her as quietly as she could. She ducked through the small opening in the plywood doghouse and found it dry and roomy. The floor was covered with new, sweet-smelling straw.

A low growl rumbled from the far corner. A large, rangy figure rose from the straw bedding and crept toward her, its hackles raised. Sarah's heart pounded. The dog was at least as large as a German shepherd but more feral looking, almost wolflike. She held her hands out for the dog to sniff. "Hey, good boy," she whispered. "What a good boy."

He snuffled at her hands, her face, and her bare legs, then gave them a tentative lick. The dog's tail drummed against the plywood enclosure with hollow thumps.

Sarah collapsed in the clean straw, almost weeping with relief. The dog gamboled around her, licking her ears, chewing at her hair, and finally curling up beside her. The heat and nutty smell of the dog lulled her into a drowsy half consciousness. Tonight, she could convince herself that her kidnapper was mortally injured, or at least nursing a whiplash. She felt secure and safe in this little plywood crate, nestled into the straw like a puppy next to the warm dog. She buried her fingers in his fur. *Tomorrow. Tomorrow, first thing, I'll get help.* Despite herself, she drifted into dreamless sleep.

32

Beans looked across the room at Cam Kristovich's passive face, as serene as an alpine lake. He had shown up every morning for the past four days promptly at nine, leaving promptly at eleven. He arrived with a small blue-and-white Coleman cooler, which he set on the floor near his desk. Out of it, he pulled a can of Coke and an Almond Joy and arranged them near the keyboard.

"Is that breakfast, Cam?" Beans inwardly shuddered. His own diet wasn't the best, but he drew the line at starting the day with a candy bar.

"No, my mother made me a breakfast of two scrambled eggs and a Jimmy Dean sausage patty. This is my first snack." Cam booted up the computer and with four clicks was watching the first of the posted security videos, his pale-blue eyes flicking across the screen.

Glad to know that the young man was ingesting some real food, Beans went back to his review of poultry farms in the Anchorage Metro area, or lack thereof. Large-scale chicken and egg production were much cheaper in the Lower 48, even figuring in shipping costs, and most of the farms had disappeared. A handful of artisanal farms produced organic eggs and chickens for limited commercial distribution, but he suspected most of the chicken and egg production in the area was for private consumption. There was very little info on backyard farmers, who weren't required to register or inform anyone of their private flock. Farm and pet supply outlets were a helpful resource, but incomplete and anecdotal.

Beans sighed and leaned back in his chair. The discovery of the trace evidence on Hannah Fernandez's feet was a huge breakthrough but no slam dunk. He glanced out the window at the streams of melting snow that streaked the glass. True to Herc's prediction, a freak warming trend had hit the Anchorage area with the force of a blast furnace. Huge drifts of snow that had only a few days ago lain like parked cars against curbs were now collapsing mounds of slush. The highway department had reported numerous incidences of flooding and water over roadways.

His front yard was the consistency of a mud-colored Slurpee. He had been annoyed to find that a leak had developed above his guest bedroom and set a plastic garbage can in the middle of the floor to catch the dripping snowmelt. He'd left a message with a roofing contractor but didn't expect a call back anytime soon. Beans suspected that this unusual temperature spike was just enough to fool cabin-feverish Alaskans into thinking spring had arrived. He was willing to bet there would be another crippling cold snap and more snow. True breakup, he thought, was still weeks away.

His deliberations were interrupted by a call from O'Reilly.

"I practically had to put on hip waders to come in from the parking lot this morning."

"Where are you?" Beans asked.

"FBI headquarters. The local yokels here found me a tiny desk in the corner next to the men's room."

"Come to APD after eleven. You can use Cam's desk after he leaves."

"Cam, your savant bus driver?"

"Yeah, he's looking at all that security video, since your colleagues can't spare the time to do it."

"Assholes," she muttered under her breath. "In the meantime, I've downloaded the registered sex offender list for the state of Alaska. No surprise that Alaska is in the top ten nationwide in terms of sex offenders per capita."

"Yeah, but you know what state is number one?" Beans grinned. He knew the answer to this one.

She sighed. "My own home state of Oregon. Anyway, I'll see if any names jump out at me."

"Can't hurt. I'll send you the bowhunter list as well as the poultry farmer list to cross-reference."

"Good plan. I'll see you at the shop after your savant leaves for the day."

"Okay. In the meantime, I'm heading out to see Liakos again—following up on a hunch."

He stood and stretched, then wandered over to the whiteboard and the Anchorage map with its six colored pins—which could have been thrown at a dartboard by a blindfolded person, he thought, frustrated. Next to it were the photos and the particulars of the three young women.

Nilsson: abducted 12/10. Found 12/13.
Morelli: abducted 12/22. Found 12/24.
Fernandez: abducted 1/28. Found 1/30.

Twelve days between Jolene's and Toni's abductions, then more than a month before Hannah was taken. *Why?* What the was the pattern? What was he missing?

Spiro Liakos' garage was almost unrecognizable from the last time Beans was there. The door was up and the building practically bursting with a jumble of vending machines, ladders, and machinery attachments.

Beans stood in the doorway and called, "Hello, Mr. Liakos?"

Liakos came stumbling out, tripping over the corner of a snowplow attachment. "Ouch, fuck this thing. That you, Detective?" He kicked the snow blade, which clanged morosely.

Beans followed him through a rabbit warren of trails to the plywood-enclosed office.

"Look at this place! I got shit coming out the yin-yang, and you know why?" The little man swept his arm to encompass the chaos that was his garage.

"No, why?"

"It's this weather! It's taking a huge bite out of my snowplowing business."

"You have a snowplowing business?"

"Of course! Mount Olympus Plowing!" Liakos said, as if his business enterprises were headline news.

It dawned on Beans then that this plowing business, run out of Liakos' garage, was one of the gyppo outfits Herc had been referring to—small operators that paid sub-union-scale wages, and most likely under the table as well.

"I thought you were in the vending machine and coffee stand business."

"Of course! But I have Mount Olympus Plowing that in the spring and summer becomes Mount Olympus Window and

Gutter. See?" He pointed to a precarious pile of scaffolding stacked against a wall of the garage.

"Wow, you're a busy guy."

"Oh yeah. And I got a laundromat in Wasilla—Aegean Coin-Op. All cash, even the snowplow business," he said, grinning. "You know, when I first came here from Greece, what's the first thing I noticed?"

"It was really cold?" Beans suggested.

"Yeah, yeah. But everybody has a pickup truck! Ford, Dodge, Chevy, whatever—everybody drives a big pickup. So, I hire guys with their own half-ton or whatever, they attach my plow, and I send them out to plow driveways, parking lots, condo association streets—all the small private shit the DOT don't touch. And you know the beauty?"

"No, what?" Beans began to fidget in the lopsided office chair.

"No credit. Payment due on completion of job. Same with window washing and gutter cleaning."

Beans wondered if Liakos did roof repair as well but thought he would save that for another occasion. He leaned forward to get Liakos' attention. "Mr. Liakos," he said.

"Please, call me Spiro."

"Okay, Spiro, I have a few more questions for you, if you don't mind."

"No, no, please ask." He waved his hand.

"The day that Toni was . . . taken, was she originally scheduled to work that day? Or did she fill in for someone?"

Spiro stood and pulled the previous year's *Sports Illustrated* swimsuit calendar from the wall. "Let's see, that was the twenty-second, right?"

"Yes, that's right." If Beans' instinct was true—that the perpetrator was targeting mixed-race women—this could be a breakthrough in the case and exponentially advance their knowledge of the killer's MO.

Spiro peered at scribblings in the tiny squares under Miss December. "Looks like Toni was scheduled to work—yeah, she was scheduled to work from six to noon that day. Bambi was taking over after that until closing."

Beans' spirits sank. There was no real pattern, then, based on the ethnicity of the victims. He was grasping at straws but asked Liakos, "And Bambi, which one is she?"

"Bambi Myerson. This one here." Liakos pointed to a headshot of a pretty honey-haired girl with large blue eyes, definitely Northern European.

"Okay, maybe not working on that day—but do you have any young women working for you who are mixed-race? Like half Asian, or Native—or half Latino?"

Spiro looked thoughtful, then flipped through the piles of paper on his desk. "I did have one who was half Japanese. Lovely girl, Melanie Yano. Here she is." He pulled out a composite portfolio shot of a striking young Eurasian woman. "She quit just before Christmas to move to LA."

But why Toni? "If she was still working for you, would she have had the morning shift that day Toni went missing?"

"Yeah, probably. Wait, you think he might have wanted her instead of Toni?"

"We don't know anything for sure yet. Just covering our bases. And keep this to yourself, okay?"

The last thing he needed was for Spiro to tip their hand. He changed the subject. "Have the baristas noticed anyone strange or inappropriate hanging around the coffee shop?" *Other than Bobo*, he almost said. Bobo was probably the strangest-looking guy in the Anchorage Metro area, but Beans wasn't going to say so. He was, after all, Spiro's brother-in-law.

"No, not really. Bobo was hanging around for a while keeping an eye on things. But he was freaking the girls out, so I'm having him stock the vending machines now."

In the last few days, women working at coffee kiosks had begun taking matters into their own hands. Many kiosks that previously had been staffed by a single barista were now staffed by two women, especially for the closing shift. Many baristas had begun packing firearms at work.

"You have them be careful," Beans said. "We've got some good forensic evidence now, but we haven't arrested anyone yet." Even to himself, he sounded lame and ineffectual.

Spiro shook his head. "This is a really scary thing. I remember reading about Bundy. The Green River Killer too, and Hansen. Very, very scary. And bad for business," he added.

33

Sarah Yancey was jolted awake by a metallic clang. She felt blindly around her in the dark, her hands groping piles of straw and the plywood walls of the dog enclosure. Her watch glowed the time: 7:10. It took her a few seconds to realize that the clanging sound was the kennel door she had latched the night before, swinging open. The dog that had curled up beside her last night was whining and pacing at the fence.

Then, a woman's voice. "Come out where I can see you." It was an even voice, not aggressive but definitely no-nonsense.

Sarah crawled out on her hands and knees and rose slowly, blinking in the glare of a flashlight beam. She held her hands up when she saw that the woman standing in the kennel's doorway held a flashlight in one hand and an ancient Winchester rifle in the other.

"Please, don't shoot," Sarah pleaded. "Please, I need help."

"Who are you? What do you want?" The woman was only a few years older than Sarah, with large brown eyes—pretty, but underfed looking. She wore yoga pants tucked into gum boots and a fleece-lined parka over a flannel shirt. Her curly chestnut hair tumbled out from under a tattered ball cap, and she looked at

Sarah with an air of curiosity. A black-and-white dog with a fluttering tail stood at her side, equally curious.

Sarah realized then how awful she must look. Her boots and the hem of her coat were slathered with mud. Her hands and legs were filthy and bloody; her face must look the same.

She rubbed her hands on her coat. "Please, I need to call the police. I'm Sarah, Sarah Yancey. Someone—a man—took me from my work. I'm a barista." She opened her coat to show the woman the black teddy underneath.

The young woman's mouth fell open. "Oh lord. Not another one. Come in, come in. Are you hurt?"

Sarah shook her head, but the motion made her feel like her brain was pinging against her skull. She suddenly felt unsteady on her feet. The woman slung the rifle over her shoulder and, with an arm around Sarah's waist to steady her, guided her across the slushy yard toward the A-frame. The simple house that had been in total darkness the night before was now bright and welcoming. The black-and-white dog gamboled around them, running ahead, then circling back to nudge at Sarah's hand.

"She alerted me of a stranger on the property this morning," the woman said, nodding at the dog. "Then she followed your tracks up into the woods. I saw your footprints in front of Zero's kennel and figured you must have holed up here."

If she followed my footprints, so could he. Sarah tried to convince herself that a quick call to the police would end this nightmare as she stumbled toward the house with her rescuer.

In the warmth of the A-frame, the woman, who said her name was Raisa, sat her down at the kitchen table with a glass of water and a cup of coffee, both of which tasted wonderful to Sarah. While Sarah wolfed down a piece of buttered toast, Raisa explained that her landline had gone down when the sudden thaw washed away a transmission line.

"And I got shit for cell reception here unless I get up higher," Raisa said. "I'm going to have to drive you in. The car's out front." She pulled open a drawer and fished out a key ring.

Relief washed over Sarah. "I can't thank you enough—"

Pounding on the front door made both women jump. The black-and-white dog named Willow stared at the door, growling.

More pounding, then a man's voice, harsh and loud. "Raisa! I need to talk to you!"

Sarah's heart leapt to her throat. *It's him.*

"My asshole neighbor." Raisa moved toward the door. "He hates Willow, and the feeling is mutual."

Sarah caught her arm and pulled Raisa toward her. "It's him." Sarah's voice was a hoarse whisper. "He's the one who took me."

Raisa's eyes widened. "Eddy Dodds?"

"I recognize his voice. He's the fucker who drugged me— threw me in his truck."

"Raisa! Come on, I know you're up. The lights are on. And I can hear that chicken-eating dog." The man's heavy boots clomped on the front porch.

Raisa crept to the front door and peered out the peephole. "Yeah, it's Dodds, all right. Face looks a little beat-up."

"It's from the airbag when he hit the moose."

"What? Never mind, fill me in later. I'll have to tell him something." Raisa called out, "What the fuck, Eddy! Do you know what time it is? What do you want?"

"Open up!"

"Jesus, Eddy, I'm sicker than a dog. Just tested positive for COVID yesterday. You don't want to be near me for another week at least." Raisa coughed violently. She peered out again, then said quietly to Sarah, "He's still on the porch. Looks like he drove the ATV over. And he's got some kind of fancy pistol. Definitely out-classes my old peashooters."

Adrenaline surged through Sarah's veins again. This hap-pened a lot when she was called out on a fire, and it was when she thought the clearest. She glanced toward the back door where they had come in.

"It's me he wants. I can't put you in any more danger. If you can distract him, I'll go out the back."

"There's no way you'll find your way, not before daylight, and that's hours from now." Raisa picked up the rifle that she had ear-lier pointed at Sarah. "We'll head up to the duck blind and make our call from there. Can you climb a tree?"

The woman asked this question as casually as if she were inquiring about cream in her coffee.

"Sure. I grew up with three brothers." Sarah wondered with a pang if she would ever see them or her fiancé Wyatt or her parents again.

"Good. We'd better go. He'll head around back in a minute." Raisa filled her pockets with cartridges, then pointed to a second rifle, a battered old .22, propped in the corner near the back door. "Can you handle a rifle?"

"Yes, ma'am." Sarah smiled, for the first time in what felt like days. She'd been raised outside Fort Worth, Texas, and sure as hell knew how to fire a gun. "Even this old piece of shit."

Raisa gave her a handful of cartridges and smiled back. "It's better than nothing." The two women, armed with rifles, and Willow the dog exited the back door with only the slightest click of the latch.

34

Another restless night was interrupted by a call from Dispatch: *Report of a dead body, just off the runway at the Big Lake Airport. Caller was practically hysterical. He said it was another barista.*

Beans threw on clothes and drove the fifty-plus miles to Big Lake in a sleep-deprived trance. *Another girl?* By the time he arrived at the snow-shrouded airport, Chuckie and his team were already there, flashlights in hand, standing in a silent circle around a mound of snow.

One of Chuckie's technicians said, "Oh, for fuck's sake."

Chuckie sighed. "Seriously?"

Beans approached, jamming a piece of spearmint gum in his mouth. "What have we got?"

Chuckie pointed at the figure that had been posed in the snow. At first glance, Beans thought it was a Jolene lookalike with long dark hair and very little clothing, and his stomach lurched. He wondered why the techs hadn't set up the crime scene lighting until he knelt to take a closer look.

The figure in the snow was not a dead body but a department store mannequin, wearing a tropical-print bikini and a dark wig.

It had been posed in an awkward fashion, as if it had been thrown from a moving vehicle. Someone had applied bright-red lipstick clumsily so the mannequin's mouth looked like a bleeding wound.

"Some sick bastard's idea of a joke." Chuckie ran his flashlight beam along the plowed runway. "Probably drove an ATV right on the runway. Dumped the dummy without leaving a trail. What kind of asshole would do this?"

Kids on a burner phone, probably, with too much time on their hands, Beans thought. Or anyone with too little patience with law enforcement's inability to stop these killings. He gnawed on his wad of gum until his jaws ached.

By the time he arrived back home, it was five o'clock and he knew trying to get another hour or two of sleep would be an exercise in futility. Arriving early in the office for a change, Beans was in the elevator when his cell phone rang. The caller ID read *APD*.

It was Carmen Fernandez, who sounded very far away, although she was in the same building. "Beans?" She took a deep breath. "Another girl has gone missing."

Sarah Yancey had been last seen at Petting Zoo Espresso, a coffee kiosk less than five miles from the beet field where Hannah Fernandez was found. She had apparently closed the kiosk at eight the previous night as scheduled, as it was clean and secured when the morning shift opened up. Sarah's Toyota Tacoma pickup was parked around the back of the kiosk, also locked, the hood cold.

Sarah was a part-time firefighter and was supposed to have reported for an early-morning shift today. Her station chief repeatedly called her cell, which rang until it went to voice mail. He finally sent a young fireman to Sarah's condo, but there was no response there.

By the time Beans arrived at Petting Zoo Espresso at eight fifteen, a cadre of burly firefighters had accumulated, a show of support for their missing colleague. They hovered near their vehicles, trying to stay out of the way of the crime scene technicians who were processing Sarah's truck and the kiosk.

One of the first pieces of evidence pulled from the melting snow just outside the kiosk door was a hypodermic syringe, half full of a clear blue liquid. Technicians bagged it for processing, but Beans was convinced that it contained Rohypnol, the same drug used on the other baristas. Sarah's cell phone, its battery almost dead, was found on the counter of the coffee kiosk—but her purse was not. Beans had a sickening feeling of foreboding.

Sarah's firefighter colleagues were only too glad to talk about her. She was dependable, responsible, and had never missed a shift, they said.

"And she's tough, strong. She could kick our asses in any physical test. The only reason she wasn't on full-time is there wasn't a position for her yet," a sandy-haired young man said.

Beans took a description down for the BOLO. Sarah was five eight, about a hundred and forty pounds. She was half African American, half white (here Beans' cop sense tingled—another mixed-ethnicity woman). She had wavy dark hair that fell past her shoulders, golden-brown skin, and arresting green eyes.

"She is a stone-cold fox," the sandy-haired firefighter said, nodding.

"Sarah was only gig-working at Petting Zoo," a shorter, balding firefighter added. "She said the tips could be awesome."

Sarah's fiancé was a Navy Seal, currently deployed somewhere in a secret-ops mission overseas. No one knew of anyone who would do Sarah any harm—a familiar refrain. Beans took down all their names and information and promised to contact them if necessary. Right now, he was still hoping she would show up alive—*the same way I'd hoped Hannah Fernandez would show up alive.*

A warm wet wind blew across the parking lot and fluttered the damp blue-and-white Petting Zoo banner. Lumps of melting snow stood in muddy puddles. If there was any evidence other than the syringe, it had likely been obliterated by tire and boot prints of customers and Sarah's well-meaning firefighting and barista colleagues.

Can't we catch a fucking break? Beans looked up into the flat gray sky. Since the discovery of Hannah Fernandez's body, tension at police headquarters had amped up several notches to near-meltdown levels. Lieutenant DuBois said the media was "crawling up his ass" and he needed something of substance to tell them soon. To make it worse, with coverage of Hannah, the ass-crawlers had started repeatedly using the dreaded term *serial killer.*

And now I have to tell them a fourth girl is missing. Beans pulled out his phone and called O'Reilly to fill her in.

"Holy Jesus," O'Reilly breathed when he told her about Sarah Yancey.

"And hey, we got a syringe."

"Our pool of potential evidence is getting deeper by the day." She paused. "Unfortunately. You talked to the girl's family?"

"Carmen did. Parents are in Texas. They told her they last saw Sarah at Christmas, so it's not likely she's heading back there, and certainly not without her phone. They're concerned, of course, but Carmen talked them into staying put for now."

"Keep me in the loop. I'm still working the lists," O'Reilly said. "I'll get back to you shortly."

Beans hung up with O'Reilly and slogged through the parking lot to the Explorer. As he unlocked his door, his cell began to ring. The caller ID again said *APD*.

"Carmen?" he asked.

"Hello?" a flat inflectionless voice intoned.

"Hello, this is Beans."

"Hello?"

"This is Beans, and this better not be you flicking me shit, Heller." Beans could barely keep the irritation from his voice.

"This is Cam Kristovich."

"Oh, sorry, Cam. What's up?"

Silence on the other end of the line.

Oh, right, be very literal and clear. He reworded his question. "Why did you call me, Cam?"

Over the phone, he could hear Heller in the background yelling, "Beans! Get your ass over here, pronto!"

Cam sounded like he was reading a script. "I think I found something."

35

Beans steered the Explorer through the slushy streets to the freeway. Melting snow dislodged by the warm breeze fell like small avalanches off the trees bordering the road, some splashing onto the hood of the car or spattering off the windshield.

An intersection loomed in front of him, a fork in the road that tugged at him like a memory. It was the turnoff toward Raisa's house. If he turned right here instead of continuing on to central Anchorage, winding surface streets would eventually take him to Raisa's A-frame in the woods. For several reasons, there would be no stopping by Raisa's house today. He pressed his foot on the accelerator and sped past the intersection, mud and ice spraying behind his tires.

Cam Kristovich sat behind his desk at Anchorage Police headquarters, his spine straight, staring ahead at his computer screen. In front of him was a half-eaten Almond Joy bar balanced across the top of a can of Coke and a yellow legal pad with precisely lettered notes. Ed Heller peered over Cam's shoulder at the grainy video as it jumped across the monitor.

"What do you have, Cam?" Beans shrugged off his raincoat and draped it across his chair.

"Oh, this kid is a genius." Heller was awestruck.

"I bookmarked certain frames and recorded the counter number and time and date stamps here." Cam pointed at a neat list on his yellow legal pad.

"Show me." Beans looked over Cam's other shoulder.

With a couple of clicks, Cam started the security video supplied by the management company of the strip mall across from Snow Bunny Baristas, where Jolene Nilsson had worked. He fast-forwarded through jerky pedestrians scurrying through the snow and cars sliding in and out of parking spots in front of the dog groomers, the cleaners, and the teriyaki restaurant. Then he stopped the video. Coming into the frame was a large light-colored truck with a snowplow attachment.

"Here." Cam pointed at the screen.

The truck moved through the frame, pushing mounds of snow in front of it.

"Okay, there's probably a bunch of these guys plowing parking lots," Beans said.

"Yes, but look at this." Cam zoomed into a small detail on the back of the snowplow.

"Is that some kind of sticker?" Beans squinted at the monitor.

"Yes." Cam zoomed in as far as the computer would allow. The decal was oval, white with a black border, with three words—EAT WILD SALMON—in barely discernible black capital letters. The decal was applied at a haphazard angle, as if slapped on by a child.

"This snowplow appears several more times on these dates and times. At these counter numbers." Cam pointed to his legal pad again. "Other trucks and plows appear. They do not have the decal."

Beans was amazed that Cam had recognized this level of detail. Because of the location of the decal, it appeared on the video only when the truck appeared at certain angles.

"Look here." Cam clicked on the next link. This video showed the exterior of the Kwik-E-Mart, the convenience store from which Toni Morelli had been abducted. Cam cued the video up, and a white pickup truck with a snowplow attachment lumbered into view, clearing snow from the pavement in front of the pumps. As it turned, the back of the plow came into view. Cam froze the frame and zoomed into the oval image adhered to the back of the plow. Again, the tilted EAT WILD SALMON decal emerged in grainy resolution.

"I'll be damned," Beans said.

"The plow comes here"—Cam pointed at his notes again—"four times in the week before Christmas."

"Show him the day of Toni Morelli's abduction. The twenty-second," Heller said.

Cam fast-forwarded until the date and time stamp read December 22, at 05:37 AM. Kamal Hazim was alone in the brightly lit store, stocking cigarettes on the shelves behind him. An older-model red Subaru Outback slid into a parking space along the side of the store, and a blond woman wearing a trench coat stepped out, fishnet hose covering what was visible of her long legs.

"Oh. Toni Morelli." Beans' heart rate quickened. He had seen the video before, several times. Every time he was struck by how lovely and alive the young woman was, so vibrant, her golden hair swinging behind her as she flung the door open and smiled.

Even on the grainy distant security video, he could tell that Kamal Hazim's body language changed when Toni walked in. Hazim smiled and reached behind him for a pack of cigarettes, rang them up at the register as they chatted, and handed Toni a key at the end of a long flat piece of wood. She strode out of the store, rounded the corner of the building, and disappeared.

"Keep watching," Heller said.

For thirty-seven seconds, Hazim checked the cash in the register and arranged pepperoni sticks and breath mints on the wire racks near the counter. Then, at the top of the screen, the white pickup with the decal turned into partial view, pushing snow like an afterthought, and vanished from the frame. Cam paused the video with a click.

Beans exhaled in the silence that followed. "Any way we can get a tighter bead on the license plate?"

"I tried. The back plate is partly covered by snow. The front plate is covered with the plow," Cam said.

"We'll work on that next. What about the video around Buffalo Gals?"

Again, this video did not show the kiosk itself, but it covered the parking lot of the hardware store adjacent to it.

"It's three weeks before the truck with the decal shows up again." Cam fast-forwarded to the three incidences in the week prior to Hannah's abduction where the pickup truck with the decaled snowplow was at work, clearing the parking lot. On the night Hannah disappeared, it was there, barely visible through the thickly falling snow.

"Okay, the plow with the decal wasn't near Buffalo Gals for three weeks. That's why the nearly monthlong interval between Toni's and Hannah's abductions." Beans' pulse began to quicken.

"That truck is at every scene, multiple times. He has to be our guy." Heller slapped the desktop.

"I've requested security video from the ATM across from Petting Zoo," Beans said.

"You will not see the snowplow in that video from yesterday," Cam said.

"Why is that?" Heller asked.

"There is no snow," Cam said simply.

"Right, duh." Heller looked embarrassed.

"But maybe we'll get a better view of the truck. We need that plate number." Beans pulled out his cell phone and called O'Reilly.

"Send me what you got," she said. "I'll make these prima donnas refine those plate images if I have to hold a Glock to their heads."

"Meanwhile," Beans said, "Heller, can you see if you can sweet-talk the woman at Far North Properties? See if she'll tell you who she contracts with to plow the strip mall parking lot across from Snow Bunny. I get the impression lots of backyard guys made extra money this winter plowing with their pickups. She can't stand me, but she may respond to your rugged charms."

"Ha!" Heller rolled his eyes.

"I'll send you her contact info. I'll talk to Kamal Hazim and the manager of Ralph's Rentals across from Buffalo Gals and see who plows for them." Beans turned to Cam. "Cameron, excellent work!"

For the first time, Cam looked pleased, nodding quickly, although he didn't smile.

"Let's total up your hours, and I'll put in a time card for you. I'm sure we can pay you a little something, although don't expect too much. We don't have much of a budget."

Cam looked offended. Small lines crossed his brow. "I did not do this for money," he said, his voice flatter than usual.

"I didn't mean to insult you, Cam. It's just our way of compensating you for a job well done. I'm not sure we would have recognized the decal pattern without you."

"I did this for Buffalo Gals Hannah. I did this for my friend."

Heller and Beans glanced at each other, both feeling like shit.

Cam looked at his digital watch. "It is only nine twenty-one, but I think I am finished here." He stood, packed his half-eaten Almond Joy bar and empty Coke can in the cooler, and put on his coat. He slipped off the lanyard with his solemn ID photo and laid it on the desk.

"Yes. Again, I can't thank you enough." Beans extended his hand, and as usual, Cam hesitated a moment before taking it. He repeated the same exercise with Heller, nodded to them both, then walked out the door.

"Well, he put us in our place." Heller slumped in his chair.

"No shit." Beans picked up the phone. "Hello, Spiro? Detective Beans here. Fine, fine, thank you. There's something you can help me with. How many guys plowed for you this winter?"

36

Spiro Liakos hesitated before saying, "I got four guys plowing for me, the same four who run the Mount Olympus Window and Gutter in the summer. Why?" His voice took on an uncertain tone.

"So, you've got how many plows there in your shop?"

"Two. Why?"

"And this is your full inventory of plow attachments?"

"That's all I own, sure. A couple of the guys plow with their own gear, though."

"Do your guys ever switch plows in the middle of the season?"

"Not with my plows. I sign them out with one plow each winter, and they better damn well bring it back in the same condition. What they do with their own gear is their business."

"This is important, Spiro. I want you to go out to your garage and look at each plow attachment carefully, back and front. Do either one of them have a decal on it that says EAT WILD SALMON?"

"What?" Spiro asked. "A decal?"

"Right, a decal that says EAT WILD SALMON on it. Look on the backside too, the side that faces the truck. The sticker's kind of crooked, like it was just slapped on."

Spiro snorted. "What the hell does eating wild salmon have to do with snowplowing?"

Beans rolled his eyes, glad that Spiro couldn't see him. "Probably nothing, but humor me, okay? Go out and take a look at each plow and let me know if the decal is there."

"Okay, hold your horses. I'll be right back." The receiver clattered to the desktop.

"I'll hang on." Beans could hear the creaking of the door opening and Spiro's footsteps retreating into the garage. He stared at the grainy frozen video on the screen and the oval sticker on the back of the plow. "He's checking," Beans said to Heller, who was on hold with Far North Properties while staring transfixed at the same image on the screen.

More clattering and thunking as Spiro picked up the receiver again. "Nope, no EAT WILD SALMON sticker. No stickers at all, actually."

Beans slumped in his chair. "Are you sure?"

"Sure, I'm sure! I double-checked, but I think I would know what's on my own damn snowplows."

"Yeah, I guess so. Thanks for looking." Beans couldn't keep the disappointment from his voice. "I also would like a list of all the guys who work for you in the plow business, and their contact information."

Spiro's voice was wary. "Am I supposed to ask you for a warrant?"

Beans sighed, exasperated. *A fourth girl is missing, and now Spiro wants to play law and order.* "Yes, you could if you wanted to. You could if you wanted to delay the investigation, sure you could. In the meantime, more girls could go missing."

"Okay, okay, sheesh. I'll email it to you in a couple of minutes. There's only four guys on my list, but Sandoval Plow and Garden has twice as many guys on their payroll."

Beans sat up straight. "Sandoval Plow?"

Heller nodded and gave Beans a thumbs-up. "Thank you, ma'am," he said into the receiver. He hung up the phone and handed Beans a hastily scribbled note that read *Far North uses Sandoval.*

"Yeah, they're based out of Eagle River too, only a few miles from my place," Spiro said. "Sandy has way more customers, but hey, there was more than enough business to go around this year."

Diego "Sandy" Sandoval, who ran a successful plowing and landscaping business, was happy to cooperate in any way he could. He employed eight plow drivers in the winter, the same eight employees who worked in the landscaping business in the spring and summer months. Like Spiro's crew, some plowed with their own equipment, and some attached plows supplied by Sandoval.

Crossing his fingers, Beans asked if any of his plows had an EAT WILD SALMON sticker on the back.

"I'm not sure. I only have two plows back here in my shop. The others are driver owned. I can check these two. Hold on."

After a few minutes of hold music, Sandy came back on the line, a little short of breath. "I'm sorry, Detective. The two plows that I have here are clean, no decals. I can call my drivers and ask them."

"No!" Beans said, more abruptly than he had intended. "No, please do not contact your drivers at this point. I would appreciate a list of your employees who plow for you and their contact information, though."

"No problem," Sandy said. "It's on its way to you in just a few."

"Oh, and Mr. Sandoval?" Beans found himself crossing his fingers. "Do you plow for the Kwik-E-Mart on Raspberry Road?"

Sandy sounded surprised. "Well, yeah, we've been working with Kamal Hazim for several years now—"

"And how about Ralph's Rentals on Boniface?"

"Sure, Ralph's a longtime customer of ours—"

"Thanks, Mr. Sandoval!" Beans punched his fist in the air. "And please—I need the employee list as soon as possible."

"I'll email it ASAP," Sandy said, and rang off.

O'Reilly called from FBI Anchorage headquarters. "Our techs said, and I quote, 'These are fucking horrible images.'"

"They're nothing if not consistent," Beans said.

"Even with our enhancement technology, they say they can only pick out the first two digits, and some possibilities for the third."

"Okay, shoot," Beans said.

"First digit is almost definitely A."

"Got it."

"The next one is probably E."

"So far, so good."

"Here's where it falls apart. There's a lot of mud and snow on the rest of the plate. The third digit could be a three or an eight, or even a five?" O'Reilly said.

Not great, but that might be enough to go on. "Okay, we'll see if this is enough for DMV to work with. Thanks, Isabelle. Let me know if there are any more breakthroughs."

"I'll keep looking to see if there's a better view in one of the later shots."

Beans was sure Sarah Yancey was living on borrowed time. The discovery of the half-full syringe was encouraging, indicating she might not have received a full dose, but where was she? Typing as fast as he could, he ran a DMV search for late-model light-colored Ford F-150 four-door trucks with the first two digits of A and E. The first search yielded more than thirty trucks in the Anchorage Metro area.

"Ah, shit," he said, under his breath. He would narrow the search to AE3, then AE5, and AE8.

His cell phone pinged with a text message from the facilities manager at the bank across the parking lot from Petting Zoo Espresso: *Attached is link to video in time window requested. Let me know if I can be of further assistance. Good luck.*

With half his attention drawn toward his DMV database search, Beans clicked on the link to the bank's security video. The counter started at 19:45 the night before. The video camera was positioned above the bank's ATM machine, so the Petting Zoo kiosk was in fish-eye perspective, near the edge of the frame and at quite a distance from the lens. Bank customers of different ages and ethnicities jerked through the video as Beans fast-forwarded through it. He saw Sarah Yancey in the kiosk, smiling, serving coffee—and yes, the firemen were right, Sarah was a stone-cold fox. Then the light went out in the kiosk.

He sat up straight and looked at the counter—20:13. He watched as a bearded young man in a beanie smiled into the camera and took out some cash. Then, as a middle-aged Asian woman frowned and pressed buttons, a large white pickup truck passed slowly in front of the now-dark Petting Zoo kiosk. There was no plow attached, so the front plate was unobstructed.

"Holy Mother . . . ," he breathed. He froze the image, then enlarged it. There it was, the entire plate number. AE8 2359.

He stood bolt upright, and his chair fell backward with a crash, startling Heller.

"I think we got it." Still standing, he typed the plate number into the DMV database.

Heller looked over his shoulder as the search result popped up. The truck was registered to Dodds Poultry Farm, PO Box 49, Chugiak, Alaska.

Heller and Beans stared at each other. "Jesus," Heller said.

"It's him. A poultry farmer. In Chugiak, not far from where Hannah was dumped. It's him."

Heller did a quick search for an address for Dodds Poultry Farm. "It's been out of business for at least ten years," he said. "Shit. There are a couple dozen Doddses in Anchorage Metro."

Two emails popped up on Beans' screen, one from Spiro Liakos, the other from Diego Sandoval, both with their employee lists attached. Beans glanced quickly over Spiro's list and saw nothing useful in his four names. But Diego Sandoval's list yielded Edison Dodds at PO Box 49 in Chugiak.

"That's him, but where the hell is he?" Beans said.

Internet search results included an old *Anchorage Daily News* story on the sorry condition of the state's poultry farmers, as one by one they were being forced out of business by the high costs of operating in Alaska. The reporter had interviewed Franklin Dodds and his son Edison at their farm in Chugiak. The article included a photo of both Doddses on the front porch, Franklin seated in a wheelchair with a white hen on his lap, a smiling Edison standing beside him. Franklin Dodds was a dried apple of a man, wizened and scowling. Edison was much more robust, with a cherubic baby face that almost seemed photoshopped onto his husky body.

"Here!" Heller pointed at his computer monitor. "Tax assessor's records say the now-defunct Dodd Poultry Farm was located at 14759 Chugiak Highway."

"Fourteen-seven-five-nine Chugiak Highway?" Beans stared in disbelief at the address.

"Yeah, that's what it says." Heller got his coat off the back of his chair. "Let's go."

"Fourteen seven-five-nine Chugiak Highway?" Beans repeated, stunned. "That's right near . . . Raisa's address is fourteen seven-nine-one Chugiak Highway."

"You're kidding me," Heller said. "Your Fish and Wildlife lady?"

Beans grabbed his coat and darted toward the door. "I'm driving. Call for backup, will you? And have O'Reilly meet us there."

37

Willow led the way through the darkness, her white-tipped tail flickering like a flame. Raisa followed the dog while Sarah pulled up the rear, each of them with a flashlight in one hand and a rifle in the other. The only sound was the splashing of their boots through the melting snow.

Sarah recognized the trail as the one she had staggered down to escape from Dodds the night before, and she shivered. She envisioned him leaping out from the scraggly underbrush or firing at them, invisible and deadly, from the silent darkness.

They had almost crested the rise when Raisa took an abrupt right down a rougher trail still covered with large patches of dirty snow. Sarah's watch glowed the time: 9:20 AM. There was no cell or internet service, as Raisa had said. For now, her smartwatch was only good as a timepiece.

"This way." Raisa motioned with her rifle and strode through what seemed like impassable brush. To Sarah, the dry branches cracked and popped loud enough to sound like bones breaking. They went another fifty feet, and Sarah was surprised and relieved that, where they stood, they would be all but invisible from the main trail .

"You first," Raisa said, handing her one end of a rope ladder.

It was only then that Sarah realized they were standing at the base of a huge spruce tree. Up at the top of the ladder, perched in the spruce's upper branches, was a small, almost camouflaged tree house.

Sarah peered up, amazed. "This is the duck blind?"

"The guy who used to own the property called it that. But he mainly came here to smoke weed. Go ahead, it's skookum as hell—all cedar construction."

Sarah stuck the flashlight in her pocket, slung the rifle over her shoulder, and scrambled up the ladder. In a few seconds, Raisa was standing beside her in the small treetop cabin, pulling up the rope ladder after her.

"That was way easier than climbing a tree," Sarah said. "What about Willow?"

The dog paced around the base of the tree, whining.

"Willow, out!" Raisa called to the dog through the hole in the floor, and Willow scampered off into the darkness. "She'll alert us if Eddy gets close." Raisa pulled out her phone. "This is the highest spot on the property. Good, three bars." She punched in 911.

"There's an armed man after us!" Raisa rattled off her name and location. "I have Sarah Yancey with me. The missing barista. She got away . . . No, I can't . . . contact Detective Beans with Anchorage Homicide."

She quickly punched in another number and waited as it rang. Finally, "Beans! No, no listen! The barista guy is *here*, at my house! . . . Listen, it's Eddy Dodds, my creepy neighbor, for God's sake! And he's got a gun . . . And Sarah? The missing barista? She's here with me . . . yeah, she's okay, we're both okay for now . . . I don't know where he is. We snuck out the back . . . I called 911 . . . they'll probably call you next. We're on the ridge in the old duck blind—" She rolled her eyes. "Oh Jesus, don't start on me, Beans. Are you on your way? Please say you are . . . Okay, good, you're not far. We've got rifles and maybe could hold him off for a little bit. He's got some kind of hand cannon, not sure what, but fuck, Beans, just get here, will you?" She sounded annoyed, but in the glow from the cell phone, Sarah could see that the woman was shaking her head with a small smile on her face.

Raisa let out a deep breath. "Help is on the way."

Sitting on the dusty floor strewn with dead leaves and dried-up spliffs, Raisa loaded her rifle with the cartridges from her pocket. She stood watch out the screenless window and Sarah did the same, straining to spot any movement in the filmy darkness of approaching daylight, while Sarah filled her rescuer in on what had happened—how the man she now knew as Eddy Dodds the snowplow guy had drugged her as she was leaving the shop and brought her here. It was only his collision with the moose cow that had allowed her to escape.

"You've helped me so much, and now I've put you in danger too." Tears pricked at Sarah's eyes. "I'm so thankful, and I'm so, so sorry."

Raisa gave her a sarcastic smirk, barely visible in the slowly brightening day. "This would all be over by now if I had a decent cell phone carrier."

Sarah smiled back.

Just then, furious growling and snarling from the bottom of the ridge set the other dogs barking and lunging against their kennels, chain link clanging.

"Willow," Raisa said, and cocked her rifle. Sarah did the same and aimed the barrel of her rifle in the direction of Willow's barks.

Then came the sharp report of gunfire, a crack that echoed through the woods, and a pitiful yelp.

"Oh, Willow." Raisa sighed and looked away. "My poor girl."

38

Beans eased off the gas as the Explorer hydroplaned across a dark puddle of standing water. The car yawed in a cascade of water until he brought it under control.

"Whoa!" Heller said, bracing himself against the dash while punching the speaker button on his phone. "O'Reilly? Heller. We think we've got him—white male, in his thirties, named Edison Dodds. Delta-O-D-D-S, at fourteen seven-five-nine Chugiak Highway."

"What? What was the name again?" O'Reilly's voice cut in and out.

"Dodds. Delta Oscar Delta Delta Sierra."

"Shit." The sound of clicking on a keyboard. "I got a Dodds who came up in my cross-checking of the poultry farmers with sex offenders. Yeah, here he is."

"Edison Dodds? DMV has him at early thirties, six four, two hundred and fifty, brown hair, brown eyes."

"No, no." O'Reilly took a deep breath. "Not Edison. Franklin Dodds. Deceased in November of last year at age sixty-seven. The thirteen-year-old victim's family wanted to keep it quiet, so he got away with minimal jail time, but he still had to register as a sex offender back in 2002. Shit, not Edison—his father."

"What the . . . ?" Heller stared at Beans.

Beans' eyes met Heller's. "We're on our way. Heller's calling for backup."

"I'll meet you there." They could hear a jangle of keys.

"O'Reilly," Heller added, "figure that he's armed, and not just bows and arrows. Bring some of your fed buddies."

Heller hung up with O'Reilly and picked up the radio.

"Tell Dispatch no sirens. We want to surprise this asshole, if possible," Beans said, swerving to miss another ocean of standing water in the road. Heller steadied himself before calling for backup.

Beans' cell phone began barking. *Raisa.* "Raisa? Get in the house and lock the door. Don't open it to anyone . . . what?" He pressed the phone closer to his ear. "Yeah, Edison Dodds, the poultry farmer . . . Sarah Yancey? She's there? Is she okay? Are you okay?" Beans gaped at Heller as he listened in disbelief to Raisa's frantic voice. "Where are you? . . . Are you safe? Where are you now? . . . Oh, right, up in Doobie's tree house." He sighed. "Okay, sit tight. We're less than a mile away."

He hung up with Raisa and gripped the steering wheel, propelling the Explorer faster through the semidarkness. Streetlights were few and farther between now, and Beans was grateful for the flashing blue rooftop lights that illuminated the sodden highway.

He glanced at Heller. "Sarah Yancey somehow got away from Dodds and made it to Raisa's. They slipped out the back door and headed for higher ground, where there's cell reception. How many times did I tell her to switch carriers?" He pounded the steering wheel in frustration.

"Where is Dodds now?" Heller asked.

"He's probably going through the house looking for them. They're hiding out in the woods. They have rifles, and Raisa's a helluva shot, but Dodds has a handgun, God knows what else."

"A gun and a crossbow?" Heller shuddered.

"Oh Jesus." The starburst-like puncture in Hannah Fernandez's chest swam in front of Beans' vision like the aura before a migraine. *Can I make this car go faster?* Now they were rushing to save not only Sarah Yancey but Raisa as well.

"What do we know about Edison Dodds?" Beans asked, trying to shake Hannah's image from his mind and focus on the road in front of him.

Heller looked down at his phone. "No recent arrests. Only priors were juvenile offenses, and those were for"—Heller winced—"animal cruelty. These happened while he was in foster care."

"Foster care? Where was the mother?"

"Looks like the mother, Lilith, left home a while ago, when Eddy was about twelve."

"About when Franklin was charged with child rape," Beans said. He was getting a queasy feeling in his stomach.

"With the mother gone and the father a convicted sex offender, it's no wonder he was put into foster care."

"And Franklin Dodds is dead?" Beans asked.

"Yeah, just about two months ago," Realization dawned across Heller's broad face. "Just about when our first barista, Jolene was killed."

Beans stomped on the brake and swerved suddenly.

Heller's head hit the passenger window with a loud thump. "Ow! What the fuck, Beans!"

The Explorer fishtailed on the wet pavement and skidded to a stop inches behind a white Ford extended-cab pickup truck that suddenly loomed out of the semidarkness. The truck was dark and abandoned, stalled out in the lane. Beans flicked on his emergency flashers. *White Ford F-150 pickup. AE8 2359.*

Half in the road and half in a ditch was the carcass of a moose cow, crumpled and bloody. The front grille of the pickup was crushed, the hood buckled. Airbags had deployed and lay draped across the dashboard like rumpled bedsheets.

"Blood in the front seat and on the driver's bag," Heller said. He used his sleeve to open the rear door and bent to loop his pen through the shoulder strap of a small tan purse. "Probably Sarah's."

Beans looked up at the wooded hillside. He knew that the duck blind was well concealed, but from someone who knew the woods almost as well as Raisa? He said a silent sutra for her safety, and for the safety of the young woman with her.

A few hundred yards from the truck, he turned down the long driveway leading to Raisa's A-frame, dimmed his headlights, and pulled into a break in a thicket hedge that offered some cover, but with a view of the house. The house itself was ablaze with light; it looked like every light in the house was turned on. Raisa's Land Rover was parked in front. Behind it, a mud-spattered Polaris ATV angled across the driveway. In the kennels behind the house, the sled dogs were silent.

Beans and Heller sat in the car for a few seconds, watching for movement in the house. No sign of life in the brightly lit rooms.

"He can't possibly still be in the house. It's too damn bright. Where's our backup?" Beans asked.

"In transit, according to Dispatch," Heller said.

"We don't have time." Beans pulled bulletproof vests from the back seat and handed one to Heller. He strapped his on, then reached under his seat and pulled out his Glock. "I'm heading up to the ridge."

"Might be a trap." Heller fastened the vest on.

"Nah, my guess is that he's panicked that he lost Sarah. He's looking for the two women. Cover me." He pointed at the right side of the house. "I'm going around back."

"What if he's got an accomplice? I should go with you." Heller opened the passenger door.

"The profile says he's a loner." *I hope to God he is.* "Stay here and coordinate the backup."

Beans felt Heller's eyes on him as he racked the slide on his Glock and clipped a handheld radio to his belt. He opened the door and looked at Heller, who nodded, his own gun drawn and propped against the hood of the Explorer. Beans ran around the front of the car and crouched in the shadows around the house, avoiding the bright squares of light cast from the windows.

In the last moments before he slipped into the woods, Beans wondered if Heller still doubted his ability to draw and fire his weapon if he needed to. He knew that today's events might settle that, one way or the other.

39

Two painted yellow poles flanked the driveway with a chain between them loose on the muddy ground. A painted wooden marker with the faded numbers *14759* stood half-hidden in the leafless scrub. Agent Isabelle O'Reilly killed her lights and drove over the chain, splashing down the long driveway to Edison Dodds' house.

"Where the hell is everybody?" She frowned. Had Heller given her the wrong address? And where was her FBI backup? They should be right behind her. She pulled out her cell phone, but her screen read *No Service*. She sighed and pocketed the phone, wishing she had waited to be issued a department vehicle with a two-way radio instead of taking her rental Nissan.

The driveway eventually opened up into a compound with a two-story house in front, a detached garage to the side, and a large barn with enough parking for a dozen cars. The lights from the main house were on, but all the other structures were dark.

She'd passed the wreckage of the white Ford F-150 pickup truck and the moose carcass on the way here, but there was no sign of Dodds. He might be in the house, injured. Neither Beans'

Ford Explorer nor the backup they were expecting was anywhere in sight.

O'Reilly parked the Nissan to the side of the driveway, an area obscured from the house by a stand of brush and hemlocks. She tightened her vest and drew her Glock. She stood for a few seconds and listened for the sound of cars splashing up the driveway, but she heard nothing.

"Oh, hell with it." Standard procedure was to wait for reinforcements, but until backup showed, she would do some stealthy reconnaissance.

The front steps had been replaced by a wheelchair ramp and a low railing. She listened at the door, but there was no sign of activity inside the house. She looked into the front room from between the gap in the faded curtains: avocado-green love seat, harvest-gold sofa with a crocheted afghan folded neatly on the sofa back. A milk-glass table lamp cast halfhearted light over the small room. A frayed braided rug partly hid the worn painted floor. Stainless-steel grab bars had been installed in the hallway to what she assumed were the bedrooms. The vase of white roses on the coffee table made her shudder.

She turned the doorknob with a gloved hand. *Locked.* All the other windows were curtained and dark. She would wait for reinforcements before trying to gain entry to the house.

The large, detached garage was unlocked, and the side door creaked as she pushed it open. She pulled her flashlight from her belt and shined it around the room. An oil stain darkened the floor where the F-150 probably parked, and at the far side of the garage was a dusty older-model Buick Regal, dark blue. Wooden shelves lined one side of the garage, laden with auto maintenance supplies—motor oil, antifreeze, windshield washer fluid.

On the other side of the Buick, next to where she guessed an ATV usually parked, judging from the width of the tire tracks, her flashlight beam caught a dark-yellow piece of machinery. A snowplow, dented from weeks of use, badly in need of a paint job. On one side of it was the white oval sticker EAT WILD SALMON.

"I'll be damned." *Gotcha.*

The driveway extended alongside the garage and led to a large parking area in front of the red barn. Compared to the other structures on the property, this building looked recently painted and better maintained. The main barn doors were locked, but she found a side door that opened when she turned the knob. She shined her flashlight into the dark, cavernous space. What looked like stacked bleachers surrounded an arena, its floor covered with stained sawdust, and the barn was filled with the acrid odor of pine and chicken manure. She found a light switch and turned on a dim, bare bulb that hung from the doorway.

Tiered benches surrounded the arena on three sides. On the fourth side were black-shrouded crates, stacked three high. As quietly as she could, O'Reilly flipped back a corner of the black canvas covers. An angry yellow eye glared at her, and a raucous squawk made her drop the heavy fabric. Heart pounding, she slowly picked up the cover again and shined her flashlight inside. The rooster in the cage pecked at the wire enclosure and fluttered his wings, screaming and gripping the cage with his talons. He was the largest rooster she'd ever seen, deep rust and green, glimmering feathers reflecting light like an oil slick. The other roosters in the cages, at least a dozen of them, joined in the chorus, shrieking and cawing in a frenzy.

"Well, hi, big boy." She felt a strange sadness for the bird, a fighting cock that would duel to his death with sharp blades tied to his talons. The rooster lunged at her, making her step back. *Interesting sideline to the poultry business*, she thought as she flicked the lights off.

She left the barn and crossed a gravel pathway to the small chicken coop. Was this all there was left of what had once been a thriving enterprise—a dozen sleepy hens with their beaks folded under their wings? The coop was not as clean as the barn and smelled like a combination of chicken shit, straw, and grain. The coop was way too small to hold a woman in addition to the hens. But she sensed she was getting close.

Outside the chicken coop, she breathed deep lungfuls of clean air. It was then that she noticed the barn's root cellar and its new, unpainted door. A lock and chain hung from it. *He could have kept them down there.*

She pulled at the heavy wooden door, and a dim rectangular shaft of light stabbed into the darkness. She held her Glock in front of her. "FBI!" she called out as she descended the stairs, but the room was silent.

She flicked on the switch near the door, and a bare bulb illuminated the low-ceilinged root cellar, which took up about a fourth of the barn's area. Most of the space was cluttered with sagging wooden and metal shelving with crates of rusted equipment parts, hardware, and tools.

She picked her way between snags of chicken wire and dented feeding troughs to the far corner of the cellar. Hidden from view from the stairway was a white Frigidaire chest freezer, humming in a corner next to a rusted drill press and band saw.

She holstered her weapon and lifted the lid to the freezer, expecting to find dried-out moose steaks or salmon fillets. Instead, nestled inside, legs folded to her chest, was the pale frozen body of a young woman, eyes closed, as if she were napping peacefully, wearing only a black bra and matching panties. Slightly above her left breast was a single triangular wound, black and dry, almost exactly like the one they had found on Hannah Fernandez.

"Oh my Christ!" O'Reilly whispered.

She guessed the petite woman had been in her late twenties or early thirties at the time of her death. The only mark on her white face was a large gray bruise on her left temple. A dried rose lay across her body. The long black hair that fanned around her face, like the rest of her folded corpse, was crusted with frost. Her dark lashes, now icy white, feathered her pale, desiccated cheeks. Even in death, in this eerie cryogenic state, she was beautiful. O'Reilly was struck with horror by the woman's resemblance to Jolene Nilsson. The unheated basement suddenly felt stiflingly hot and airless.

She slammed the freezer shut and scrambled up the stairs, fumbling for her phone with shaking gloved fingers.

"Oh shit shit shit." She held her cell phone up, trying to get some kind of cell or Wi-Fi reception. Her phone detected a secure Wi-Fi network called *Bigcock90*, which she assumed was Dodds'. She made a gagging sound under her breath. She headed for the slight rise behind the house and finally showed two bars—not great, but it would have to do.

She got Heller after six rings. "Hellboy, where is everybody?"

"We're at Raisa Ingalls', next door." Heller spoke in hushed tones. "Backup is arriving any minute."

"I'm at Dodds'. You guys have got to see this. There's another body—repeat, there's another body here."

"What? Isabelle . . . wearing a vest? Wait for us . . . Take . . . We think he might . . ." Heller's voice cut in and out.

"Yeah, yeah, I'm wearing a vest. Listen, I'm losing you. Let me get to where—"

A gloved hand pressed across her mouth, and her breath left her in a muffled shriek. Arms like metal cables grabbed her around her waist and lifted her above the ground, her feet pedaling frantically in the air. Her phone slipped from her hands and fell into the slush at her feet. She tried to reach for her gun, but her arms were pinned by a man who smelled of cloying aftershave. Panic rose like bile in her throat. Worse than that was the sinking feeling that in her lifetime of making risky ill-advised decisions— joining the FBI instead of the family CPA business, getting that ridiculous tattoo—exploring the Dodds property without backup would be the last impetuous mistake of her life.

40

Five minutes earlier

The dog came out of nowhere, a black-and-white snarling blur, teeth glinting. It hurled at Edison Dodds like a missile, knocking him off his feet. Jaws clamped onto his left forearm. Pain shot through him, faster than adrenaline, a horrible, excruciating high. Then it began snapping at his head, and he raised his wounded arm to protect his face. The dog's growl was deep in its throat, rumbling like an approaching train.

It was all he could do to raise the little runt's handgun and squeeze off a round.

The dog flew back, yanked away like on a pulley, yelped, and lay still. Eddy watched the blood pool in the dirty snow. A very nice-looking pelt, all in all. Maybe he'd come back later to get it. He'd clean it and skin it and give it to that she-wolf Raisa. *See how she likes her chicken-eating dog now.*

He struggled to his feet. His arm throbbed and dripped a bloody trail into the snow. The whole day had been a clusterfuck from the moment he took the girl from the Petting Zoo.

He'd never expected her to be so strong. He hadn't gotten the plunger all the way down like with the others. The minute he jabbed her with the needle, she'd started to fight him like a heavy-weight champion. *Jesus, she was strong.* He only pushed the plunger in partway before it fell out. It was enough to knock her out to get her in the truck, but he knew it wouldn't last.

And then the fucking moose. He cringed thinking about the front-end work that the rig would need. Undrivable. Fucked up in a major way. And worst of all, the woman Sarah got away. She couldn't have gotten far. That bitch Raisa must be helping her.

And I can't go back to get the Polaris. The place is probably stinking with cops. What a hot fucking mess. This was supposed to go easy, like the others. Who knew that the half-breed was going to be some kind of MMA wrestler, for chrissakes?

But then he remembered the Buick, twenty years old, a little dusty but otherwise pristine, good tires, only thirty-five thousand miles on it. He started it up every couple of weeks and had replaced the fluids just before the cold snap.

He stumbled back toward the house. The cut on his forehead from the airbag started weeping, and he kept having to blink blood out of his eyes. No matter. He could navigate blind through these woods. He knew them like the back of his hand. When he was a kid, he and his dad had crept through the woods at night, faces blackened, creeping up on game with their crossbows, set-ting crippling traps. Killing shit in the dark. That was before Dad was caught with Shelly from his American History class and Eddy went to live with the Underhills.

Now, his best shot was to get to the Buick. He could fire it up and blow this place. He could get so lost in the Interior that they would never find him. That thought brought him some comfort. He liked living in the woods with his crossbow and rifle, shooting game to eat. Shooting men to keep them away.

As he neared the chicken shed, the place where he'd held the other women without problems—except that boxer bitch Sarah—he heard a woman's voice.

"You're breaking up. Let me get to where . . ."

She was little, almost as small as the first one, the one he loved the best. Jolene. She had long hair that spilled out of a dark ball cap that said *FBI*.

Fuck me, the feds. He moved without a sound toward the woman on the phone.

He took her totally by surprise, covering her mouth and lifting her off her feet, gripping her to him. Her phone fell to the ground. A man's voice said, "O'Reilly?" He smashed the iPhone under his boot and heard a satisfying crunch as the screen cracked.

She was feisty for a little one, but he tucked her under his good arm, feeling the bulletproof vest like a medieval corset between his body and hers. She shrieked and tried to reach for his eyes with her fingers, her nails, but he knew better after that Morelli girl and held her fast.

She began screaming, "Beans! Heller! Beans!"

He slapped a gloved hand over her mouth. This woman had beautiful red curls. In the dim light, they looked like molten lava. He might have to save a few as a souvenir. He moved his hand from her mouth to finger the curls at her neck. He felt her shudder against him.

"Heller! Beans!"

This woman would just not stop yelling until he pointed the gun at her. "Can you *please* shut the fuck up?" She was hot, but Jesus, she was *loud*.

She nodded, her eyes wide, those red curls bouncing.

"Good. Me and you gonna do some cruising in the Buick."

He pressed his aching forearm against her neck and staggered toward the shed for some duct tape, her lavender scent oddly arousing.

41

eans had been halfway up the rise when feral snarls and growls stopped him short. Then a man's high scream and a single shot echoed across the hillside. A dog's pitiful yelp, and a chorus of Alaskan huskies baying and howling.

His radio crackled.

"You okay?" Heller's concerned voice sounded far away.

"Yeah, I think he got one of the dogs."

The melting snow had almost eradicated any footprints, but this hillside was familiar territory to him. He took long strides up the slushy embankment to the well-concealed duck blind. The rope ladder was hanging from the opening, swaying slightly.

His hand on his Glock, he peered into the dark opening above his head. "Raisa? Sarah?" No answer. He scrambled up the rope ladder and looked around the small tree house. No sign of either woman, but there was evidence they had been there. The dust had been disturbed by smaller, female boot prints, and a rifle cartridge had rolled into a dark corner.

His phone call to Raisa went directly to voice mail. He radioed Heller, who answered in a tense whisper: "Say they're okay."

"They're not here. Raisa's not answering. I bet she went to her dog, damn it. I'm heading down there. Might be out of range for a while."

"Copy that. But if I hear any more shooting—fuck the backup, I'm on my way."

Beans followed the trail toward the sound of the shot, keeping as low as possible, using scrub and leafless trees for cover. A patch of green caught his eye, a parka that he recognized as Raisa's. At the base of a small spruce, blood mixing with the mud and melting snow, was the black-and-white Karelian bear dog Willow, covered with Raisa's familiar green jacket. The dog raised her muddy head. Her tail fluttered when she recognized Beans.

"Oh, I'm sorry, girl." The dog whimpered and tried to stand, then fell back to the ground. She had a gunshot wound in her hindquarters that he hoped wasn't serious, although she'd lost some blood. He noticed a dark blotch on a nearby patch of snow. *Blood, but whose? Where is Raisa? Sarah?* A few feet away was another blotch on another melting lump of snow. Cautiously, his boots splashing in the dissolving snow, he crossed over a section of downed fence and followed the trail of blood down the other side of the hill to the Dodds Poultry Farm.

The splotches were farther apart as the snow dissipated near Dodds' barn and outbuildings. Stamped into the mud were smeared prints, larger boot prints and noticeably smaller ones. He noted the familiar larger Sorel boot prints—probably size 11.5, the same that had been cast at the Chambers farm, Hannah Fernandez's dump site. The smaller prints were probably a woman's—*Sarah's? Raisa's?*

Two dark figures struggled against the stark gray of a shed—a large man wearing a baseball cap and a smaller figure, a woman.

Both figures staggered into a shaft of watery light. It was Dodds, dwarfing the person he dragged around the corner of the shed. A bright flash of red hair caught the light, and Beans recognized the smaller figure.

His heart sank. *Isabelle?*

Her wrists were duct-taped together in front of her. More tape covered her mouth. O'Reilly struggled against her restraints, but Dodds outweighed her by at least a hundred pounds. He had the muzzle of a pistol pressed against her head as if drilling it into her skull. He buried his nose in her hair and appeared to murmur something as she strained against him.

Beans couldn't risk a shot, not with Dodds holding O'Reilly to him like a human shield. "Edison Dodds, this is Detective Beans with Anchorage Homicide," he called out from behind a stand of trees.

Dodds turned and fired off a round that splintered a chunk of tree trunk by Beans' head.

"Where is Sarah? Sarah Yancey?" Beans called out.

Dodds snorted. "Hell if I know. Probably with my she-wolf neighbor."

Good. "Come on, Dodds. Put down your weapon. Let her go. You really don't want to be on the hook for a federal agent."

Dodds tightened his grip on O'Reilly. He fired another shot that sent a spray of shredded wood into the air. A sharp splinter nicked Beans along his right eye, and he flinched. A trickle of blood oozed down the side of his face. He swiped at it. "Tell me about the women." Beans desperately wanted to keep him talking.

"Jolene," Dodds said. "Oh, Jolene." It came out singsongy, like from the Dolly Parton song.

"Jolene Nilsson, Snow Bunny Baristas?"

"There's only one Jolene." There was a dreamy note to his voice.

"Of course. Tell me about her."

"She was . . . she was just like Lily. The most like Lily of any of them."

"Lily?" Beans scoured his memory for a barista named Lily.

"She was so pretty, with those smiling eyes. She made me laugh."

"Who is Lily, Dodds?"

"Dead, long dead." Dodds sighed, and O'Reilly's red curls fluttered under his breath. "I followed her once, found out where she lived."

"Lily?" Beans asked.

"No, Jolene!"

"Okay, so you found out where she lived."

"Yeah, so later, when she wasn't there, I got in through a window. I looked through her stuff."

"Did you take anything?"

"No! I'm not a thief!" Dodds' boyish face reddened.

"Did you leave her something, then?" Beans asked.

"Yeah, sure. I left her a rose, because that's what you do with girls you like, right, give them flowers?"

An elaborate romantic fantasy? O'Reilly's unsub profile ran through his head. "Okay, then what?" Beans asked. O'Reilly had stopped struggling and appeared to be letting Dodds give Beans his full attention. She would be biding her time, waiting for her opening. He felt a rush of pride for the young woman—smart, skilled, and now patient.

"Then I brought her here."

"How?"

"What do you mean, how?"

"How did you get her to go with you?"

"I gave her a shot of the blue stuff."

"What stuff?"

"You know, the roofie. I dissolve the pills in a little water and put it in the needles. Works great to make them sleepy."

Rohypnol. "So, she went to sleep. Then what?"

"Then I brought her here," Dodds said.

"And you killed her."

"I made her a frozen angel." His voice was no longer wistful but matter-of-fact.

"Frozen angel? What does that mean?"

"What does that mean, Jellybean?" Dodds' voice was mocking.

He'd seemed so amiable and willing to talk about Jolene, then, like flipping a switch, he had turned juvenile, imitative. Beans lowered his hands but kept them at his sides. He took a deep breath. "So, what now?"

"What now?" Dodds' forehead wrinkled as he considered the question.

"Where are you going with Agent O'Reilly?"

"Me and her are going on a little road trip. She'll drive, of course. Or she could make the trip in the trunk."

"Where?"

"That's for me to know and you to find out," Dodds sang, half dragging O'Reilly beside him.

"Eddy Dodds, you motherfucker!" a familiar voice screamed. "You. Shot. My. Dog!" *Raisa.* Beans heart leapt to his throat when he saw her emerging from the woods in her camo beanie and gum boots, the stock of her Winchester on her shoulder.

O'Reilly faked a stumble over an invisible rock, for an instant loosening her captor's grip on her. A rifle shot rang out, and a ragged hole appeared in the shed wall just above Dodds' head. Beans ducked for cover and pulled out his Glock but couldn't get a clear shot. She stomped on Dodds' arch, then kicked him in the groin. When he folded forward with a muffled cry, she swung up with her bound wrists and bashed his nose with a sickening crunch. The pistol that he had held at her head discharged as it fell to the ground.

Another rifle shot from Raisa rang out, sending up a spray of mud in front of Dodds. He loped off like a wounded caribou toward the side door of the barn, his nose cascading blood.

"Dodds! Stop! Police!" Beans fired a round above Dodds' head, then took off running. *Damn it, Raisa should have stopped at one shot.* Dodds staggered clumsily across the melting snow.

Beans took careful aim at the retreating man, Redbird's high, panicked voice an indelible memory, shrieking, "Take the shot!" Beans held his breath and pulled the trigger, aiming high, and felt the recoil as Dodds' baseball cap flew into the air. Dodds screamed and grasped at his head but didn't stop as Beans had hoped.

Beans ran past O'Reilly as she ripped duct tape off her face. "Ouch, shit! He's going through the barn, heading for the garage, the Buick. Go! And Beans, he's got my gun." She looked contrite, angry.

"Whose is that?" He pointed to the pistol that Dodds had dropped.

"It's mine now. I'll get Heller. We'll cover the other door."

"Find our backup!" Beans sprinted to the barn.

One of the two side doors to the barn was ajar. Inside, it was dark and eerily quiet. As he groped for a light switch, a bullet zinged by, making him duck for cover behind a bale of straw.

"Dodds! Anchorage Police! It's over. The barn is surrounded. Drop your weapon. Come on out."

Gunfire exploded and another two bullets whizzed by Beans, slamming into the wall behind him. A dark figure scurried along the wall, toward the opposite door. Beans took aim and fired, causing the shadow to dive for cover. In the dim light from the clerestory windows, he saw a blur of movement near a stack of crates covered by drop cloths. Keeping as low as possible, he crept around the perimeter of a large open area that appeared to be some kind of arena and approached the wall of crates.

"Come on, Dodds. Throw out your weapon."

Suddenly, the wall toppled, cascading in front of him like a collapsing tower of children's blocks. They weren't crates but metal cages, which burst open with deafening crashes and spilled their contents—shrieking, cackling creatures with talons.

42

Like demons released from hell, they tore at his face and scalp, ripped at his hands as he tried to fend them off. As one crazed, glassy eye loomed near him, Beans realized that these were large frantic fighting roosters, spooked to a frenzy by the flapping tarps and toppling crates. Furious and agitated, they attacked anything that moved.

A shot rang out, and the rooster stabbing at his face was flung away by the force of the bullet, gold-and-green feathers fluttering to the ground. Beans knew that shot had been meant for him and not for the bird that now lay twitching and bleeding across the arena.

Dodds let another bullet fly, whizzing by Beans' ear. "I like Red's gun." His voice was cheerful, victorious.

Beans dodged copper-and-emerald-colored roosters as they swooped at him, strafed his head, and flapped in and out of the milky light from the overhead windows. He shot one as it flew toward his face, but their shrieks and lurching attacks threw his aim off and gave him a vague feeling of the barn spinning around him. He shook his head, trying to regain his equilibrium. "Dodds! Just drop the weapon."

Dodds answered by toppling another stack of wire crates, releasing more frantic birds. A crate narrowly missed Beans' head, crashing into him. Before he could clear the blood from his eyes, a huge rooster flew at him. Raising his arm to fend it off, he managed to grab it by one foot. A ragged spur punctured his palm as pain shot up his arm, but he held it fast. Even as blood dripped down his fingertips, he grasped the bird's other leg and held the rooster upside down, where it flapped its wings feebly and calmed.

Squinting through the veil of blood that oozed from his scalp and forehead, he saw that Dodds still had O'Reilly's gun trained on him. "Are you kidding me? Cops and FBI have the place surrounded, Dodds."

"So, where's Red, then? Where's the cavalry?"

Good question. The rooster hanging from Beans' hand wriggled.

"Well." Dodds peered down the barrel of the Glock. "Time's a-wastin'. Drop the gun and kick it over here." He moved his index finger onto the trigger.

The side door burst open, and Heller bellowed, "Police! Drop your weapon!"

Dodds' finger jammed reflexively on the trigger, and the bullet went wide, embedding with a thud into a bale of straw to Beans' right.

At that moment, Beans hurled the rooster as hard as he could toward Dodds. Now upright and wide awake, it flew at Dodds' head, jabbing viciously at his face. The rooster's claws found purchase on Dodds' cherubic cheeks, and its sharp beak stabbed at the frantic man's eyes. He shrieked in a high-pitched voice, trying to scrape the furious bird from his face, spraying the barn with random shots.

Beans raised his Glock and fired. Dodds' body jerked, and the gun flew from his hand. *That'll wreak havoc with my karmic balance. Or maybe not.* "That was for Jolene," he said under his breath. Dodds tried to move toward the gun, but Beans kicked it away.

Heller and O'Reilly rushed in, guns drawn. Heller looked from Beans' bloody face to Dodds, who writhed on the ground, clutching his shoulder, the irate rooster continuing its attack. Heller nodded to Beans. "Not bad for a Buddhist."

"Where the hell is the backup?" Beans holstered his weapon and bent to handcuff Dodds.

"Highway was flooded, so they had to divert to surface streets. They should be here now." As if on cue, sirens came whooping up the driveway. Heller shrugged. "They were supposed to be on silent approach."

"Makes no difference now." Beans swiped his bloody forehead with the sleeve of his coat and smiled at his colleague. "We got him, Hellboy."

"Get this fucking chicken off my face!" Dodds screamed.

An army of policemen and paramedics descended on the barn. The EMTs determined that Dodds' bullet wound was less serious than the rooster-inflicted lacerations to his eyes and face. They bandaged him up, sedated him, and loaded him into an ambulance. With lights flashing, the ambulance and its police escort crunched down the gravel drive and headed to the hospital. A sedan-load of dark-suited FBI agents showed up just in time to get an earful from O'Reilly.

The surviving roosters strutted in the parking lot, picking fights with each other or jabbing at the tires of the emergency vehicles. Beans sat at the rear door of an ambulance, getting his wounds administered to by a deadpan paramedic named Dean, while a rooster pecked at Beans' shoelaces.

"Can't remember the last time I was called to a poultry attack," Dean said. "I'll clean and dress your injuries for now, but the one on your scalp might need stitches. Get that puncture on your hand looked at too. Always danger of infection with these types of wounds. When was the last time you had a tetanus shot . . . no idea? Then I'm giving you one now. I also want to give you some antibiotics . . . any allergies?"

Beans shook his head.

O'Reilly was suddenly beside him, smiling. "How you doing?"

He smiled back and a jolt of pain zinged through one side of his face, where Dean was applying some kind of antiseptic ointment. "Ow! Okay, I guess. And you?" He pointed to the plum-sized bruise on the side of her face.

She rolled her eyes. "I'm fine. What hurts the most is my pride. I was disarmed by a guy who had his ass kicked by a chicken."

"Not your average fryers." Beans looked down at the deep scratches on his hands. He didn't want to imagine what his face looked like. His coat and the front of his shirt were spattered with blood and chicken shit. He sighed, resigning himself to the fact that he would hear chicken jokes in the squad room for the next few months, maybe even years.

"The body in the freezer?" Beans asked.

"Chuckie's with it now. He thinks she's been there a while. No positive ID yet."

"We need to talk to that son of a bitch Dodds." Heller came from the police unit, carrying a gray sweatshirt. "Who'd have thought he'd have another one on ice?"

"We can't talk to him until at least tomorrow, according to the docs."

"Shit. He doesn't need his eyes to talk to us, does he?" Heller grumbled. He handed Beans the sweatshirt, an extra-large with a Red Dog Saloon logo silk-screened on it. "Might be big, but it's clean."

"Thanks. And Sarah—Sarah Yancey?" Beans asked, unbuttoning and peeling off his bloodstained shirt and pulling the baggy sweatshirt over his head.

"Sarah's at Dodds' neighbor's—Raisa?" O'Reilly said.

"Raisa Ingalls."

"Right, the lady with the rifle. She saved my ass, that's for sure. What a gutsy move." O'Reilly shook her head in admiration.

He couldn't keep the pride from his voice. "She's a gutsy lady."

She looked at him sideways, like an inquisitive bird. "She a friend of yours?"

"Yeah. A good friend." The minute he said it, he knew it was true. "How's her dog?"

"Raisa and a couple of uniforms rushed her to the vet. Hopefully, she'll be okay. From what I hear, the dog is as much a hero as her owner."

Again, Beans felt a swell of pride in his chest. Oxy addiction or not, most twenty-year police force veterans didn't have the balls Raisa did. Her warning shot above Dodds' head had been just that—a warning shot. She was a good-enough markswoman to have killed or maimed him if she wanted to. As it was, she'd provided a distraction and given Isabelle the time to get away.

He wanted to feel jubilant that Dodds had been apprehended, that the last victim had survived, that the killing of baristas would stop, but the thought of the three dead young women left him feeling heavy-hearted. He thanked Dean and stood, shoving a squawking rooster aside with his foot. "Okay, let's talk to Sarah Yancey."

43

Tall and green-eyed, Sarah Yancey was a stunning combination of her parents' African and Irish American genetics, Beans thought. She sipped on a cup of coffee in Raisa's warm and brightly lit kitchen, wearing an oversized fisherman's sweater that looked oddly nostalgic to Beans. It took a few minutes for him to recognize his own well-worn sweater that had been forgotten at Raisa's a few years ago.

Sarah was a level-headed and observant witness. At closing the previous evening, Edison Dodds had come from behind and jabbed something into her neck as she was unlocking the kiosk to get her phone. She fought him off the best she could, but the next thing she remembered, she was in the back seat of a moving truck, drifting in and out of consciousness.

"I was out of it most of the time, but I caught his face in the rearview mirror. I recognized him as the guy who plowed the drive-through. I never knew his name, but he'd stop and chat every now and then. Hell, I even gave him a free peppermint mocha on Christmas Eve." She shuddered. "Thank God for the moose. Airbags went off, and I guess he was stunned. That's when I got away."

When Edison Dodds tracked her to Raisa's house the next morning, she explained, the women had crept out the back door and made their escape. After Willow was shot, they waited up in the duck blind until they were pretty sure he was gone, then Raisa wanted to check on Willow. "After that, we didn't know if Dodds went back to her house to get the ATV or to his house, so we went deeper into the woods just to be safe."

"So the two of you came out when you heard the commotion rather than staying in hiding?" *Raisa is gutsy for sure, but sometimes half-crazy as well.*

Sarah nodded. "She heard your voice and gunfire and thought you might need some help." She smiled. "She said she's a better shot than you anyway."

Beans sat back in the kitchen chair and smiled back. "She could be right."

"You know, when she handed me that rifle, I would have gone into battle for her. I owe her my life." Sarah wiped tears from her face with the sleeve of Beans' old sweater. "She's my hero."

Investigators began the painstaking task of examining all venues of the Dodds Poultry Farm crime scene. The two-story farmhouse at the front of the property appeared to be frozen in the 1970s. The only fixtures that appeared new were the stainless-steel grab bars and an articulating hospital bed, stripped of linen, in the master bedroom.

A wheelchair and a battered dresser took up opposite corners of the master bedroom, while a commode sat, lid up, near the foot of the bed. A large flat-screen TV had been installed on the wall opposite the bed. When it was powered on, the Outdoor Network came on at a dead-raising volume. Beans assumed that this had been Franklin Dodds' room until he passed away, a paraplegic at the time of his death, having fallen off a ladder nearly fourteen years earlier. His primary caregiver until his death had been his son, Edison. The room was neat, with just a thin layer of dust, and smelled like bleach.

The front room looked like it was rarely used. Frayed furniture slumped beneath crocheted throws. Not a single photograph graced the side tables or hutch. The most notable thing in the room was a fragrant bouquet of white roses, bursting from a florist's vase on the scarred coffee table. It seemed to be the only living thing in the house.

In the kitchen, the loudly humming Whirlpool refrigerator held preloaded syringes of blue liquid, presumably Dodds' homemade Rohypnol solution. Other than the syringes, the refrigerator contained a six-pack of Bud Light, half-used jars of condiments, eight chicken-shit-speckled eggs, and a carton of rancid takeout Mexican food.

How many more women would Dodds have abducted and killed? Beans had to steady himself with an aching gloved hand against the kitchen counter. Exhaustion, lack of sleep, and the rooster attack had given him a reeling sense of vertigo.

This only got worse when he climbed the stairs to the second floor. The bedroom was a shrine to Edison's hunting prowess. Pelts of a variety of animals adorned the walls—beaver, mink, muskrat, otter, raccoon, coyote, and wolf. Beans recognized a couple of cat pelts and the distinctive coat of a harlequin Great Dane. Smaller pelts were tacked above the dresser—rats, voles, and a family of baby skunks.

On the floor beside the bed was a large brown bearskin, head attached, teeth bared. Beans had a sinking feeling of déjà vu and realized that he had seen a similar bearskin on the floor of

Zachary Ingalls' study. *Another hunter fallen from grace, fallen from the sky.*

The room next to Dodds' bedroom had a carved wooden sign on its door that read *The Arsenal*. In it, every conceivable kind of bow hung on racks and hooks on the wall, along with quivers, bolts, and feathered arrows. Against another wall was a glass-fronted display case containing a half dozen rifles.

Ironically, this weapon-filled room was probably the coziest in the house. An overstuffed sofa and recliner faced a flat-screen TV above a credenza that held an old DVR, various *Fast and Furious* DVDs, and a few framed photographs of Dodds in camouflage gear posing with various kills. No other human being populated the photographs—just a smiling Edison Dodds with his dead animals.

He didn't look that unhinged, Beans thought, examining a photo of Dodds with the glassy-eyed corpse of a Dall sheep. Taller and huskier than average, with brown hair and eyes and a pleasant, gap-toothed smile, Dodds wouldn't stand out as a serial killer of young women. *But they said that about Ted Bundy.*

His bathroom was almost clean, with a rust-colored hard-water stain around the toilet bowl. A Costco-sized canister of Old Spice and a small spray bottle of rose water sat on the sink next to the shaving cream and toothbrush.

Beans needed some air. The Old Spice, the roses, the dusty funk of animal hides—all of it was stifling. He went out the back door and took a deep breath, feeling the cool air cleanse him. To his right, the parking area in front of the barn bustled with police and crime scene vehicles. Animal control officers wearing protective gear rounded up the surviving roosters and reincarcerated them in cages.

He stepped off the porch and walked past the barn, where CSIs were digging slugs out of the wall. Heller and more technicians were processing the inside of the barn, which should take them well into the night.

O'Reilly radioed in from the shed adjacent to the chicken coop, where technicians were vacuuming every speck of debris off the floor. "This has to be where he held them." She shouted to be heard over the whine of the vacuum. "The techs have already pulled a long blond hair from the blanket on the cot—it's got to be Toni Morelli's. There's blood on the blanket. A good-sized blood-stain on the floor too. Forensics will be busy until Easter."

That's where he held them, but where did he kill them? Beans couldn't ask Dodds—he was in surgery, where doctors were trying to save his right eye. "Okay, you sick bastard, where did you do it?" he asked out loud. No answer from the silent plastic bear and elk targets, riddled with holes, that peered with faded painted eyes out of the nearby woods.

Just past the shed where Dodds had held the women was a small clearing, muddy with melted snow, ringed by spruce and hemlock. He stood in the center of the clearing, turning, looking around him. A large black spruce, two feet in diameter at its base, towered at the far end of the clearing, looming over the others. As Beans neared it, he ran his eyes down its trunk and stopped about two feet from the ground.

Here the bark was splintered and punctured, clearly by arrows or bolts. Some of them had been removed, so only deep scars remained. Others had been sawed off at bark level, so the arrow-head and some of the shaft remained in the tree. Impaled by one of the bolts was a torn shred of stained blue fabric, no larger than his thumbnail, quivering in the breeze.

"Shit!" Beans jumped back. *The pale-blue velvet of a Snow Bunny Barista outfit.* He got on the handheld radio. "I know where he killed them."

O'Reilly flew out of the shed and sloshed toward the clearing, joining him by the black spruce. She peered down at the holes in the tree and the swatch of pale fabric. "Why so low? These women were at least five feet tall."

"Remember, they were sedated and couldn't stand. My guess is he propped them up and tied or bungee-corded them to the tree, then fired the crossbow. The ground here at the base is probably saturated with blood—though you can't tell with all this mud."

O'Reilly nodded. "The bark! The bark on their clothing!"

Beans nodded. "I bet it's a match to this tree. Also betting that this fabric matches Jolene's outfit." He pointed to the tiny scrap of velvet.

To his surprise, O'Reilly's eyes began to fill with tears. He looked away as she brushed at her eyes with the back of a gloved hand. "They must have been terrified."

Beans put a hand on her shoulder. "I tell myself that they had enough sedative in their systems to be unaware of what was happening. That's how I sleep at night."

He didn't tell her that his sleep was still torn apart by nightmares of Jolene with her torso flayed open, Toni tangled in the burning truck's seat belt, and most recently Hannah with the ragged hole in her heart. Beans reached into his pocket for a piece of sugar-free gum to quell his nausea and offered one to O'Reilly. Sniffing, she took it. They chewed in silence for a while.

O'Reilly spoke first. "Can blood evidence be retrieved from the tree, do you think?"

"Probably on the bark. And the bolts probably pulled some blood into the trunk itself. We won't know until we dig them out. Looks like at least three people were killed here."

"At least? You mean there might be more?"

"I'm guessing one of these bolts belongs to Jolene and another to Hannah. Chuckie extracted Toni's arrowhead from her body, but I'm betting she was killed here as well. There's still one bolt unaccounted for"—he pointed to the broken shaft—"still embedded in the tree."

44

"Who is the woman in the freezer, Edison?" Beans asked from Dodds' hospital bedside the next day.

"Lily, of course. Lilith Dodds, my mother."

Beans and Heller glanced at each other, trying hard not to look surprised.

"You didn't call her Mom?"

"She was seventeen when I was born. She's always been Lily."

Both of Dodds' eyes had been injured in the rooster attack, but the cornea of his right eye had been so badly punctured that, even after hours of surgery, doctors weren't sure he would see from that eye again. It was covered now with a fist-sized wad of gauze and bandages. The dog bites on his left forearm had been stitched and bandaged, as were the wound from Beans' bullet and the additional rooster lacerations to his face and scalp. His nose, broken from O'Reilly's volleyball dig with her bound hands, was now purple and swollen, as was his left eye. Despite his injuries, Edison Dodds looked triumphant, grinning one-eyed from his hospital bed, while an IV drip administered antibiotics and fluids.

"How did she get there?" Beans leaned forward, opening his notebook.

"My father. Franklin 'A-Is-for-Asshole' Dodds put his child bride there. Almost twenty years ago, when she was still fresh." Edison Dodds blinked at Beans with his one good eye.

Edison said that just after his twelfth birthday, Lily had caught Franklin with Edison's junior high classmate. "He'd bring her to the shed—you know the one. Take pictures of her." He shuddered. "It was disgusting. Lily called Shelly's folks and had them haul their little whore daughter off. Dad was lucky to only do minimal time. He still had to register as a sex offender, though.

"It was just Lily and me while Dad was paying his debt to society. Those weren't bad times, even though the chicken business was in the shitter. Then one morning, not too long after Dad was let out, Lily was gone. He said she'd run off with some crab fisherman from Dutch Harbor."

With his mother gone and his father drunk most of the time, Edison had been shuttled around the foster care system until he graduated from high school.

"Week before graduation, he fell off that ladder and became a fucking potato." Dodds scratched his head with his bandaged hand and grimaced. "I've been taking care of that prick since I was seventeen. Time flies when you're fucked, huh?" Dodds flashed a gap-toothed grin.

"And Lily. All those years in the Frigidaire. I only found her last November when I accidentally ripped the door off the root cellar with the snowplow."

From a corner of the hospital room, Dodds' public defender, an overweight pasty-faced attorney named Todd Crenshaw, raised his hand. "Surely my client is not being accused of killing his own mother." He doodled on his yellow legal pad.

"Not at this point, but a woman's body in your client's freezer—well, that's significant," Beans said. "And there's the fact that she looks very much like the first victim."

"Fair enough. Continue." Crenshaw waved Dodds on.

"Just one moment." Beans set his cell phone to record. "Before we go any further—it is February seventh at ten thirty AM. Present at the Providence Medical Center are Edison Dodds, Attorney Todd Crenshaw, and Detectives Ed Heller and DeHavilland Beans. Go ahead, Dodds."

Dodds rubbed his good eye with a bandaged hand and continued:

So, I found Lily in the freezer and went tearing up the stairs, fucking terrified, and ran to the house. Dad was in bed watching the news.

"Where you been, boy? It's my dinnertime."

I was out of breath, and maybe I was crying. "Lily's in the freezer, Dad. She's in the freezer."

"Did you get the chickens fed?"

"Did you hear what I said? Lily's in the barn cellar, in the freezer."

He looked all pale and bony, in his white undershirt and flannel pajama bottoms. His gray hair was standing up like straw. He poured a couple of fingers of whiskey into a tumbler he kept on his nightstand. He took a sip and smacked his lips. "Well, son, how do you think she got there?"

I sat down hard in a chair in the corner of his room. It was like my legs couldn't hold me. "You put her there." My voice was a whisper.

He slammed the tumbler down on the table, and I jumped. "Damn! I didn't raise a fool after all!"

"But why?" I knew he'd never forgiven her for the Shelly business, but Jesus.

He shrugged. "She was about to leave me, take you with her, the faithless whore. Couldn't let that happen, could I? I put an arrow through her thievin', unfaithful heart."

He said just after he'd done his time for that Shelly fiasco, he found Lily loading the Buick with suitcases and my Schwinn. You gotta understand, nobody leaves the old man. He whacked her on the side of her head to calm her down. Then he strapped her to that black spruce and fired an arrow through her—right through her heart with a single shot. Good luck and fine marksmanship.

Since it was January and the ground too frozen to bury her, he put Lily in the freezer with the intention of burying her after breakup. The following Valentine's Day, he got drunk and threw a pink rose into the freezer with her.

He never got around to burying her. He figured as long as the power didn't go out, she could stay there forever.

The night he told me all this, he died of a massive stroke. Just as well. Saved me the trouble of putting the arrow through him myself.

Beans heard the hollow sound of the PA system paging medical personnel, the clatter of carts, and the hushed conversation of nurses in the hall. In the ensuing silence, he shut off the record function.

"She was going to take me with her," Dodds said. "All those years, I thought she had dumped me . . . left me with the old man. Turns out she wanted me to be with her all along." He sighed. "Take a look in the Buick's trunk. My Schwinn's still there."

The rasp of Dodds rubbing at his two days' growth of beard was startling in the quiet of the hospital room. Beans unwrapped a stick of spearmint gum and folded it into his mouth, a preemptive strike against the nausea he knew would come. "Okay. Let's talk about the baristas."

45

"Lily was so perfect. So, so perfect," Dodds said, closing his eye as if to conjure her image on the backs of his eyelids. "Stuck in a Frigidaire all that time. She was a little freezer burned and dried out but almost exactly the way I remember her." He smiled.

The expected wave of nausea washed over Beans. "What about the baristas, Eddy?"

Dodds seemed not to have heard him. "That image of her, under that layer of frost, the dried-out rose beside her—I couldn't get it out of my mind. Night and day, it was like a slideshow, only the same slide, over and over.

"Then after I had Dad cremated—ha! Hellfire was fitting for him—I saw Jolene for the first time when I plowed the parking lot across from Snow Bunny. My God—I thought it was Lily. The long dark hair. Young and beautiful. Half-Native, just like Lily. I followed her home and found out where she lived. I got in through a window when she wasn't home and looked through her stuff. Jolene didn't have the same black underwear, but I guess you can't have everything. I left her a pink rose. I wanted her to know I was thinking of her."

Beans sensed Crenshaw shuddering across from him.

"Eddy, as your attorney, it's my duty to caution you—" Crenshaw began.

"Don't you think that ship has already sailed, Todd?" Dodds went on in a conversational tone. "Then I knew that wasn't enough. I needed to freeze her in time, like Lily."

"So you took her," Heller prompted.

"So I took her." Dodds nodded. "And brought her to the same tree where Dad did Lily." He made a *thunk* sound like an arrow hitting something solid. "One arrow. Just as good as the old man."

"Then what?"

"Put her in my truck and took her out in the pristine snow, just where you found her."

"You didn't figure on the wolves coming to ravage her, did you?" Beans voice was sharp, an accusation. Heller tossed him a warning glance.

Dodds frowned, and a disgusted look crossed his face. "Damn, it's a lucky thing I took a picture."

"You did?"

"Sure, with my phone. Posed her in the snow. She looks like a frozen angel, like Lily, she does." Dodds smiled.

Frozen angel. Like a menu item at Dairy Queen. Beans took a deep breath to keep his growing revulsion under control. "Did you engage in any sexual activity with Jolene Nilsson?"

Dodds looked shocked. "No! I'm not a pervert!"

The room lapsed into a stunned silence. After a couple of beats, Beans said, "Let's talk about Antoinette Morelli."

"Oh, the blonde, the dancer." Dodds frowned. "That could have been a bad mistake."

"What do you mean?"

"There was a girl who worked at Arctic Foxes earlier—a Melanie something—a Chink name, I think. I saw her when I was plowing the place across the street earlier. She had long dark hair and looked a lot like Lily. I was ready to make her into a frozen angel. But then she quit, and the blonde took her place.

"At first I thought, I'm fucked. This girl doesn't look at all like Lily. But when I was at the drive-through, getting coffee one morning, I saw the tattoo of a bird on the inside of her wrist."

"She told me it was in honor of her mother, maiden name Brighthawk, almost full-blooded Cherokee. I told her she didn't look very Native American, being blond and all, but she said her hair color was out of a bottle."

The photo in the townhouse of Toni Morelli as a teenager sprang back to Beans' memory. *Coltish girl with a mouthful of braces. Long black hair. Disneyland. Happier times.* Toni Morelli, a temporary blonde, whose cosmetic alteration hadn't saved her life.

Dodds nodded. "I'm glad I got a picture of her too. If I squint real hard, she could look like a frozen angel like Lily."

"We found some tissue under her fingernails. She scratched you, didn't she?"

"Oh yeah! Fucking hellcat! She got me here." He pointed to the dried scabs on his neck. "Bled like a son of a bitch."

Crenshaw sighed and shook his head. He stood and whispered into Dodds' ear, but loud enough for Beans to hear. "Diminished capacity might be the best chance you have, Eddy."

Dodds waved him off. "Sit down, Todd."

Beans went on. "Tell us about Hannah Fernandez."

"Oh, the little chiquita. It took a while to find her. Another lovely frozen angel, like Lily." Dodds sighed nostalgically.

He denied engaging in sexual activity with any of the women, looking insulted when asked. He'd briefly considered dressing them in Lily's clothes but decided that was distasteful.

Beans, Heller, and O'Reilly had agreed ahead of time that having "Red" present during these initial interviews would be distracting to Dodds. O'Reilly would be part of the FBI Behavior Analysis team that later would conduct more-in-depth interviews with him, but she wanted the detectives to find out why Dodds had left the bodies where he did.

"You had acres of property in which to dispose of their bodies," Beans said. "This is Alaska—you could have left them anywhere they might never have been discovered. But instead, you left them along a public trail, in a park, and on private property."

Dodds blinked his blackened eye, and his answer chilled Beans. "I didn't want them to spend years alone in the cold and darkness, like Lily. I wanted someone to find them."

The radiator in the corner hissed in the otherwise silent room until Beans spoke. "Okay, let's talk about Sarah Yancey."

"Oh, let's not!" Dodds looked tired and petulant.

"My client is exhausted, Detective. Can we continue this tomorrow?" Crenshaw asked.

"No, no, I'm okay." Dodds drew a deep breath. "Not much to say about the one that got away."

"We've already taken a statement from her, but we need one from you as well."

"Another mistake. I had no idea that woman was so strong. She never really went under. Then I hit the moose, and you know the rest. My bitch neighbor and her dog from hell protected her. But I did get a shot off at the dog. Is it dead?" Dodds looked hopeful.

"No, the dog will survive."

"A clusterfuck all around." Dodds sighed.

Beans' hand throbbed where the rooster wound had been reexamined, treated with antibiotics, and rebandaged. Although his face and scalp wounds hadn't required stitches, they stung when he showered, and he avoided mirrors except to painfully shave. Far worse than these superficial injuries was the burning anger he felt at Dodds' total lack of remorse toward his victims. When he thought of how these three young women had been cruelly murdered by this grinning, cycloptic maniac, he could barely meet the man's eye. *Karmic balance be damned. I should have aimed lower.* And even worse than the anger was the gnawing feeling of guilt that he and his colleagues had been unable to stop this psychopath until he had killed three women. He was relieved when a ward nurse poked her head into the room and terminated the interview.

"Good." Dodds beamed, rubbing his hands together. "It's almost time for tapioca pudding."

"Jesus, Mary, and Joseph," Beans heard Heller murmur under his breath as they left the hospital room. They nodded to the armed guard at the door and continued toward the elevator. As they waited for the doors to open, Heller shook his head and said, "Twenty years on the force, and I thought I'd seen it all."

46

It was past noon, but neither Beans nor Heller felt like eating. After their interview with Edison Dodds, the last thing on their mind was lunch. They drove back to headquarters in silence, the Dalai Lama action figure spinning and swaying from the rear-view mirror, seeming to look from one detective to the other with a questioning stare.

Beans pulled into a space in the slushy parking lot but left the engine running, hands on the steering wheel, staring at an undefined point in space. Their session with Dodds had left him numb to his surroundings, as if a bomb had gone off beside him. Heller was no better, staring at the roof of the Explorer and chewing on his lower lip.

A sharp rap on the passenger window made them both jump. Beans' foot slipped off the brake, and the car lurched forward before he put it in park. A young Asian man peered through the window and smiled at Heller, revealing a gold incisor.

Heller rolled down his window. "Manny? Manny Concepcion?"

"Yeah, hi, Detective." Manny nodded at Beans as well. "Hello."

"This is Detective Beans," Heller said.

"Yeah, I know. I saw your guys' pictures in the news. You're big heroes, huh?" The young man grinned, the sunlight glinting off his gold tooth.

Heller unclicked his seat belt. "You want to go inside and talk?"

Manny's smile faded. "Nah, maybe not. I'm not real comfortable in police stations. Can I just . . ." He motioned to the back seat of the Explorer.

"You're not packing, are you, Manny?" Heller asked.

"Oh, Detective." Manny opened his coat and turned around, then lifted his pant legs to show he wasn't wearing an ankle holster. "Don't you trust me?"

Beans unlocked the back door, and Manny climbed in.

The young man chuckled. "This isn't the first time I've been in the back seat of a cop car."

Throughout the investigation into loan shark Sevy Concepcion's disappearance, his close-knit Filipino family had given police only minimal information on his business dealings, treating Heller like the outsider he was. Sevy's youngest brother Manny, dim-witted but fiercely loyal, was considered a beloved pet by the entire family. Heller had told Beans that even his own relatives affectionately referred to Manny as "a box of rocks," the goon who could provide muscle when needed but little else.

Heller leaned over the seat and smiled. "You got something for me, Manny?"

"Yeah, well, maybe." Manny fidgeted in the back seat.

"Okay, well, I'm ready to hear what you got to say." Heller reached into his pocket and pulled out a pad and pen.

"Sevy was there, just before he went missing. There at Dodds' farm," Manny blurted out.

Heller shot Beans a glance. "Why would he go there? You told me earlier that there haven't been fights there since before the holidays."

"There's a shed there that nobody goes into. Sevy stores stuff there."

"Stuff?" Heller asked.

Manny shrugged. "Some weed. Coke. A few pills. Not a lot, and just until he could get it to his guys, you know."

Heller sighed. "So why didn't you tell me this earlier, Manny?"

"My old man doesn't know about the drugs at all—shit, he would have killed Sevy if he knew about that operation. My pop wants no part of 'that dirty stuff,' he calls it. But he worked hard to build his own business, you know?" Manny shook his head. "I couldn't risk you guys nosing around and shutting down his operation."

"We've been all over that farm," Heller said. "Where do you think Sevy is?"

Manny leaned forward. "Hell if I know. But that son of a bitch Dodds does."

* * *

"Stupid fucking Flip." Dodds picked at the gauze on his bandaged eye.

"Tell us what happened," Heller said. Heller, Beans, and Dodds' public defender Crenshaw were once again at Edison's bedside.

"What's in it for me?" Dodds' shrewd dark eye darted between the detectives and Crenshaw.

"My client requests leniency in sentencing in exchange for his cooperation," Crenshaw said, sounding bored again.

"Don't expect anything on the baristas," Beans said, "but there might be some room with Concepcion."

Crenshaw shrugged and nodded at Dodds.

Dodds said, "Okay, Concepcions have always run the business end of the cockfights. I get a percentage for the barn, they get the rest. Helluva deal for everybody. They're in and out all the time—Sevy and his brothers or cousins, or whatever.

"Sevy came into the shed that day. He found Jolene tied up on the cot, in la-la land. He fucking freaked, let me tell you. Jabbered in that crazy language. He went for his gun, but I grabbed it. It went off. *Bam!* Got him through the head. It was an accident, but he was seriously dead, man."

Crenshaw emitted a loud sigh but didn't tell Dodds to stop talking. Beans and Heller exchanged glances.

"I felt bad at first. I didn't have nothing against Sevy—he's my roofie connection, you know—and his old man always treated us fair. But then I started thinking that it wasn't so horrible that he was dead, since he was a witness, right? I drove his Lincoln to the airport, wiped it down, and left it there. Like he took a flight somewhere. Caught a shuttle back downtown."

"And what did you do with Sevy?" Heller asked.

"The old man shot a bull moose once just for the rack. He cut off a chunk at the haunch for meat but didn't want to deal with the rest of it. So he slit open the carcass, dug out the guts, and filled the cavity with rocks. Then he drug it out and sank it in the pond. I mean, there's no room in the freezer, right?" Dodds tilted his head.

Crenshaw looked a little green. "Oh my."

"You did the same with Sevy?" Heller grimaced.

"Had to chop a hole in the ice, but it was thawed enough underneath. He's there."

*　*　*

Beans paced on the slushy bank of the pond at the back of Dodds' property. Police divers waded into the frigid water, pulling their masks down over their faces. The water level was well over the divers' heads, high with runoff from the melting snow. More police in a small skiff poled their way across the pond, feeling for any foreign object on the bottom. Beans jammed his hands into his coat pockets, looking for a stick of gum. He would need it if body retrieval efforts were successful.

Chuckie appeared at his elbow, carrying his bag of instruments. "Good news is that there shouldn't be advanced decomp, not at these temperatures. Where's Heller?"

"On his way. He's finalizing Manny's statement."

Chuckie shook his head. "One-stop shopping with that Dodds guy. Unbelievable. This should wrap up Heller's case too."

Just then, a neoprene-covered head bobbed above the water like a harbor seal and a voice called out, "We got something here."

Divers pulled up an adult Asian male, preserved enough in the icy water to be identified as Sevy Concepcion. A gunshot wound blossomed out the back of his head, just as Dodds had said. Rattling around with the rocks in his abdominal cavity was a crushed iPhone in a pink Hello Kitty case. Jolene's cell phone.

"Anything else?" Chuckie mumbled to himself as he bagged Sevy's remains. "A FedEx driver? A couple of Jehovah's Witnesses? Jimmy Hoffa?"

As it was, in addition to Sevy Concepcion, divers found the skeletons of a headless moose, a bear cub, a coyote, a German shepherd, and a beaver.

It was dark by the time Chuckie had loaded Sevy's body into the van and headed for the morgue. Beans stayed until after the last police officer and technician had gone. As he turned toward his car, he heard frantic clucking and shrieking from the hen house. Turning on his flashlight, he headed toward the small chicken coop. Two golden eyes suddenly leaped from the darkness.

"Shit!" Beans jumped back, startled.

The flashlight beam revealed a fox, the scraggly remains of its white winter coat still clinging to it, with a speckled squawking hen in its jaws. Beans stamped his foot and waved his arms, yelling. The fox seemed to look at him accusingly, then slinked into the darkness, not relinquishing the bloody dying chicken.

The chicken coop door had been left unlatched—an oversight by one of the techs, Beans assumed. He threw some feed down for the still-ruffled hens and gave them fresh water. He secured the coop door behind him and followed his flashlight beam toward his car.

His phone barked in his pocket. The display read *Mom*.

"Your grandfather died about an hour ago." *While I was watching them pull Sevy's gutted corpse from the frozen pond*, Beans thought. "The care facility called your grandma. They said he slipped away very quietly." Mari's voice sounded thin and reedy. "I guess it's the merciful thing."

"I'm sorry, Mom. How are you doing? How is Grandma?" He thought about his frail Japanese grandmother, alone for the first time in sixty years.

"I'm okay. I said my goodbyes to him when I was down there. Your grandma's sad, of course. But I think she's relieved. Your Aunt Naomi and Uncle Roy are with her now."

"Will there be a service?" Beans unlocked the Explorer and slid onto the seat. Now that the case was pretty much wrapped up, he could accompany his mother to the Bay Area if she needed him.

"No. Mom said he never wanted any fuss. He'll be cremated and sit in an urn in their house until they both can be interred at the Veteran's Cemetery in Sonoma. It's what he wanted."

Mari said she would fly back down to spend time with her mother during her school's spring break. "I'll help her clear out some of Dad's stuff. He never seemed to throw anything away."

Sitting in the darkness, Beans thought it was an emotional shortcoming on his part that he felt nothing, no sense of loss at the death of a blood relative. Still, he would observe the Buddhist mourning period of forty-nine days, saying prayers every seven days for a grandfather he'd known only as a stern judge of his family's weaknesses.

He started the Explorer and turned up the heat. Mari said, "Oh, you're in the car. I'll say goodbye, then. It's late, and I still need to call your sister. Sleep well, baby."

"You too, Mom."

As he turned onto the highway from Dodds' farm, a wave of exhaustion broke over him. He had averaged no more than five hours of sleep a night since mid-December, when Jolene Nilsson was found on the snow. Now with their killer caught, maybe the dead girls would no longer haunt his dreams.

47

The highway on the way to Ingalls' Homer house was iridescent with snow runoff and antifreeze. With the warming weather and clear roads, Beans took the rare opportunity to drive faster than he normally would this time of year. The duffel bag containing the bows, arrows, and bolts that Beans had borrowed from Zach Ingalls slid back and forth on the back seat of the Explorer, clacking and rattling every time he changed lanes.

Part of him was reluctant to make the long drive while the mountain of evidence in the high-profile barista case was still being processed. Even without Dodds' bizarrely cheerful confession to the abduction and killing of the three young women, the kidnapping of Sarah Yancey, and the accidental shooting of Sevy Concepcion, the sheer volume of physical evidence was damning.

After Dodds happily turned over the passcode to his phone, techs extracted photos of Jolene Nilsson, Toni Morelli, and Hannah Fernandez from soon after they had been placed on the snow—in Jolene's and Toni's cases, well before scavengers ravaged their bodies. There were also several photos of Lilith Dodds in subzero slumber in the Frigidaire.

That was just the tip of the iceberg. Hair matching that of Jolene Nilsson and Hannah Fernandez was found on the pueblo-patterned blanket in the shed. A long dyed-blond hair matching Toni Morelli's was discovered clinging to a splintered leg of the cot. In the slushy mud surrounding the black spruce, CSIs found a broken fingernail torn from Toni's hand. On the floor of Dodds' pickup truck was a small gold crucifix on a broken chain that had belonged to Hannah Fernandez.

The plastic Dalai Lama figure swung rhythmically from Beans' rearview mirror as he drove, seeming to dance a jig to spring. The landscape around him was shrugging off winter like a threadbare coat. Here on the Kenai Peninsula, vague smudges of green were visible on some of the deciduous trees lining the roadway. Or maybe he was projecting his own hopeful feeling of renewal, of starting again.

He had called Raisa two days ago, the first time he had spoken with her since Sarah Yancey's abduction. He wanted to see how she was, and wanted to return some of the archery supplies that her father had loaned him.

She was silent for a couple of beats, and he was afraid he had upset her. He was ready to stammer out an apology when she responded. "Oh. Oh, I'm fine. I'm fine, Beans." He thought she sounded surprised but pleased.

She told him that she and Oksana were hosting an informal celebration of Zachary Ingalls' life at his house in Homer that Saturday. "We would love it if you could come," Raisa said, and again she sounded sincere.

Still, it was with some trepidation that he turned up the long driveway to Ingalls' log mansion. Cars were parked on both sides of the gravel lane—more than a couple of Mercedeses and BMWs and a Tesla SUV. Even in death, Ingalls ran with an elite crowd, Beans thought.

He nosed into a parking space and opened his door, then was greeted immediately with black-and-white enthusiasm by Thor the Bear Dog. After some happy ear scratching, Beans pulled the duffel bag from the back seat and strode up the drive, Thor bounding around him.

On the front porch, another black-and-white dog rose slowly to her feet, her tail waving like a fan. Willow, her right hindquarter shaved and stitched, yipped in greeting from within the plastic Elizabethan collar.

When Beans looked up from petting Willow, he found Raisa standing next to him, her brown-eyed gaze warm and steady.

"Looks pretty good, doesn't she?" Raisa said.

"She looks great!" Beans said, as the dog bumped into his legs with her plastic cone.

"The vet says when she's healed up, she probably won't even limp."

"Brave girl, good girl." Beans scratched the base of Willow's tail.

There was an awkward silent moment after he set the duffel bag on the porch when he wasn't sure whether or not to hug Raisa. The decision was made for him when she moved easily into his arms and embraced him.

"Come in." She smiled and took his arm.

Inside, with the fire roaring in the river-rock hearth, the log house was more welcoming than he remembered. Oksana, the Second Stepmother, traffic-stopping in a body-hugging black sheath, seemed happy to see him as she pressed his hand between both of hers.

The large front room was teeming with well-heeled men and women, drinks in their hands, reminiscing about the great outdoorsman Zachary Ingalls. Beans thought he recognized a features reporter from a local television station and the host of a fishing show on the Outdoor Network.

Raisa handed Beans a cup of coffee and motioned him toward the dining room, where a huge buffet had been laid—caribou steak, salmon, moose burgers, and an endless array of salads and side dishes.

"Hungry?" Raisa asked. "I thought Oksana went way overboard with the catering, but judging by the turnout, it looks like she was spot-on."

Beans said he might have a bite later but right now would enjoy the coffee and conversation.

"I'm so glad you're here," she said, refilling her coffee.

"Really?" He searched her face.

She motioned him toward the study. "Let's go in here, where it's quieter."

"I don't want to pull you away from your guests."

She rolled her eyes. "Massive egos and roving hands. Oksana can handle them."

The relative coolness and quiet of Zach Ingalls' man-cave was refreshing. They settled onto the same leather sofa they'd sat in a few years ago, the stuffed animal heads looming above them, when Zach Ingalls was still very much alive. Beans asked if there was anything new on Ingalls' homicide case.

"No, nothing. The feds are working through diplomatic channels, but you know how great our relationship with the Chinese is these days."

"I wanted to tell you, really, how sorry I am about your dad. He was a big help with this case." This was an exaggeration, but it couldn't hurt for Raisa to think well of her father. The glassy eyes of a stuffed pronghorn antelope seem to glare down at him at the sound of his white lie.

"I know he could be an asshole." She teared up and wiped her eyes with the heel of her hand, like a child. "But he was my dad."

Beans reached for her hand. "He was very proud of you."

She squeezed his hand, then reached for a tissue. "So, how's the Eddy Dodds case coming?"

"Crazier and crazier."

"Mother in the freezer or not, what kind of crazy would make someone kill innocent young women like that?"

"Good question."

O'Reilly had theorized that finding his mother's idealized frozen remains had likely traumatized Edison to the point of dissociation, where he'd felt compelled to repeat the icy tableau over and over. Although there was no evidence that he had had sexual intercourse with his victims, FBI psychologists on the case believed that his behavior could have eventually escalated to that level.

"And you should have seen the rack on that motherfucker ..." Alcohol-fueled voices from the other room jolted Beans' attention back to Zach Ingalls' study.

Raisa rolled her eyes. "Let's get out of here. Say, Dad's shorthaired pointer had puppies just before he ... died." She hesitated, then gave Beans a sad smile. "Isn't that stupid? I can't even say he died—there, I said it! Anyway, Sadie had a huge litter of pups. Want to see them?"

Raisa refreshed their coffee, and they headed down the gravel path to the heated metal building that housed the dog kennels.

Thor romped alongside, and Willow, looking mournful from inside her cone, followed more slowly.

"Isn't this great? It feels like spring." Raisa spread her arms and took a deep breath.

Sadie, a liver-and-white German shorthaired pointer, wiggled her cropped tail in greeting. Nestled at her side were nine nursing puppies, four like Sadie, four solid liver, and one tiny black-and-white puppy.

"Isn't that funny? The puppies' sire is solid liver, and here pops out this little black-speckled guy." She picked him up, cooed to him as he yawned, and handed him to Beans.

The little puppy snuggled against his chest and soon fell asleep. Beans was reminded of an earlier time, a more innocent time, when he and Raisa had shared a kiss, holding her warm puppy between them.

Raisa seemed to sense his wistfulness and said brightly, "We've got a prospective buyer for Dad's property."

"Already?"

"One of the blowhards getting drunk on Dad's liquor." She pointed back to the house. "His money's good, though."

"Oksana didn't want to keep it?"

"No, she's going back to Vladivostok—at least that's the plan for now."

"What about the dogs?"

"I'll take Thor, since he's Willow's littermate, but the buyer will take the others. He's a good dog man—has field trial champions of his own. He runs a hunting-and-fishing excursion company like Dad's, only on a smaller scale."

"He'll take the pups too?" The puppy against Beans' chest made snuffling noises.

"The little shorthairs will be sold as soon as they're weaned."

"Even this little guy?"

"He's smaller than the others. He'll probably be sold as a pet. Why? Do you want him?"

"I might," he blurted out. "I mean, I hadn't thought about it until just now. I know it's a huge commitment."

Raisa smiled. "Tell you what. They can't leave their mother yet for another four weeks or so. Think about it. I promise we won't sell him before we check with you first."

What was he thinking? On the one hand, he had a large fenced yard, and he could build a kennel so the dog could stay outside on warm days. It would be nice to have a running and hiking companion. But was he ready for a dog? His old childhood mongrel, Muktuk, had died in his arms when he was home for spring break his junior year in college. Since then, he hadn't had the time or the inclination to own a dog. But then, he reminded himself, he hadn't intended on owning a cat either.

"Thanks, I'll think about it. Please don't let him go without calling me." He wondered how Archie would react to a canine housemate.

Raisa nodded and picked up one of the brown pups. Stroking its soft ears, she said, "Hey, you'll never guess who called me yesterday. Go ahead, guess."

"Sarah Yancey."

"You butthead." She laughed. "You talked to her."

"How do you think she got your number, now that it's working again?"

"Okay, smartass. She invited me to her wedding—isn't that cool? I think the Eddy Dodds episode convinced her to seize the day. She and her fiancé decided not to wait until September. They're getting married at Alyeska next weekend."

"Good for them." Beans really was happy for Sarah. She was a brave young woman who deserved the brightest future. *The same with Raisa, he thought. Another young woman who deserves nothing but the best.*

"What do you think I should get her for a wedding gift?" Raisa touched her nose to the puppy's.

"You're asking me? Remember, I'm the one who bought you a Ninja blender for Valentine's Day."

They both laughed, then fell silent.

Raisa cleared her throat. "I feel awful about that night—you know which one. My God, I was out of control." Her voice fell off.

"It's okay," Beans said, and it was. "I'm as much to blame. I was pretty clueless."

"No, I was wrong to blame you for why I was so . . . fucked up." She shook her head. "I'm so sorry."

"Me too," Beans said.

After a few moments of silence, Raisa said, "So, I've been working with an osteopath, getting off the pills. I'm doing yoga again too."

"Sounds great," he said. She did look healthier and happier than she had in a long time.

They talked about the dogs, the weather, and the Dodds case as they returned to the main house. It felt normal and relaxed, like they were on steady ground again.

"So, the three girls and Eddy's mother all died there?" She shuddered.

"And a drug dealer who was in the wrong place at the wrong time."

"What?" Raisa's eyes widened.

"Sevy Concepcion, loan shark and drug dealer who was shot accidentally. Collateral damage."

Raisa shook her head, only somewhat ironically. "I used to think it was a good neighborhood."

Back at the house, Beans mounded a plate with buffet delicacies and engaged in a lively conversation with a bleary-eyed Catholic priest and an equally inebriated taxidermist. After dessert and hearing a few drunken tributes to the departed Zach Ingalls, he stood to leave. He had a long drive back to Anchorage and wanted to start while there was still some daylight.

He saw Raisa talking with Oksana and caught her eye.

"Oh, Beans." Oksana took his hands in hers again. "Thank you for coming. And Raisa says you will—"

"Might," Raisa interrupted.

"Might take one of Zacky's puppies? He would have liked that."

Beans wasn't sure about that but appreciated the sentiment. "Zach was . . . larger than life. I'm so sorry for your loss. Raisa says you'll be returning to Russia?"

"Yes," Oksana said. "My mother, she is ill and wants me back."

"I hope I'll get to see you before you leave." He accepted a perfumed kiss on the cheek.

After Oksana walked away, Raisa rubbed the crimson lipstick off his cheek with more vigor than he thought necessary.

"Ow," he said. "Don't forget about the rooster wounds."

"Sorry," she said under her breath, rubbing the napkin more gently against his skin. "It's just that, since Dad's been gone, she's been on the prowl. I really am fond of her, but sometimes she's such a barracuda."

Raisa walked him to the Explorer, the exuberant Thor and the more deliberate Willow trotting alongside. This felt right, Beans thought, calm, devoid of drama. Sometime after that disastrous night at his house, all the tension between them had dissipated, like air released from a crazily overinflated balloon. It was a welcome relief but at the same time felt sad and flat, the giddy buoyancy of their up-and-down relationship gone.

"Thanks for bringing Dad's stuff back," Raisa said.

"Thanks for the loan," he said.

"And I won't forget about the puppy. You get first dibs."

Before either of them had a chance to overanalyze the moment, Beans took Raisa in his arms and gave her a long hug. He felt her tremble a little and smelled her sweet tea tree smell. Then he gave her a soft kiss on the forehead and smoothed her hair.

"Be well, Raisa."

She smiled at him with just a slight glistening in the corner of her eyes. She stood on her toes and kissed him on the cheek, just where Oksana had. As she did, she pressed a small metal object, still warm from her pocket, into his hand.

It was his house key that had been in her possession for two years, returning to roost like a migratory bird. She headed back toward the house before he had a chance to respond. He rolled down the window and stuck his head out.

"Thank you," he said.

She turned and hooked her hair over her ears, an achingly familiar gesture. She shook her head and smiled. "I hung on to it for far too long."

He nodded and turned in the circular driveway. As he passed the house, Raisa stood on the porch and gave a brief wave that had a finality to it, Willow and Thor flanking her like sentinels.

It was after ten o'clock by the time Beans arrived home, and he was again bone-tired. Still, it was a good kind of exhaustion, the kind of loose-limbed euphoria he felt after running a few miles. He hadn't realized how heavily his unresolved issues with Raisa had been weighing on him. It was a bittersweet end, for sure, but one that was necessary.

Archie greeted him with irritated yowls as he walked in the door.

"Yeah, yeah, I know. Way past dinnertime." He reached down to stroke the cat, but Archie sniffed at his hand, then backed away, every hair on his tail standing on end. His eyes narrowed and he emitted a soft hiss.

"I get it, I smell like a dog. I admit it. I'm a faithless whore." The comment escaped him before he realized that those were the words Edison Dodds had said his father had used to describe the young wife he had killed and stuffed in the freezer. It would be a long time before this case worked its way out of his system, he thought, as he spooned cat food into Archie's bowl. Archie got over his sense of betrayal long enough to wolf down his dinner and eye Beans suspiciously.

Checking the day's mail, he was surprised to find a small box sent from his grandparents' home in Fremont, California. Inside the box was a note in his grandmother's spidery script:

Dear Havi:

I found this in your grandfather's dresser drawer. Maybe he had intended it as a Christmas gift? Anyway, I thought I'd send it on. I know it's hard to believe sometimes, but he loved you all. Please try to remember him fondly.

Love,
Grandma

The tissue-wrapped bundle beneath was addressed to *DeHavilland* in what Beans assumed was his grandfather's careful printing. Under the wrapping was a small wooden toy, lovingly carved to look like a revolver. Scabs of old varnish marred parts of its finish, but most of the little gun had been smoothed by years of handling. The initials *BY* had been carved into the handle.

Beans didn't have to compare it to the old black-and-white photo to know that this worn toy gun had once been carried in his grandfather's child-sized holster. Why had his distant, disapproving grandfather chosen to leave such a treasured childhood possession to him? And why now? He was surprised by the wave of sorrow that washed over him. He tried to imagine little Ben Yamane pacing off the dusty yard of the internment camp in a mortal showdown with the forces of evil, armed only with a make-believe gun.

48

Isabelle O'Reilly surprised him by reaching up and kissing him on the cheek as they stood in the watery sunshine outside the offices of the Anchorage Police Department. This was the same cheek that Oksana Ingalls had pecked at with her dark-red lips and Raisa had kissed in a soulful goodbye.

O'Reilly's kiss was gentle and warm, and her smell of lavender made it even more sweetly incongruous. "See you, Beans." She gave him her sparkling Amy Adams smile. "It's been a pleasure."

"Likewise," he said. "You'll be back, though, won't you? You still owe us drinks at Muldoon's."

"Of course. I'll be here with the whole dog-and-pony show from Quantico. There's much more to be learned from Edison Dodds. We still need to dig into his family history." She squeezed his arm. "In the meantime, keep me in the loop, okay?"

Which loop? In the last few days, the body from the pond had been positively identified by the family as Sevy Concepcion. Blood evidence on the floor and walls of the shed also matched Sevy's remains.

The families of Jolene Nilsson, Toni Morelli, and Hannah Fernandez had been notified that a suspect had confessed to the killings. Jolene's father said they were putting her cremated remains into the family graveyard in Manokotak next month and took comfort in knowing that her killer had been apprehended. Ray Morelli broke down and wept. Hannah's mother gripped her rosary and said a silent tearful prayer.

Sarah Yancey was called "The Girl Who Lived" by the national press—the young woman who'd magically survived her own deadly version of the Dark Lord. She declined all media interviews, saying through a spokesperson that she was on her honeymoon at an undisclosed location and was unavailable for comment.

The news services ran the huge headline BARISTA KILLER SUSPECT CONFESSES TO SHOOTING OF SEVERINO CONCEPCION. It was a news bonanza for the Anchorage media. The local NBC affiliate dubbed Beans and Heller the knights in shining armor for all scantily clad baristas and hapless loan sharks. Neither detective had any interest in being a media darling, and they managed to slough press relations duties off onto Lieutenant DuBois.

Details began emerging of Edison Dodds' horrific childhood, so dysfunctional that Dodds was portrayed as a damaged but strangely sympathetic character by some advocates for the accused. His own mother, Lilith, had been impregnated by the much older Franklin Dodds, an occasionally employed gold miner, when she was sixteen. Lilith's father, a Baptist minister, threw her out of their home in the Kuskokwim village of Aniak and never spoke to her again.

By Edison's account, Lilith, herself still a child, loved her baby, treating him more like her little brother than her son. Such was not the case with Franklin Dodds, whose treatment of his son was erratic at best, cruel at worst. After the failure of the chicken farm, his branding as a sex offender, and the disappearance of Lilith, Franklin Dodds became an abusive alcoholic, and Edison was removed from the home.

Edison's five years in the foster care system did nothing to stabilize his already unstable temperament. He lived with three different families, each giving him up when their household pets died grisly and untimely deaths.

Remembering the way Eddy had selected and stalked his victims, Beans himself found it hard to be sympathetic to Dodds's cause. *Unfortunate and crazy he might be, but stupid he's not.*

The Sevy Concepcion homicide case was quickly closed. The district attorney and defense agreed to a lesser charge, given the circumstances of Concepcion's accidental shooting and the near certainty that Dodds would spend the rest of his life incarcerated. As Manny had suggested, two quart-size plastic bags of Ecstasy and cocaine were found stuffed into bales of pine shavings in Dodds' shed.

After seeing O'Reilly off, Beans bumped into Heller in the lobby of police headquarters. "Hey," Beans said, "never had a chance to tell you—thanks for having my back at Dodds'."

Heller looked at him strangely for a minute, then pointed at his left cheek.

"Uh, you got, um . . ." Heller smiled.

"Shit," Beans said, and yanked a handkerchief out of his pocket. O'Reilly's lipstick, damn it—how many people had smirked at the red lip marks on his face?

"So, about that," Heller said.

"About what? Did I get it all?" Beans rubbed at his face.

"Yeah, it's gone. About that having-your-back thing."

"Uh-huh."

Heller motioned to a couple of leather chairs as far as possible from the rush of workers leaving for lunch break.

Beans sat and jammed his handkerchief into his jacket pocket. "What's up?"

"I'm wondering if you'd want to make it a more permanent thing."

Beans grinned. "Why, Ed, this is so sudden."

"Shut up," Ed said, looking chagrined. "I know we didn't start off on the right foot, and that was my fault, mostly."

"But not all," Beans admitted.

"No argument there. What do you think about working together, at least on a trial basis?"

"Have you talked to DuBois about it?"

"Not yet. I wanted to run it by you first. What say you?"

Beans held out his hand. "Let's do it."

Not surprisingly, DuBois was smug when they approached him. "You remember, right, that teaming you two together was my idea all along?"

"Was it?" Heller looked at Beans. "Do you remember that?"

"Nope, first I heard of it," Beans said.

"Get out of here." DuBois smiled as they left his office. "Assholes."

Heller had a dental appointment, but after he returned, they would merge their case files and prioritize them. He left the office whistling under his breath. He was especially cheerful since they had convinced DuBois to hire on Cam Kristovich as a part-time consultant. DuBois conceded that Cam's special skills had been vital in solving the barista case and that he could be a valuable asset to the department. Heller, ecstatic that the young man would take over CCTV viewing duties, not to mention pivot table designing in Excel, could hardly wait to tell Cam.

For the first time in months, since before Jolene Nilsson's body was found, Beans felt a load had lifted. Since the resolution of the barista case, he had slept deeply and restfully, interrupted only by his recurring childhood nightmare—alone, once again, in Lindbergh's burning truck. On top of that, breakup seemed to have truly arrived early in Anchorage, and the air was fresh and clean. He grabbed his coat and headed out.

He was standing at the curb, waiting to cross the street, when a city bus passed in front of him. Thinking the driver might be Cam Kristovich, he looked up in time to see an advertisement for the Anchorage Ballet glide past on the side of the bus. It was a large black-and-white photo of Amy Chandler in an arabesque, her serene face turned to the camera. *Shostakovich Ballet Suites 1–4*, the headline read. *Presented by the Anchorage Ballet, April 15 through 30.*

Her larger-than-life face drifted past him, her long leg extending past the articulating center of the bus, supported by the athletic arms of Brady, her new roommate.

He had almost forgotten how beautiful she was, luminous even under all the makeup and costuming. He stared at the bus as it snaked down the street, gazing at her image so long that he missed the walk signal. He convinced himself that Archie was just about out of his foul-smelling salmon and sweet potato cat food and strolled the five blocks in the spring sunshine to Back to Nature Pet Supply.

At the pet store, he picked out Archie's cat food, then on impulse walked down the dog toy aisle. He selected a squeaking plush toy in the shape of a peanut, about as long as his femur. He asked himself if that meant he was going to adopt Raisa's pointer puppy. Well, maybe, but not necessarily. *Then why the hell am I paying twenty bucks for a supersized dog toy?* He sighed to himself, pulled out his credit card, and resigned himself to the fact that he was going to be a dog owner.

He left Back to Nature with a huge shopping bag, the peanut-shaped dog toy peering out the top with cheerful embroidered eyes. It was now one thirty and he was starving. And coincidentally—again he asked himself who he was fooling—he found himself at Snowtown Bistro.

Amy Chandler stood behind the counter, smiling and chatting with a teenage busboy who was clearly infatuated with her. Beans entered the restaurant and set the shopping bag on the floor with a piercing squeak from the femur-sized peanut.

Amy turned, a puzzled look on her face, then recognized him.

"Hi," she said. She wore a lilac-colored sweater over a black turtleneck. Her hair fell down her back in a long dark braid.

"Hi," he said. "I saw you on the bus. Not *on* the bus, but on *a* bus, on the *side* of a bus." *Oh God, even Cam Kristovich is more eloquent.*

"You'd be surprised how many people have said that to me. Maybe not exactly like that." Her steady blue gaze searched his face.

Beans sighed. "Am I screwing this up?"

"No, not at all." Her smile was warm and welcoming. She set a mug in front of him on the counter. "Coffee?"

Acknowledgments

Thank you to my dear friend and occasional collaborator Becky Warden. Without her creative input and support, I'm convinced that DeHavilland Beans *and Cold to the Touch* would have never come to life.

Many thanks also to members of my critique groups, past and present—the aforementioned Becky, Sherry Decker, Carol Morrison, Judith Kirscht, Serena DuBois, and Dennis Ford—for good times and priceless feedback. Bob Ray and Jack Remick's creative instruction, encouragement, and bodies of work have been truly inspirational. James E. Wadsworth's *The Writer's Guide to Archery* was a wealth of information and a valuable resource—any inaccuracies in archery specifics are definitely mine. Dr. Judith A. Berg gave me expert medical and pharmaceutical advice, for which I am very grateful. Again, any lapses in accuracy are very much on me.

Heartfelt gratitude to the incredible team at Crooked Lane Books, but especially to my editor extraordinaire Sara J. Henry, who championed *Cold to the Touch* from the start.

And last but certainly not least, thank you to my husband, Jon Black, who has put up with me with patience, love, and good humor all these years.